"Jude, I'm your man, financially speaking, if you'll have me."

She appeared uncertain, as if she was going to turn him down.

"I really do know what I'm doing. All you need to do is...give me a chance," Liam finished.

And then she completely surprised him. "I guess I could." She looked up into his eyes. "You really will try to understand, right?"

The question made her seem so vulnerable, as if she'd trusted before and her faith had disappointed her. Guilt stabbed him. He'd made a deal with her father even though he hadn't been comfortable doing it. Liam didn't like keeping secrets. And yet here he was, working undercover for Dr. Foster.

But why should he feel guilty? The foundation, and Jude, would benefit from his advice. And once he helped her, just maybe this normally strong, determined woman would accept an invitation for dinner.

An unexpected breeze kicked up from the woods. Strands of Jude's hair tickled Liam's nose.

Most likely she wouldn't go out on a date with him. How could he forget that she loved another man?

Dear Reader,

In my last book, I told the story of Alexis, the firstborn daughter in the series, The Daughters of Dancing Falls. As firstborn, much was expected of Alex, and she more than met expectations in grades and accomplishments.

In this book, I concentrate on Jude, the middle daughter, whose life was fraught with mistakes and risks. Writing this story, I thought a lot about middle children. Had my sister not died very young, I would have grown up a middle child. I discovered that middle children often act out, because they feel underappreciated or have a difficult time finding their niche in the family. But I also discovered one very interesting fact. If you look at pictures of three siblings, the middle child is usually in the middle of the photo. That should make the "middles" feel special. They are the center, the focus of the picture. "Middles" unite. You are the center of the family. You ground the others with your determination and will to stand out on your own merits.

I hope you enjoy this book about the middle child in the Foster family. I certainly enjoyed writing it for you.

I love to hear from readers. You may contact me at cynthoma@aol.com or visit my website, www.cynthiathomason.net.

Cynthia

HEARTWARMING

The Bridesmaid Wore Sneakers

———

Cynthia Thomason

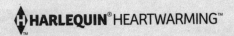

Recycling programs
for this product may
not exist in your area.

ISBN-13: 978-0-373-36800-6

The Bridesmaid Wore Sneakers

Copyright © 2016 by Cynthia Thomason

All rights reserved. Except for use in any review, the reproduction or utilization of this work in whole or in part in any form by any electronic, mechanical or other means, now known or hereinafter invented, including xerography, photocopying and recording, or in any information storage or retrieval system, is forbidden without the written permission of the publisher, Harlequin Enterprises Limited, 225 Duncan Mill Road, Don Mills, Ontario M3B 3K9, Canada.

This is a work of fiction. Names, characters, places and incidents are either the product of the author's imagination or are used fictitiously, and any resemblance to actual persons, living or dead, business establishments, events or locales is entirely coincidental.

This edition published by arrangement with Harlequin Books S.A.

For questions and comments about the quality of this book, please contact us at CustomerService@Harlequin.com.

® and TM are trademarks of Harlequin Enterprises Limited or its corporate affiliates. Trademarks indicated with ® are registered in the United States Patent and Trademark Office, the Canadian Intellectual Property Office and in other countries.

Printed in U.S.A.

Cynthia Thomason inherited her love of writing from her ancestors. Her father and grandmother both loved to write, and she aspired to continue the legacy. Cynthia studied English and journalism in college, and after a career as a high-school English teacher, she began writing novels. She discovered ideas for stories while searching through antiques stores and flea markets and as an auctioneer and estate buyer. Cynthia says every cast-off item from someone's life can ignite the idea for a plot. She writes about small towns, big hearts and happy endings that are earned and not taken for granted. And as far as the legacy is concerned, just ask her son, the magazine journalist, if he believes.

This book is dedicated to Lisa Beaumont, my rugged and beautiful stepdaughter, who, like the heroine in this book, finds as much comfort in the company of four-legged creatures as she does the two-legged variety.

PROLOGUE

Eight years ago

"An Old Soul with a fighting spirit." That was how Jude Foster's mother often referred to her. Well, if caring about people and creatures and causes made her an old soul, then Jude was happy to have earned the title. Just because she didn't go out with friends a lot and chase guys...just because she didn't care a bit for the community college courses her father had encouraged her to enroll in—none of that meant she didn't have a fulfilling life.

True, she was twenty-three years old and had never been in love. So what? Her mother also told her that her heart would find its match eventually, and in the meantime she didn't mind avoiding all the angst and heartache her sisters constantly talked about.

If she could just convince her dad that she wasn't college material, that she truly hated the idea of cleaning teeth for the rest of her life. All she needed was a new goal, one she could present to her father as a viable alternative to scraping molars.

Jude left the medical associate's degree building of Munson Community College and released her usual sigh of relief. Somehow she'd managed to muddle through nearly three semesters of training in the dental hygienist school, doing just well enough to keep from flunking out.

She certainly couldn't attribute her modest success in college to her own drive and purpose. Jude simply wasn't a student, never would be. No, she was doing this for her father, who'd spent the first two years after Jude graduated from high school trying to interest her in a field that required higher education, while she worked the cash register at Winnie's Western Wear. They'd settled on this path, or more accurately Martin Foster had settled on it, and the rest had been a history just short of drudgery. If she finished this semester and got through one more, she could clean teeth. Wow, the prospect excited her not at all.

She came around the corner of the student

union building and decided to skip lunch today. She could be home in thirty minutes and spend her afternoon at the barn with her docile and delightful mare, Honey. Maybe they'd ride on the property. Maybe they'd go all the way to Bees Creek. Either way, the thought of a gallop through the countryside made Jude forget uppers and lowers that hadn't been flossed in months.

She was about to cross the paved road that ran between the union and the students' parking lot when she noticed an old pickup truck broken down on the side of the asphalt. The hood was up, and a frantic hand waved the air where smoke was billowing from the engine. She couldn't see the man's face, but he was dressed in old jeans, work boots and a long-sleeved T-shirt that showed off admirable muscles.

Never one to pass by a trouble spot if she thought she could lend a hand, Jude went up to the truck. "Can I help?" she asked.

The man rose from the hood, wiped steam from his forehead and grimaced.

Jude's mouth almost watered, probably from a lack of lunch, she told herself.

He was gorgeous. Long, dark hair that

reached nearly to his shoulders. A strong face with storybook masculine features that included a square jaw, high cheekbones, a slightly crooked nose. The only part of that face that didn't blend well with the other features were dark, curling lashes that immediately captured Jude's attention.

"Have you got a cell phone?" the man asked. "I need to make a phone call."

The guy didn't have a cell phone? Wow, maybe she'd entered a time warp and had been transported back a few decades. The truck, at best a relic of the eighties, fit the scenario in her mind. She fished her phone out of her backpack and handed it to him. "Do you know how to use this?"

He gave her a questioning look. "Of course. I just forgot mine when I left the house this morning."

He punched in a number. "Richie, it's me. Tell Pop the truck broke down again. I'm going to need a tow." He paused, listening. "I know. I tried that." Another pause. "Yes, I made it to the college, but I'm going to have to unload all this produce by myself and carry it into the kitchen."

For the first time Jude noticed a plastic tarp

covering the cargo area of the truck. Between the rope tie-downs she could see assorted vegetables and fruits.

"Don't bother," he said to the person on the phone. "By the time you could get here, I would already have it mostly delivered. Just tell a tow to be here in an hour."

He handed Jude her phone. "Thanks. Can't believe I left my phone at home." Glaring at the truck, he added, "I should know to keep it handy when I'm forced to drive this piece of…" He stopped, looked at Jude. "Sorry."

She'd noticed his left hand when he gave her the phone. No ring.

"No problem," she said. "I heard you tell that other guy…"

"My brother, Richie."

"Okay, Richie, that you would unload this produce. I assume it's going into the building next door to us here."

"That's right. My family farm furnishes fresh vegetables to the cafeteria. Usually I drop it off at the loading door in the back. Looks like I won't be doing that today." He frowned at the truck. "She conked out on me and won't go another inch. Can't let the stuff sit in the truck and spoil."

"No, you wouldn't want to do that." She dropped the backpack from her shoulder and tossed it into the truck cab. "This should be safe here." And if it wasn't, she really didn't care.

"What are you doing?"

"I'm going to help you carry this produce to the union. Me and anyone else I can draft to give us a hand."

"You?" His facial expression was less than confident. "I can do it, really. I don't want you straining anything."

She knew her slight figure belied her strength. And she also knew her strength. A girl didn't haul hay bales and water buckets without building up some muscle tone. She began untying the knots in his tie-downs. When she'd cleared a bushel basket of tomatoes, she hoisted it easily from the truck. Staring at the man's shocked expression, she smiled and said, "Come on, let's go."

Jude succeeded in nabbing a half dozen volunteers she knew from hygiene classes. The entire truck was emptied in a half hour.

"Wow, thanks everyone," Mr. Gorgeous said when the job was done. The other students left, but Jude, gratefully accepting an apple, munched and waited for the tow to arrive. When it did, she asked the man what he intended to do to get back to his farm.

"I'll ride in with the tow driver. My brother will pick me up."

"I might be able to take you," she said. "Where is your farm?"

"Bees Creek Township," he said.

"Amazing," she said. "I'm going right by there." Never had a lie come so easily.

"Well, then, I appreciate the lift. You'll really save me some time." He stuck out his hand. "I don't think a young lady should offer a ride to a stranger, though. My name's Paul O'Leary."

"Jude Foster. Nice to meet you."

They rode to Bees Creek in Jude's trusty Volkswagen with its ragtop and five-speed transmission. By the time they pulled into the driveway of an old farmhouse, which bore the signs of many coats of paint, Jude was in love.

CHAPTER ONE

DESPITE BEING A WIDOW, Jude Foster O'Leary was content with her life most of the time and even happy on occasion. Unfortunately she'd only experienced a very short period being happily in love. And on this last Saturday of November, at her sister Alex's wedding to the love of her life, Jude had to work at keeping a smile on her face. That was because she'd only been married to Paul O'Leary for two years before he was killed in Afghanistan, and while she was truly happy for her sister, she couldn't help being miserable for herself.

Paul had left her with an infant son who just turned six a few weeks ago. Jude adored Wesley, even though his appearance was enough like his father's that sometimes her eyes hurt just looking at him. And she loved the animals she cared for. She loved and respected her father, and she'd always been close to her two sisters, Alex and Carrie. But as anyone who's ever been in love, or suffered the loss of love, can attest, all that isn't enough.

Alex was the one in white today, while Jude and Carrie, along with Alex's daughter, Lizzie, wore floor-length shimmering pink dresses, perfect for the other two ladies, not so much for Jude, who never chose to shimmer for any occasion. Now that the ceremony was over, the bridal party occupied a banquet-length table affording a view of the guests at Fox Creek Country Club. The Fosters had lived in Fox Creek, Ohio, for three generations, so Jude knew most everyone in attendance.

Except the tall guy in the perfectly fitted three-piece suit whose sandy blond hair was meticulously styled in an I-don't-have-to-try-to-look-like-this way. Jude normally didn't fixate on men, but when this guy had walked by the table earlier, Jude noticed several details, including the overhead chandeliers reflecting their twinkling lights in his polished shoes. She picked him out of the crowd again as she played with her shrimp cocktail.

"Hey, Carrie," she said, gently jabbing her younger sister in the arm. "Who's the slick reality show bachelor sitting at the farthest table to the left?"

Carrie adjusted the glasses that made her look like an adorable nerd. "I've seen him before," she said. "Also that man next to him." She drummed her fingers on the table. "I know now. That's Lawrence Manning. He's a dermatologist at the hospital where Daddy works. They've been friends for years."

Jude coughed. "That young guy is a friend of Daddy's?"

"No, silly. I'm talking about the older guy. I think the younger one is his son. I remember meeting him a couple of years ago when Daddy and I were at a restaurant near the hospital. His name is Ethan or Liam, or…something old-fashioned."

Liam Manning. The name raced to the forefront of Jude's mind, but not in a good way. "It's Liam," she said. "I remember him, too. We were at a party together when we were kids, maybe ten years old. He was a horrid little monster back then."

Carrie exaggerated fanning her face with her hand. "Well, he doesn't look like a monster now."

Unless monsters came with too-perfect bodies, perfect bronzed skin and aristocratic noses.

"I think you should ask him to dance, Jude," Carrie said.

"Me? I don't think this orchestra knows any Western line dances. And I'd only fall over my feet trying to do anything else."

"Don't be silly," Carrie said. "You're graceful on a horse, why not the dance floor?"

"Because grace isn't a transferrable quality," Jude answered. "I think you should ask him to dance. You're the one with light feet."

Carrie gave her the cute, conniving smile that Jude had admired for years. "You saw him first."

"I don't care. I don't want him. I was mostly admiring his shoes. Besides, he's probably married."

"I don't think so. I believe I heard Daddy say that Lawrence's son got a divorce."

"Oh." Jude continued looking Liam's way.

"Doesn't matter, anyway. Looks like neither one of us will get the chance to dance with Mr. Charming," Carrie said. She watched her father approach the young man. "I wonder what Daddy's up to."

Her father walked up to the Mannings' table and put a hand on Liam's shoulder. Martin leaned over, spoke to Lawrence and then into the younger man's ear. Liam nodded, stood and followed Martin out of the room.

"Now, where could they be going?" Jude said, suddenly suspicious of her father's motives. "What does Daddy have in common with that guy? He must be thirty years younger than Daddy."

"I'm sure it doesn't have anything to do with any of us," Carrie said. "Are you going to eat the rest of that shrimp?"

Jude wasn't so sure. Most of what her father did outside his office was about his family. She absently slid the shrimp bowl over to her sister. Martin Foster was a wonderful, generous, supportive father, but she'd bet her sister Alex's shiny new diamond ring that Martin was up to something. And when Martin Foster was up to something, one of his daughters was usually the reason.

"NICE PARTY, SIR," Liam said as he allowed himself to be led toward a quiet alcove away from the festivities. He had a pretty good idea why Martin Foster was taking him away from his table. His father had warned him that Martin wanted to talk to him today about a business matter. The whispered message in his ear confirmed that when Dr. Foster said he needed a few minutes of Liam's time.

"Thank you, son. It's nice to see my Alexis so happy."

Liam sat in a comfortable wing chair and thought about the prime rib he'd signed up for. Though he wasn't friends with any of the Foster daughters, and didn't socialize with Dr. Martin Foster, he'd driven down from Cleveland to accompany his own father to the wedding. He figured the prime rib would be the best part of the afternoon and he didn't want to miss it.

At first Liam didn't know why his father had insisted he come. Dad had lots of friends among this crowd. Liam was an outsider to Dr. Foster. He recalled only one brief meeting at a restaurant with Martin's youngest daughter, Carrie. But when his dad mentioned that Dr. Foster might need his services, he donned his best suit and showed up. Liam was good at what he did, and if Dr. Foster needed financial advice, Liam didn't mind charging for his expertise.

Martin took a seat next to Liam. "Did you know I asked your father to bring you today?" he said.

"Yes, he told me something about your concerns when I got here today. I don't know a lot, and frankly I was confused because I don't know Alex, and I'm not part of the medical crowd."

"This isn't about Alex. Your father tells me you can do more with a dollar than most people can do with a hundred," Martin said. "Is that so?"

Liam smiled. "I'm not a magician, sir. A dollar can only go so far today, and there's not much any of us can do to stretch it. But I like to think I know a bit about managing money."

"Of course you do! A person doesn't graduate with honors from the Wharton Business School without having a great deal of economic savvy."

So Dr. Foster knew something of Liam's background. "Is that what this is about, Dr. Foster? Do you need some financial guidance?" Liam knew that Dr. Foster was taking care of his ailing wife. Perhaps his insurance was running out and funds had become limited. He took out his wallet and fished out a business card. "You're welcome to call my office anytime, and we can set up a meeting."

Martin absently took the card and slipped

it in his shirt pocket. "I won't be coming to your office, Liam. And I don't need help with my finances per se. But someone in my family certainly does."

"Oh?"

"Do you remember my daughter Jude?"

"No, sir, I don't believe we've met."

"Well, you have, but it was twenty years ago. You don't remember a young blonde with her hair in pigtails?"

Liam could almost picture a rangy preadolescent in braids, but he wasn't sure.

"She doesn't look much different today," Martin said. "Still has the pigtails. She's the sister in the middle up on the dais. The one who looks as though she'd like nothing better than to get that dress off and get into a pair of jeans."

"I'll be sure to notice her when we go back inside. Does this meeting have something to do with Jude, then?"

"It does, and I should warn you. Jude can be headstrong, stubborn. I can count the times she's taken my advice on the fingers of one hand."

"I don't follow, sir. I don't know about children, since I don't have any."

Martin gave a wise nod. "Count your blessings for now, son. Here's the thing. I want you to take her in hand, Liam. She's the CEO of a private charitable foundation, and every year the foundation's bottom line gets worse. Jude is penny-wise and pound-foolish if you get my drift. If I let things go on as they have been for the last few years, working to keep her afloat, I might be facing bankruptcy."

"Bankruptcy?"

"Well, maybe that's an exaggeration."

Liam knew Dr. Foster's reputation. He was the best cardiologist in the Cleveland district, and patients came from the tristate area to seek his advice. Bankruptcy? Liam didn't think so. "Foundations are supposed to exist on donations and grants. Are you telling me your personal finances are mixed up in this particular charity?"

"I funded it when Jude set it up. I gave her a considerable amount and a credit line to use while she was getting started."

Naturally any creditors would be happy to accept Martin Foster's IOU. "And you're still backing Jude up when she needs it," Liam said.

"Nothing I can't handle yet, but you know how it is, Liam. This wedding cost a pretty penny. I have expenses because of my wife's illness. I was hoping to retire soon, but until Jude's project is under control, I can't."

"What do you think I can do, Dr. Foster?"

"Teach her how to manage money."

He said it like he was asking Liam to teach her the multiplication tables.

"It's not like she spends it on shoes or purses or any of the fineries other women get so excited about," Martin said. "She barely spends a dime on herself. But she's quick enough to spend hundreds, even thousands on other things, all the dang projects and causes she's supporting."

"What kind of causes?"

"It's hard to keep up. There's stray animals, wounded vets, physically challenged children. She's even supporting a local radio station that she claims is vital to the rural farming community around Fox Creek. And the bills that keep all these charities running end up in Jude's mailbox, or mine, and often require large chunks of money from my personal account to pay them. The worst is the animal upkeep. I've paid for more hay, animal feed and vet services than I care to think about."

Liam knew the answer to his next question

before he even asked it. "Why doesn't she pay the bills out of the foundation's funds? Doesn't she get donations?"

"Oh, she does. Some. But that's where you come in, Liam. I don't know the true answer except to say when bills come due, there is often no money." Martin shook his head. "She's a wonderful girl, don't get me wrong, but she doesn't have a head for numbers and accounting."

And Liam had no desire to get himself in the middle of what was obviously a Foster problem. "Excuse me for saying so, Dr. Foster, but this seems like a family matter to me. Have you tried talking to your daughter?"

Martin sighed. "You don't know how difficult that is for me. You see, Jude lost her husband over five years ago. He was killed in the Middle East fighting for his country. Since then, she's been kind of like a lost soul, always running from one needy cause to another. Besides her son—and she's a good mother—all those good works have become her life. It's not easy for me to get in the middle of all that suffering and try to change things."

"That's tough, I'll agree," Liam said. "But

I still don't see what I can do. What makes you think she'll listen to my financial advice if she doesn't listen to yours?"

"I'm trying to tell you…I haven't given her any!"

"Maybe if you sat her down…"

"I don't have the heart, Liam. She's my baby. I love her. Oh, I've made a few suggestions, tried to guide her, but things don't seem to improve, and I don't want to drive a wedge between Jude and me. That wouldn't help either one of us. I believe there's a lot of hurt inside her, and I'm her father, the one who's supposed to help her, encourage her."

"With due respect, sir, I'm not sure I can help her. I don't even know your daughter."

"That's true right now, but I'm hoping you'll introduce yourself into her life and you, as an outside party, can show her how to manage her money better, or at least cut back on the spending. After all, son, you're the expert, and even Jude can't argue with an expert."

"Well…"

Not letting Liam finish, Martin said, "Your father can't brag enough about you. You can be a voice of reason for Jude. You don't have the problem of emotion to deal with. Once you've gained Jude's trust, I believe she'd listen to you."

"I don't know how true that is, Dr. Foster. My clients come to me willingly. I don't seek them out to try and get them to listen to reason as you're suggesting. And anyway, I have a full-time job with a financial planning firm in Cleveland. I can't take time away from my regular clients to counsel your daughter, especially when you've hinted that she's not the type to be counseled."

"You don't have to give up your clients, Liam. Just come out here on weekends and maybe once or twice during the week. Show an interest in what she's doing, get her to trust you and—"

"While I secretly examine her books?" Liam said. "That's dishonest, Dr. Foster. If not downright impossible."

"Not if you show interest in what she's doing. Don't you first try to gain the trust of anyone you educate about money? Isn't that the first step?"

"Well, yes..."

"Then this is no different. Besides, once you two meet, once the groundwork is set, I intend to tell her why I've brought you in. But it wouldn't do for me to divulge that until she trusts you. Jude is a trusting girl. She just doesn't like to be pushed around. I think she'll like you right off."

Liam didn't have any reason to believe that.

"Think of me as another client, Liam," Martin said. "I'll pay you whatever your hourly rate is." Dr. Foster held up his index finger. "Just don't bully her, son. She may be trusting, but once her mind is stuck on something, she won't let anyone tell her what to do."

Slightly offended, Liam said, "I don't think I bully anyone."

"No, I'm sure you don't. You seem like a nice young fellow. Now, just go on out there and have your dinner and then ask Jude to dance. She's a pretty girl, and aside from scoot-booting around a Western bar once in a while, I don't think she's danced with anyone since Paul left for the service." Dr Foster chuckled. "You may decide this is the most pleasant job you've ever had."

Even though Liam believed Dr. Foster truly loved his daughter but just felt inadequate to help her, he doubted that this assignment would be easy. During this conversation Liam had conjured up one very clear image of an afternoon twenty years ago at a doctors' picnic. He remembered a curly-haired pigtailed girl shoving him onto the ground when he was poking a snake with a stick. He hadn't been hurting the snake, and besides, it was a snake… But the pigtailed girl obviously decided the snake needed a champion.

That was the only contact Liam had ever had with Jude Foster, Jude Something-Else now, and he'd ended up covered in mud, and hating girls for the next six months.

"Now, go on before your dinner gets cold," Dr. Foster said. "It cost me twenty-four ninety-five a plate, and for that price, you should eat it while it's hot. And remember my involvement with you is a private matter between you and me, for now. Jude doesn't need to know yet."

Uncertain about this plan, Liam returned to his table, sat next to his father and ate his tepid prime rib.

"So you talked with Martin?" Dr. Manning asked.

"He wants to hire me for a short while," Liam said. "But I guess you already know that."

"I hope you agreed," Dr. Manning said. "There's not a better man than Martin Foster, but he's a pushover when it comes to his daughters. And Jude, the middle one, is tougher to handle than the other two. According to Martin, if left alone, without some solid, timely advice, she'll run that foundation of hers into the ground and Martin along with it."

"But I don't feel right about this whole thing. Dr. Foster wants me to keep our relationship a secret until I've gotten closer to Jude, until she trusts me."

"Sounds to me like a good way to approach this," Lawrence said. "Why alienate the girl right at the start?"

Liam frowned. "What do you know about her?"

His father smiled in a guarded way that made Liam uncomfortable. "Martin doesn't criticize his daughters for the most part, but I know he's not used to opening up to Jude. That's where you come in. And since Martin is likely to pay you well for this assignment, I wouldn't want to prejudice you with idle gossip about the girl."

"So without telling me some of that gossip you've heard, you're warning me that if I work with Jude, I might be better off to use a whip and a chair rather than a mechanical pencil and spreadsheet."

"You should talk to her tonight, see what you

think for yourself. Women have always liked you, son. You're clean, cultured, honorable…"

"Staid? Boring?" An image of his ex-wife came to mind, and he realized she might add other adjectives that could describe an Eagle Scout.

"No! I didn't mean that at all. Could be Jude will take to you like a mama bear to honey."

The analogy was not a comfortable one. Didn't bears eat honey? And besides, Lawrence's facial expression suggested that he truly might have no faith in his son being able to get along with Jude.

"You'd be doing this as a personal favor to me, Liam," his father said. "Martin and I go all the way back to medical school. I don't suppose I have a better friend than he is, and he needs help with this situation. It's gotten out of control."

"I guess I believe that," Liam said.

"Besides, you want to go to that economic conference in Stockholm this spring, don't you?" Lawrence added. "If you straighten Jude out, Martin will be so grateful, you'll be able to afford a first-class plane ticket."

Dr. Manning patted his son's back. "At the end of the night, if you want them, I'll give you my impressions about Jude. There probably are a few things you should know. Combined with what you learn yourself, you can decide what you want to do. But if it makes any difference, I'm counting on you, son. Friendships mean a lot to me."

Nothing like putting on the pressure, Liam thought. He owed his father for sticking by him during his divorce. Lawrence had called his son every day to ask how he was, and Liam didn't know how he would have gotten through those difficult days without his dad's concern. And Liam figured he could straighten out this foundation in a matter of a few visits. He was that good. Besides all that, Dr. Foster had promised he'd tell his daughter about their alliance soon.

The wedding cake had barely been cut when Liam stood in line to get his piece. He chose a small slice and turned to go back to his table. And ran into Jude.

No time like the present to get to know Martin's middle daughter.

"Excuse me," she said, stepping out of his way.

Liam stopped her by placing his hand on her elbow. She turned toward him and he stared into the softest, bluest eyes he'd ever seen. She didn't look like an obstinate, my-way-or-the-highway girl. "My fault," he said, giving her his brightest smile. "My name is Liam Manning. I don't really know many people here. Would you like to share our cake together?"

"I really can't," she said. "I have to give a toast soon."

He tried again. "We're actually not strangers. We met at a picnic years ago."

"I remember. You were tormenting a defenseless snake."

Was she kidding? "Tormenting?" he said. "I was doing no such thing. Besides, it was just a snake."

"Yeah, and if a snake bit you, one of his buddies would say, 'Don't worry about it, pal. It was just a human.'"

Oh yeah, she wasn't kidding.

"Anyway, snake torture is enough to make me wonder about you now. Like for instance, what did you and my father talk about in the hallway?"

So she'd seen them leave the party. He tried to speak, to come up with a convincing stall, but his jaw seemed to tighten up. He put down the dainty china plate that held his cake and reached for Jude's hand. "Let's dance."

CHAPTER TWO

JUDE PULLED HER hand back. "I'd rather not."
She glanced down at her elegant so-not-her
dress. "I'm part of the bridal party. I have
duties."

"But you do dance?" he asked. "And I'm sure
the bride won't mind if you have a little fun."

Truthfully, except for a modest skill at
line dancing, she wasn't much of a dancer.
Her mother had paid for the same ballroom
lessons for all three of her daughters. The
glides and swishes and dips had looked great
when executed by Alexis and Carrie. When
Jude tried to do them, she looked like a horse
who'd thrown a shoe.

"Everybody dances," she said. "But it's not
my proudest achievement."

Refusing to take the hint, he suddenly had
her hand tucked into his, and they were walk-
ing toward the dance floor. "Forgive me, but I

feel the need to convince you that I'm not the snake torturer that you believe I am."

"And dancing will do that?"

"Among other things, I hope." He continued on a path to the dance floor. "These are all your friends and family, right?"

"Yes." She made a quick summary of the guests in the room. How many could she actually call friends? "Most of them." She frowned. "Some, anyway."

"Then no one will be critical of your dancing."

She stared into glimmering brown eyes that seemed lit from within by tiny gold sparklers. What man had eyes that perfect? She shouldn't trust this guy. "Don't count on it," she said.

They stopped on the fringe of the dance floor. Jude couldn't think of a way to escape.

"Everyone's having fun," he said. "And you just pointed out that you're an important member of the wedding party. Joining in and adding to the general spirit of the occasion is part of your job, isn't it?"

She couldn't argue. Alex had told her, "It's just one day, Jude. I'm counting on you. You can at least pretend to have fun." If spinning around the dance floor one time would endear her to Alex, she could do it. Besides, *pretending* to have fun was what she did. She was good at it. Liam held up one hand to hold hers and slipped his arm around her back. And then, when he should have been gliding or whatever, he just remained still, staring into her eyes.

"What?" she said.

"Weren't you taller?" he asked. "When I watched you walk down the aisle a while ago, I could have sworn you were tall. Now I wouldn't peg you at more than five and a half feet."

"I was tall then."

"What?"

She raised the hem of her gauzy, satiny concoction of shiny pink, showing her bare legs almost to her knees. Laced securely to each foot was a simple but expensive running shoe. She almost laughed out loud when she saw his shocked expression.

"If you want me to put the stilts back on, you'll have to walk me over to my table where they're hidden under the drape. But then I won't dance, so it's a catch-22."

He fidgeted with the layers of dress in her

hands, trying to smooth the fabric so it covered her legs again. Was he embarrassed to be seen with a woman who'd abandoned her high heels? Too bad. Jude had never enjoyed the fashion sense of her two sisters, even though they'd tried. The shoes for the wedding had cost her fifty bucks, and they would end up gathering dust in the back of her closet.

"No, no. It's fine. The shoes are fine," he said, returning his arms to dance position. "We'll dance a few minutes and then adjourn to the tennis courts outside where we can play a couple of sets."

She almost smiled. After about thirty seconds of keeping time to the five-piece orchestra, Jude had decided that maybe she was a dancer after all. Or maybe Liam Manning was so accomplished at leading that she didn't feel like the wallflower with two left feet. His arm pressed with authority on her back, and her hand felt light as a feather in his. His feet seemed to move with precision, stepping around and between her own so that her toes were protected while she managed to follow his unspoken directions.

At one point, he grinned down at her. "See? You're dancing like a pro," he said.

She chuckled. "Let's not get carried away with the flattery, Liam."

What is this guy's game? she wondered. He seemed to be a mixture of propriety and charm, and Jude still didn't trust him. She had a hard time trusting anyone who didn't smell a little musty and have straw stuck to his boots. Although Liam Manning could possibly change her mind about all that.

She didn't ask to sit down after the promised spin around the dance floor. Instead he slowed the pace to an easy-breathing, conversational level. "You never told me," she began. "What's going on between you and my father?"

"We're back to that, are we? I hope my explanation won't make you angry."

"I suppose we'll have to see about that."

Liam cleared his throat. "Your father just asked me if I remembered you from an outing twenty years ago. I told him I didn't, but then you reminded me of the snake incident. He mentioned how pretty you are and said I should ask you to dance."

She grimaced. "Oh, Dad."

"It's okay," Liam said. "You are pretty, and I would have asked anyway."

Some women might have ruffled feathers after hearing such an admission. Obviously Martin Foster didn't believe Jude could snag her own dance partner, so he decided to fix her up. But Jude wasn't terribly upset. Making certain his daughter enjoyed a dance or two was the kind of goal Martin Foster would try to achieve on a day like this. Jude hardly ever lost patience with her father. Everything he did was from love.

She nodded, accepting that she was the daughter least likely to have dance partners lined up. "I see. And are you sorry you got stuck with the job?"

He smiled again, showing a row of perfect white teeth. If she ever found herself with Liam in good lighting, she was going to study that face until she found a flaw. There had to be one.

"Not at all. Despite your reluctance to dance with me, I think we've done quite well."

So did Jude. He stopped dancing and walked with her out the door to the country club portico. "I could use some fresh air," he said. "It's unseasonably warm for November, but in that dress, you might be too cold."

"No. I'm okay."

"Good. Let's find a place where we can sit and get acquainted."

"This is as good a place as any." She hopped up on the concrete railing surrounding the patio, pulled her skirt to her knees and dangled her sneakered feet as if she were anticipating plunging them into a cool stream.

"Aren't you worried about your dress?"

"I am worried—about the next person who'll have to wear it once I drop it off at Goodwill."

He jumped up beside her. "I take it you're not a, what do they call it these days? A fashionista?"

"I suppose I'm not. I buy most of my clothes at Winnie's Western Wear, and I get my son's school uniforms at Target. Everything else I buy online. I don't have time to traipse through malls."

She clutched her hands in her lap and lifted her face to catch the breeze coming through the fall maples and oak trees. There was no place more beautiful than northern Ohio in autumn. When a strand of hair whipped across her face, she tucked it behind her ear. The elaborate French something-or-other the hairstylist had perfected for her this morning was probably hanging on by a few last-gasp pins.

She and Liam sat on the railing without speaking for a moment. They both looked into the country club where wedding guests were still dancing and lining up for cake. Wesley, who was probably as uncomfortable in a tux as she was in her pink fluffy dress, was dancing with his aunt Carrie. His head only came to her chest, but they were keeping perfect time to the music. The photographer was busy snapping everyone in the throes of Alexis's marital bliss.

"The kid in the tux who was ring bearer," Liam said. "That's the son you mentioned?"

"It is."

"Cute kid."

This guy seemed to say all the right things. Jude sighed with unexpected contentment. She felt more like herself outside, away from the festivities. And she was happy for Alexis. She deserved this wedding and this fairy-tale beginning of a new life. She and Daniel, the state's newest young senator, were perfect for each other, and despite many problems, they'd found their way back together to share a life and a daughter.

Amazing, Jude thought. Two of the three Foster daughters had been widowed at a young age. Alexis had lost her beloved Teddy almost a year ago, and Jude had lost her Paul. Well, life had turned around for her Allie-belle today, and sitting next to this dark blond, good-looking guy, Jude had the first warm flickering of hope for a happy ending for herself one day. But the feeling was just a flicker, nothing upon which to base a future. Paul was gone. He was never coming back. Part of her would never forgive him for that. Part of her knew she would never experience the same love again.

"So, what do you do?" The voice that came from beside her and interrupted her thoughts was low and just slightly scratchy as if this dressed-up man put hot sauce on everything he ate, just like she did. No way. He had to be a hollandaise kind of guy. She didn't answer right away because explaining what she did was difficult for some people to understand, so he added, "I mean, you don't like walk-ing malls…"

"I said I don't have time for shopping," she repeated. "But you're right. I don't like it, ei-ther." She turned her head to be able to read his reaction when she said, "Actually I run a small farm. In addition, I'm the CEO of a charitable foundation."

"No kidding?" Liam said. "That's interesting. Is it a national or a local foundation?"

"Local. Really local. We benefit mostly people from this area. I started the foundation five years ago and named it after my late husband, Paul O'Leary. He was killed in Afghanistan."

His eyes widened as he drew in a quick breath. "The foundation is named after your late husband?"

"That's right."

"So you're continuing work that Paul started when he was alive?"

"Not exactly. I…that is, *we* support many causes, but I always take into consideration whether I believe Paul would approve."

"So your day is basically spent in an office while you decide which projects are worthy of foundation support."

She laughed. "Do I look like a person who would be glued to a desk?" He couldn't be more wrong. Jude's day started at 6:00 a.m. By eight o'clock, it was time to rush Wesley to school, she'd fed one hungry boy and dozens of animals, checked fences, gathered eggs and milked a very large but thankfully docile cow. And that was if something didn't happen to interrupt her.

"You've oversimplified what I do," she said. "I try to be careful with the money that comes in. I analyze each proposal for its merit. And I have to answer to a board of directors, as well. So if you're thinking that I'm a wealthy embezzler…"

"No, of course I don't think that. But you did say you were the chief administrator, so the buck must stop…or leave the foundation's checking account at your desk."

Jude did make all the decisions about spending so she answered honestly, "I suppose that's true."

"Who is on your board of directors?" Liam asked. "Anyone I might know?"

"You know my father. Maybe you know my sister Carrie. My son, Wesley, is on the board, as well. I realize he's just a child, but his insights are often spot-on. He has definite opinions about children's issues. And I hope he'll want to carry on after I'm gone."

"And your father and Carrie aren't active in helping with decisions?"

"Not so much. My sister works for the US Forest Service, and she's sent all over the country. My father is a doctor, as you know. Neither one of them is a hands-on adviser."

"I'm something of an economist, and I know a bit about how foundations work," Liam said. "I might be interested in donating to one of your funds. It would be a needed tax break for me."

"We'd be happy to have your money."

"I'm cautious with it," he added, "so I'd have to know more about the charities you contribute to." He paused a moment before adding, "Maybe I can come out one day this week and take a look at the charities you fund."

Suddenly suspicious, Jude wondered if Liam had an angle. Was he an IRS investigator? They weren't usually so underhanded about their searches. And anyway, she had nothing to hide. Her father's accountant had made certain she'd filed all the proper papers with the government. Maybe he was just interested in what she did, although that didn't seem logical. The only people who paid attention to the Paul O'Leary Foundation were the ones who stood to benefit from it, or the handful of small philanthropists she counted on to keep going. Maybe Liam was hitting on her? No, impossible.

But if this educated, subtly charming "economist" wanted to see the foundation at work, why should she stop him? His money was as needed as anyone else's. "I suppose that would be okay."

She smiled to herself, thinking how Carrie would interpret this exchange. She would choose to believe that her hermit of a sister was finally encouraging a man. Nothing could be further from the truth. Other than the persistent clerk at the feed store and one of the construction workers over at Aurora Spindell's bed-and-breakfast, no fella had shown an interest in Jude for a long time. Or, as Carrie suggested, she didn't notice if one did. Jude didn't date, and she'd all but forgotten the rules and wiles of flirting.

"When should I come?" Liam asked.

She bounced down from the railing. "You're welcome to come anytime, as long as I know so I can be certain to be there. But if you come in the day, you'd best ditch the suit for a pair of jeans and some boots. And it won't hurt if you can swing a hammer and walk fast to keep up with me."

"I never knew running a foundation required such physical work."

"Did you forget? I happen to run a farm, too. Nothing happens with the foundation until all the animals are fed."

"Okay. I'll be by on Monday a bit after noon. How's that?"

"Works for me. Do you know where my dad's property, Dancing Falls, is located?"

He indicated he did.

"Just come there and drive around until you see the barn." She cupped her hand around her ear. "Did you hear that? Someone just called for Jude O'Leary's toast to the bride and groom. Guess that's my cue." She crossed the portico but stopped in the doorway. "Thanks for the dance, Liam Manning. You're very good at it, and I'm actually not as bad as I thought I'd be."

He gave her another winning smile. "My pleasure, Jude O'Leary."

There had to be a flaw somewhere in this man's character, and on Monday, if he showed up, Jude would certainly look for it. But for the rest of the weekend, she might enjoy imagining a head-to-toe appraisal of Mr. Perfect. And if he didn't show, which was more likely, no harm done.

LIAM IMMEDIATELY SOUGHT out Martin Foster. While he was trying to convince Liam to help, how could the good doctor have forgotten one vital piece of information?

"Well, how did it go?" Martin actually found Liam on the patio and put his arm around the younger man's shoulders. "I saw you two out here getting close."

Liam flinched. "Not half as close as your daughter is to the foundation she runs," Liam snapped.

"What are you talking about?"

"You could have told me that her charities are all under the umbrella of her dead husband's name! It's almost as if she's built a shrine to Paul O'Leary."

Martin managed to look guilty as he dropped his hand to his side. "I didn't think it was important. The name of the foundation has nothing to do with its financial problems."

"Sorry, but I disagree. This is too personal now. You're asking me to come between a woman and her deceased husband, a man who is probably regarded around here as a national hero."

"Paul has been gone for more than five years," Martin said. "It's time for my daughter to move on. And it's definitely time for her to be more sensible about this foundation."

"Helping lonely widows move on is generally not the job of an economist." Liam let the doctor's words sink in. "But at least now I understand what this is about," he said. "You want to heal your daughter's heart as much as you want to curtail the spending."

"I wouldn't mind it."

"Again, I feel I should remind you, I'm not a grief counselor."

Martin sighed. "I only want your services as an economist. Jude has family to help her with the rest. You leave her heart up to us." His voice mellowed. "We have an agreement, Liam. I'm counting on you. This is the first step, a vital first step in enabling my daughter to get on with her life, as well as putting a Band-Aid on the endless spending."

"But I'm a stranger to her," Liam said.

"Not really. She's met you before…"

Right. Truly auspicious.

"And she knows you're a family friend.

She'll listen to you. I know she will. Don't disappoint me now, son. If you back out of the deal, I'll just have to find someone else to examine those books and steer Jude in the right direction. And I don't want anyone else. I want you."

Liam sighed. This was a ticklish situation. Jude was doing her good deeds to honor her dead husband. That meant she wasn't exactly impersonal or impartial about her decisions. She no doubt made monetary decisions based on emotion. What would Paul want? But still, he could help her. As an outsider, he could keep an open mind, something she might have problems doing. He could influence her, help her to be rational. Liam could look at this assignment, this *favor*, as a profitable job, couldn't he, despite pressure from both Dr. Foster and his father?

Martin smiled. "Does that look mean you're going ahead with our plan?"

Liam closed his eyes a moment, took a deep breath. "Yes, I'll give it a try."

"Wonderful. So, again, how did the first meeting with Jude go?"

"We talked and it went fine," he said. "She seems like a nice girl. In fact, I'm stopping at the barn on Monday to find out more about the foundation."

"Good, good. Get her to show you the books, see where all my money's going and give her some pointers." Martin stared at his middle daughter as she picked up the microphone to speak. "Don't intimidate her, though. That's not what I want. I picked you for this job because there's a gentlemanly quality about you that I like. Jude hasn't been happy for a while, and I don't want you making it worse."

So besides throwing Liam under the bus, the good doctor was practically threatening him? But unknowingly Martin had just voiced Liam's own concerns—that he might end up making Jude's attachment to the foundation even stronger, her loneliness even worse, especially if she felt emotionally connected to every dime she gave out. "I'll certainly try," he said. "But remember, you said you would level with her as soon as possible. Monday wouldn't be soon enough."

"Not so soon, Liam. She won't open up with me looking over her shoulder. She thinks I trust her judgment, and if she believes I'm questioning her ability, it will cause a rift between us. I know my daughter. This will work much better if she gets to know you, if she appreciates your expertise in this area. Then she won't just be dealing with an interfering daddy."

Liam didn't like deception of any kind. He dealt with figures, and numbers didn't lie, but he had to agree with Dr. Foster in this case. Family situations were often delicate. Jude actually might accept criticism and advice from someone like him much more readily than she would her father. Or she might not.

"I know a lot about how foundations work, and I can help her, but I'll be more comfortable if we don't let this game play out for too long. You've got to be honest with Jude once I've set the groundwork for improvement."

"I'll tell her everything soon enough," Martin said. "But the first thing we need to do is pinpoint the problems, get her to see where mistakes are being made. And I'll step in and tell her I hired you when the time is right, a few days, maybe a week at most."

A week? Liam supposed he could play along with the doctor's plan for a week. Like Martin, Liam believed that the spending was out of control and Jude did need sound guidance. Her father obviously cared for her. Liam had promised his father, and he definitely wanted to go to that world economic conference in Stockholm… "Okay, Dr. Foster. One week. And then no more charades."

Liam was met by his father when he came back into the dining hall. "You met Jude?" Lawrence asked.

"I danced with her," Liam said. "And then we talked outside for a few minutes."

"And you're going to help Martin with this problem?"

Liam nodded. "We'll see how it goes."

"Okay, then," Lawrence said. "I told you I'd fill you in on a few details I've learned about Jude through the years. Have a seat."

"Don't worry about it," Liam said. This arrangement was already tinged with deception. He didn't want to add gossip to the mix. "I don't anticipate any big problems."

"Okay, but one word of warning. This is a business deal, son. Martin is paying you handsomely. Don't get interested in Jude romantically. Go after that pretty little one, Carrie. Martin wants her to stick around home anyway."

"I'm not interested in anyone, Dad," Liam

said. "It was just a conversation. But even if it were more, I don't think I'm in need of romantic advice. Neither one of us has been very successful in that arena."

"No, I suppose not. But your mother never approved of that daughter. Always thought she was wild and daring, even going so far as to get in scrapes with the law. She's nothing like the other two. She's not your type, son. That's all I'm saying."

"Good, because I don't think I'd like it if you were saying anything else."

He walked away from his father and tried to tamp his irritation. Suddenly he felt the oddest urge to defend a bridesmaid in running shoes.

CHAPTER THREE

"GOOD MORNING AGAIN, MAGGIE." With a breakfast tray in his hand, Martin Foster crossed the soft plum-colored carpeting and stopped at his wife's bedside. He set the tray on a nightstand and fixed Maggie's tea the way she liked it—a little cream, one sugar.

"Rebecca is going to be late this morning," he said, explaining why he would feed Maggie instead of her nurse. "But that's fine with me, gives us a chance to talk more about the wedding."

He glanced over at the twin bed situated close to his wife's larger one. Martin slept in the narrow bed every night now that the master bedroom had been converted to a sickroom. The sheets were still rumpled, but the weekend nurse would see to light housekeeping chores.

He tipped a teaspoon of tea toward Maggie's mouth. She opened, swallowed and seemed eager for more.

"Later today, I'm going to make some large prints of photos I took with my phone so you can see how grand the wedding was, how happy our Alexis is with her new husband." He hoped the pictures would stir some reaction in his wife. Maybe in some deep, quiet place that the Alzheimer's had taken her, she would recognize the family who still loved her. But probably not.

He dipped a toast corner in tea and offered it to Maggie. She chewed automatically, swallowed. He followed that bite with scrambled eggs. So far, his Maggie was eating well this morning. He wouldn't feel so badly about leaving her to go out for a while to run errands.

"Carrie's leaving tomorrow," he told Maggie. "This time, the forestry department is sending her to Michigan for an assignment. We're lucky Carrie's employers are so understanding about her asthma. They try to send her places where the triggers are seasonal so she can avoid them. The cool temperatures in Michigan this time of year should be beneficial.

"I wish I could think of a way to persuade

her to change careers and find a job that is safer for her but you know how determined she is. She's so much like you in that respect. She thinks she can take on the world, one tree at a time. Our Carrie only seems to flourish in the outdoors where every breath can threaten her health. But I'll load up her duffel bag with medications and call her every week to be sure she's taking them."

Martin raised his wife's head and put the teacup to her lips. She blinked rapidly while taking several long swallows.

"Now, Jude is another matter," he said, scooping scrambled eggs onto a spoon. "I took a big step with regard to her yesterday. I've hired a crackerjack financial planner to look at the foundation's books. Lawrence Manning's boy, Liam."

He searched Maggie's face for some sign of disapproval. If Maggie hadn't been ill, she probably would have chastised him for putting any part of Jude's future in the hands of a relative of Alicia Manning's. Maggie had never gotten on well with Lawrence's now ex-wife, whom Maggie referred to as "Fox Creek's self-appointed royalty." When Lawrence and Alicia divorced, Maggie had privately congratulated Lawrence.

"Liam is going to take a look at the books, see if he can't curb some of the spending."

He paused as if waiting for Maggie to say something. Realizing his foolishness, he said, "I know what you'd say to me if you could speak. You'd tell me I should just talk to her myself. Well, I can't. You were always the one who disciplined the girls. And as far as Jude is concerned, you always saw an inner spiritual strength in her that I never fully appreciated. 'Our little fighter,' you called her. Our Old Soul." He chuckled. "You didn't even seem upset when we drove to the police station to pick her up after some bit of nonsense, though you grounded her for weeks.

"I know she's strong. I know her heart is as big as Dancing Falls. But to me she's wounded, Maggie. Her hurt goes deep, and I can't take a chance that something I say will drive us apart." He sighed. "But I can't let her continue spending as if there's no end to the money, no matter how worthy the causes are."

Martin stroked Maggie's curly gray hair. The girls insisted that a beautician come once a week to wash and style their mother's hair.

"Liam is coming over tomorrow sometime," he said. "Supposedly the kid has a brilliant mind. He'll be able to steal a quick look at the books and figure out where Jude's going wrong. I know the simple answer. She's giving away more money than she's bringing in. But telling her to let some of the charities go would be nearly impossible for me, hopefully not for Liam. Once Jude sets her mind to helping someone, she won't quit. I guess that's the fighter in her. And she finds it just as hard to say no."

His phone rang and he took the instrument from his pocket. Checking the screen, he said, "It's Aurora from next door. I'm going to bring her up here to meet you soon. The girls like her a lot."

He connected. "Hello, Aurora. I can almost smell your cinnamon rolls from here. Save me one…" He held the phone away from his ear and grimaced. "What's that? A goat is eating your fern?"

Background noise kept him from hearing Aurora's words clearly. Her parrot was squawking up a storm. A lady guest was screaming that the goat tried to eat her skirt. And the goat—Martin didn't know which one, but he was certain it had a name, since Jude named all her animals—was braying with enthusiasm.

"I'll pick up Jude and be right there," he said. Remembering Aurora's penchant for using anything as a weapon, he said, "For heaven's sake, Aurora, don't hit the goat with a toilet plunger. Jude will never speak to us again."

Martin called his housekeeper upstairs to sit with Maggie until the nurse arrived in a few minutes. Then he dialed Jude's number as he sped to the barn. She and Wesley were waiting in front when he circled to pick them up. When Martin stopped, the two piled into his SUV. "Would you rather I take my truck?" she asked her father. "After eating ferns and skirts, the goat might—"

"No, there isn't time." Martin glanced back at his pristine SUV. "Let's just hope his breakfast didn't upset its stomach." He stared across the seat at his daughter, who was still buttoning her jacket. "And I hope to heck this goat doesn't have a hankering for parrot."

"I think the culprit is female—Eloise," Jude said, winding her long hair into a knot on top of her head. "I took a quick look around and didn't see her with the herd. She likes to wander anyway and might have discovered a new hole in the fence."

Dollar signs danced in front of Martin's eyes. He'd just repaired the fence a few months ago when Jude's dog, Mutt, invaded Aurora's property. The incident had not been a particularly favorable way to meet his new neighbor who was setting up her bed-and-breakfast business. Thank goodness Aurora hadn't held a grudge, and in fact, had become a considerate and helpful neighbor. Martin didn't know how she would react to a full-fledged goat invasion.

BY THE TIME they'd entered Aurora's property and driven around back, the situation had calmed. A middle-aged man had corralled Eloise with a cotton rope and was keeping her from further dietary damage.

Jude was the first out of the SUV. She skidded to a stop in front of her goat and placed a hand on each side of Eloise's face. "You are one naughty goat," she said. "Look at the trouble you've caused." She took the end of the rope from the man. "I'm sorry about all this," she said. "I'll remove the nuisance right away."

"No problem," the man responded. "Gives me something to talk about at the golf club when I get home to Florida." He handed his camera to Jude. "Do you know how to take a picture? I'd like to have proof that I tamed this mighty beast. Can you get one of me and the goat?"

"I should be able to," Jude said.

"And another one with you in the picture. It would be nice if it looks like you're praising me for my bravery and quick thinking," the man added.

"Sure." Martin watched in awe as Jude took the first picture and then squeezed close to the man with Eloise between them. The adults smiled. Jude smiled at the man. The goat contentedly chewed whatever had last gone in her mouth. Jude snapped a photo. Then as if realizing she'd thrown on yesterday's barn clothes in her hurry to get downstairs this morning, she backed away rather than offend the man's sense of smell. Her jeans had chicken feed stuck to the legs, and her shirt wasn't even buttoned below her waist. She quickly tied the ends of the shirt into a makeshift bow.

Aurora came across the yard and stopped in front of Jude. "I'm sorry for the panic, dear," she said. "The situation has been under control for the last few minutes."

"No problem. You are definitely within your rights to expect an absence of goat on your property." Realizing she was still the object of attention for Aurora's guests, she walked Eloise toward Martin's SUV. "Hey, Wes," she called to her son. "Help Grandpa and me get this monster into the back."

Wesley ambled over as if the last thing he wanted to do was lift the hindquarters of a goat. He'd probably been sleeping off wedding festivities when his mother woke him with an urgent call to "Get up!" this morning. Jude lowered a pair of ramps from the back of the SUV to the ground, and the three of them got Eloise inside. Then she and Martin went over to apologize once more to Aurora.

"Looks like we've got another hole," Jude said. "But don't worry, Aurora. I'll keep Eloise on a leash until it's mended."

"And you get that helper of yours, Johnny Ray, to fix it, Jude," Martin said, knowing he sounded unnaturally irritable. "I've spent enough on fence mending for one season."

"Sure, Daddy. I'm on it." She gazed around the now serene backyard scene. "Any damages, Aurora?" she asked. "Did Eloise eat someone's smartphone or chew off a finger?"

"No, nothing so bad as that," Aurora said. "Why don't you have some tea and a cinnamon roll?"

Jude looked like she was about to accept the offer, but a pointed glare from her father followed by a nervous glance at the goat-filled SUV changed her mind. "Thanks, Aurora, but I think I'll get Eloise home," she said. "Dad, you can stay and I'll pick you up in an hour."

He agreed to the plan, watched his daughter and grandson drive his vehicle around to the front of Aurora's home and then allowed Aurora to lead him inside her sunroom to a table set with a floral tablecloth and a pitcher of autumn wildflowers. His irritation suddenly vanished. Sometimes there was nothing so sweet as a glass of tea and a moment's rest at Aurora's Attic Bed-and-Breakfast.

"I don't know what I'm going to do with that one," he said to Aurora. "Her projects are getting out of hand. She must have two-dozen goats over there."

"Besides you, Wesley and the girls, Marty, those animals are Jude's family. You can understand her attachment to them." She smiled. "Not that I'm looking forward to another goat trespassing on my property anytime in the near future."

"You've been very patient, Aurora. The girls are lucky to have you as a friend." In the short time she'd lived next door, Aurora had managed to defuse several difficult situations in the Foster family. And Martin had found solace in being able to communicate with someone near his own age.

"And I'm lucky to have them," Aurora said. "Now sit down and have some tea. I want to ask you about that young fella I saw Jude talking to at the wedding yesterday. They looked so cute together. If you ask me, a little love affair is just what that girl needs to get her mind off goats."

"Aurora! A love affair?"

She laughed. "Don't be such an old fuddy-duddy, Martin. You know what I mean. Jude needs romance in her life. Do you think it might happen?"

No, Martin hadn't thought that could happen. He'd point-blank told Liam that Jude's heart was a family matter. Besides, Jude was still in love with her husband, probably always would be. Was that a healthy way to live her life? Probably not. But Liam Manning hooked up with his wild, good-hearted Jude? No way. Three-piece suits did not go well with chaps and boots. And he wasn't at all sure how he would feel if they were somehow attracted to each other.

CHAPTER FOUR

LIFE WAS FILLED with too many bittersweet moments. That was how Jude felt almost every day. Those moments happened when she visited her mother and remembered when Maggie Foster was vibrant and brilliant and loving. Or when she waved her sister Alexis off in a limousine to begin her honeymoon. Or when she thought of Paul, as she so often did, in so many ways. The freshest of the bittersweets occurred Monday morning as she shared a last cup of coffee with her sister Carrie before the airport shuttle came to get her.

"Don't forget to take your meds," Jude said. "I saw Dad stuffing your duffel with them this morning."

"I won't forget." Carrie smiled over the rim of her mug. "Does everyone in my family think I enjoy having asthma?"

Jude chuckled. "Point taken."

"Now, let's get back to the subject of Liam Manning."

"What do you want to say about Liam?"

"He's gorgeous. How's that for a start?"

"He's decent looking, I'll agree with that. But I'm not interested in him, gorgeous or otherwise."

"So why are you so upset that he might not show up at the barn today?"

"Upset? I'm not upset." Jude had confided in her sister this morning about the possibility of Liam coming out to the farm. Jude didn't believe he would and had admitted this to Carrie. Since leaving the reception on Saturday night, she'd tried to put the entire incident out of her mind. Meeting someone on a starstruck night of love and having it actually materialize into something was not Jude O'Leary luck.

"Besides," Jude said. "He was just being polite at the wedding. Dad coerced him into asking me to dance, and I guess small talk was a part of the deal."

"But he said he was interested in your charities," Carrie reminded her.

"I can't believe that's true. *Oh, here, Liam. Here are my goats. Aren't they adorable?*"

Jude mimicked her own voice. "Come on, Carrie, any interest he may have shown was just small talk."

"All right. Maybe he's not interested in your charities," Carrie said, her eyes twinkling. "Maybe his interest has everything to do with you."

Jude snorted, one of her unladylike habits. "Care Bear, be reasonable. If Liam wanted to date a Foster girl, he'd sure as heck pick you. Cute, petite, soft-spoken and smart. You'd be Liam's dream girl."

"According to who?" Carrie said. "He never even spoke to me at the wedding."

"Because, unlike me, you were never lacking a dance partner! The poor man never had a chance to whisk you onto the floor."

"I'll bet he shows up," Carrie said. "And just in case, I think you should put on a bit of makeup…" She held up her hand as if she believed Jude were going to protest the notion. "Not a lot, just a touch. A little blush, some eye shadow."

Jude leaned back in her chair and threw her hands up. "Will you look at me for once, Carrie? I mean really look! I wear makeup. I have some on now, and you can't even tell."

Carrie tried to appear guilty. As usual, the expression came across as Care Bear cute. "Oh. Now I see it. Maybe a little *more* blush…"

"I am not going to any fuss for a man who's not going to show," Jude said.

"Okay, have it your way. Be stubborn and negative and don't take advantage of this opportunity if it should happen today."

"I'm not stupid, Carrie. Even I recognize that Liam is a good-looking guy with a lot going for him. If he comes by, I'll try to be all girly and sweet."

"And phony."

Jude rolled her eyes. Pleasing Carrie was not easy.

"Just be yourself, Jude. That's the person he talked to at the wedding." Carrie got up and looked out the kitchen window. "The shuttle is coming up the drive, so I've got to go. I'll call you tonight. Let me know if you hear from the honeymooners."

Carrie slung her duffel over one shoulder, her purse over the other, and picked up her suitcase.

"Let me carry those things for you," Jude said.

"Stop it! I can manage my own things. Quit

babying me, Jude. And get a life, will you? I worry about you. Try some positive thinking for a change, and good things will happen."

"I suppose you know of a magic potion for that, don't you, Carrie, or a crystal I can wear around my neck?"

Carrie fingered her own good luck talisman around her neck. "You're impossible. Why do I even try?"

Jude hugged her sister over all her gear. "Don't worry about me, sis. I've got everything I want out at that barn with my cozy apartment above just right for me and Wes."

"You live with horses and noise, and…"

"You're wrong, Carrie. I live in peace and solitude. Remember when we had a full-time groom in that apartment? We had six horses. Now we have three and taking care of them is a piece of cake. My life is full. The only thing that would make it more perfect is if I'd have you here for more than a few days at a time."

Carrie leaned back and stared into her sister's eyes. "And Liam Manning. He might make it more perfect."

"You don't give up, do you?"

"Not where you're concerned." Carrie gave

her sister one last smile. "Take care of yourself. Talk to you tonight."

The shuttle taking Carrie to the Cleveland airport was soon just a cloud of dust. Jude missed her already. Less than two years apart in age, they'd always been close. Jude couldn't imagine her life if Carrie weren't in it. So, yes, of course she worried.

She took the mugs to the sink, rinsed them out and decided she'd go up and visit her mother for a few minutes. Then she'd head back to the barn where she was comfortable.

It wasn't perfect, but it was hers and the familiar smells of hay and leather and the tasks and nonhuman company would surround her whether Liam Manning showed up or not. Most days, that was all the positive thinking she needed to get her through.

JUDE KNEW RIGHT away that the BMW coming up the drive had to belong to Liam. It was a corporate-looking car and it only made sense that it was owned by a corporate-looking guy. She wondered if he would park next to her pickup or leave some space so his shiny sedan wouldn't be inflicted with old Dodge Ram barnyard dust.

She leaned on the rake she'd been using to spread chicken feed and waited for him to get out of the car. He'd actually shown up. If Carrie were still here, she'd be gloating big-time. And he'd even remembered her fashion advice and had on a pair of jeans. Despite the denims having a "just pressed" look, at least they were barn appropriate. His close-fitting, long-sleeved T-shirt was a common Pittsburgh Steelers variety, faded from wash-ing. His sandy hair, unencumbered by a ball cap like hers was, was neatly combed, prov-ing that the executive still existed alongside the cowboy.

She took off her cap and squinted into the sun. "Well, well, look who's here. Did you bring a hammer?"

He came toward her. "In the trunk. You'll have to show me how to use it."

She harrumphed before tossing her cap to a nearby bench and flicking her braid over her shoulder to stream down her back. Untamed wisps of curls swept around her face as usual. Jude figured she looked okay. She wasn't a complete fashion dolt. She bought denims that fit, shirts that hugged in the right places and tucked into her twenty-four-inch waistband without a struggle. And from the way Liam was looking at her, maybe he thought she looked okay, too.

"Did you have any trouble finding the place?" she asked.

His answer was lost in a riot of barking as Mutt, the family dog, raced from the barn and ran directly toward Liam. Jude expected her guest to run back to the safety of his Beemer. Mutt was a large, furry, Bernese mountain dog, a rescue who was so grateful for two squares a day and a comfy spot at the foot of Jude's bed that he loved everyone. But Liam wouldn't know that.

"He won't hurt…" Jude started to explain. But Liam was down on one knee, his fingers scrunched into the layers of fur around Mutt's face. Mutt lapped his chin with his scratchy tongue.

"Friendly dog," Liam said, standing again and wiping his mouth with the back of his hand.

"Almost too friendly," Jude said. "Sorry about that."

"I like dogs. It's okay."

Jude wasn't sure that Liam liked big, sloppy, licking dogs, but to his credit, he was handling the situation. "How do you feel about goats?" she asked.

"Goats? Can't say that I've ever sorted through my feelings about goats."

Jude snapped her fingers and pointed to the side of the barn. "Mutt...goats! Goats!"

The Bernese trotted off gleefully around the corner of the barn. A minute later the Dancing Falls goat herd appeared in all its braying, furry splendor. Two dozen of them. At least half tried to get a curious sniff of the newcomer.

"I trained Mutt to open the latch that releases the goats."

Liam frowned. "Did you also train him to put them back again?"

She laughed. "No. That's my son Wesley's job." She handed Liam a bucket filled with feed and carried two buckets herself to a pair of troughs. "Feeding time. Most of these guys will walk around the yard and nibble at leaves and grass, but my vet concocts this pellet food to add bulk. Just dump your feed into the bin."

He did and seemed grateful that lunch distracted the beasts from making a meal of a guy in creased jeans. She had to give the man credit. He was trying to fit in, though his heart wasn't in it.

"Are the goats a permanent fixture at Dancing Falls?" he asked.

"Nope. They are temporary. This is just a stopover until they reach their new destinations."

"Which is where?"

"Central America, most likely. The goats are part of the foundation. I got the entire herd about three months ago from a farmer out in Bees Creek Township. He'd been raising the goats for their milk and to use in petting zoos, but he hadn't figured that a few goats would cost so much to maintain. He couldn't pay the feed bills to keep the herd healthy, so he applied to the foundation for assistance."

"And the goats all ended up here?"

"They did. Actually I didn't trust the farmer to keep them healthy, and I figured I was much better equipped to deal with them. Dancing Falls was a good choice. We have pasture land here for them to roam."

"You haven't found someone else to care for them?" Liam asked.

"I haven't tried. I did some research and

discovered a charitable organization in Central America that provides goats to families in need. Most of these goats are milk goats. Just one can keep a family in dairy products for a long time. With my plan, I'm helping the goats as well as people who need it."

"So, why have the goats been here three months? Shouldn't they be on their way to Central America where they'll do some good?"

"I'm fattening them up. Some of them were in bad shape when they came here. Hoof disease, ribs showing. But they're healthy now. A good dairy goat gives sixteen cups of milk a day, and as soon as they're completely healthy I'm shipping them to Costa Rica probably."

"But in the meantime, you're paying the bills to feed and care for them."

She squinted her eyes at him. "Somebody has to, and the foundation is willing. By the way, you're out here because you said you might want to donate to one of the foundation's causes." She gazed over her herd of hungry goats. "How about this cause? Right now we're somewhat strapped for cash. As you might imagine, being a whiz kid and all, it costs a lot to keep two dozen goats fat and happy."

He picked up his feed bucket. "I'll think about it. Where does this bucket go?"

"In the barn. Why don't we go inside? You can meet more of the family."

TRY AS HE MIGHT, Liam couldn't manage to feel more than a passing interest in Jude's goats. They were odd-looking creatures with their sloping foreheads, awkward gait and continuously moving jaws.

Ruminate. He recalled the word from his high school biology class. These animals pulled up roots and plants from the soil, chewed it, swallowed, brought it back up and chewed again. Hardly Liam's idea of fine dining. At least he'd never eaten goat, and didn't have to hide any guilt in case Jude asked him if he had.

"We have three horses in here," Jude said, leading the way down the central aisle of the barn. "They are all offtrack thoroughbreds."

"You mean racehorses?" Liam said.

"That's right. My husband loved horses. He was an expert rider, quarter horses mostly, and when I learned of these horses being at risk, I immediately brought them to Dancing Falls. That's what Paul would have wanted. You can't imagine their condition when they were brought here."

She stopped to rub the nose of one large beast. "These horses gave so much when they were in training. It's a shame that they aren't rewarded with a nice retirement when they are no longer financially important to their owners."

Liam didn't know much about horses. His mother had made him take riding lessons when he was a kid, since so much of this part of northern Ohio was horse country. He'd learned what he'd had to, mastered a few dressage techniques on multi-thousand-dollar animals and considered his education complete. He was surprised by what Jude had just said. He always thought racehorses were put out to pasture and allowed to fill their last days with peace, contentment and a diet of rich green grass and hay.

He walked down the aisle, stopping to look into stalls. "These guys don't look so bad," he said.

"Not now. I have a vet tech come out once

a week to check their vitals and adjust their feed."

"That must be expensive."

She gave him a skeptical look. "Knowing we're a charity, the tech at least gives me a reduced price." Jude took a carrot from her pocket and gave it to a horse that had to top sixteen hands. "This guy is twenty-one years old. He probably doesn't have too long, and he deserves to live out his life in comfort."

Liam continued to the end of the barn, where a stall was occupied by a large bay. When he approached the horse, the animal reared up on its hind legs and pawed the stall gate. Liam jumped back.

"Don't go near Titan," Jude said. "He doesn't like strangers. Actually he doesn't like anyone." She went to the gate and spoke softly to the agitated animal. Slowly the horse calmed but still pawed the ground and whinnied in some sort of equine frustration.

"This animal had suffered the worst case of abuse I've come across," she said. "He was skin and bones when he got here. He'd been whipped and beaten, drugged and hit with electrical charges while he was on the race circuit."

Jude took another carrot from her pocket and held it for Titan. "Is it any wonder he's a bit cranky?"

Liam tried to feel for these animals something of the sympathy Jude obviously did. Yes, it was a shame that animals could be treated so cruelly, but the bills for caring for these creatures had to be enormous. Liam thought of Dr. Foster and was reminded that he was here to find ways to cut some of these expenses. "I can't even imagine what it costs to take care of these animals, Jude," he said.

She narrowed her eyes again. "That's the third time you've mentioned the cost. You really are a money guy."

He shrugged.

"But again, to respond to your comment, it's not cheap. Thank goodness my dad supports my efforts to fund the foundation. He's our biggest contributor, and he knows how important these causes are to me, how important they would have been to my husband."

Liam shook his head. If she only knew. Dr. Foster was no doubt a patient, kind man, a good and loving father, but no one who wasn't a multimillionaire could carry this burden forever.

She turned away from the stall and started back down to the barn opening. She stopped along the way, adjusted tack on the walls, hung a water bucket on a hook for a horse. Each movement was smooth and natural, and not wasted. Jude O'Leary was in her element in this barn. Her plaid shirt was dusted with hay. Her jeans were coated with feed and goat spit. Liam felt out of place, like the quintessential rhinestone cowboy, a phony in clean jeans.

"So, what do you think, Liam?" she asked as they came into the barnyard.

He wanted to say, "I think you're amazing," because a big part of him truly believed it. Liam would be reluctant to even take in a stray cat, and here this woman devoted her life to creatures who needed help. He wondered how many hours of her days were spent taking care of these needy animals and how many hours she spent helping other causes. She might not be the most practical woman he'd ever met, but she had to be one of the kindest.

But he was here at her father's request so Jude's good works didn't send the poor doctor into bankruptcy. It shouldn't matter that Jude's hair was the color of summer wheat in the sunshine, or that her slim body was muscled and toned from hard work. Liam liked looking at Jude. She had hard angles and soft curves, and she was nothing like the starvation-diet women he saw in the offices in Cleveland or that his mother introduced him to. She might come from money, she might have been raised on Dancing Falls, but there was nothing debutant about Jude. She was pure, unspoiled, raw, in an unembellished-beauty sort of way.

"Do you want to contribute to any of the causes you've seen so far?" she asked, interrupting his thoughts.

"I might," he evaded.

"What do you do, anyway?" she asked. "Are you an accountant?"

"Partly," he said, knowing she was understating his expertise. "I have a master's degree in economics, and I currently work for the firm of Baird and Picard, financial planners. I basically monitor trends, study performance graphs, try to separate sound investments from riskier ones." He paused before her eyes completely glazed over.

"Oh. Maybe you can help me cut some expenses. I'm not much with a pencil and calculator."

She couldn't have given him a better opening. "I'd be glad to try," he said.

"I can't pay you," she added.

"No problem. If I can help you, consider that a donation to one of the causes."

"Sounds fair. I actually do a lot of bartering to keep the foundation going. Thanks."

A dated Toyota pulled up to the barn and a kid got out. Liam recognized him as Jude's son, Wesley. Jude gave him a quick hug and waved to the woman driving the car. "Thanks for picking him up at the bus stop, Rosie," she said.

The Toyota left and Jude gave her son the typical mom attention. "How was school? Did you eat all your lunch?"

"Okay. Yes." Wesley stared at Liam. "Hey, you were at the wedding, weren't you?"

"I was. It was quite a party."

"Yeah, it was cool. What's your name?"

Liam told him.

They actually chatted about the wedding and some of the guests as if they were old friends. The kid was easy to talk to.

Jude postponed any further conversation

when she reminded her son of his chores, "Hey, Wes, you want to round up the goats and put them back in their pen?"

"Can I do it in a minute, Mom? I'd like to show Liam my science project." He flashed Liam a hopeful grin. "It's in the house upstairs. Do you want to see it?"

Liam looked to Jude for approval. She shrugged. "Sure. Okay with me."

They both followed Wesley up the stairs to the family's living quarters. Liam wondered if the faint smells of the barn would follow them into the house. He was surprised to enter a small but neat home with no earthy odors. He smiled. Of course the windows were closed.

CHAPTER FIVE

WITHIN A COUPLE of minutes, Wesley had the dining table covered with magazine cutouts, Magic Markers and a large piece of poster board. Jude filled glasses with sweet tea for her and Liam and gave Wes some fruit juice. She probably should have had a snack on hand. She figured most mothers had cookies, sodas and chips, but Jude's pantry only held healthy goodies. Wes ate enough junk food at his grandfather's house.

Magazines, mostly farm and husbandry journals, covered the old pine coffee table, a castoff from her parents. A throw depicting galloping mustangs hung loosely from the back of a plaid sofa, another freebie from her parents' early marriage days.

Now that Jude actually studied her surroundings, she realized that there were very few pieces in her apartment that she could call her own. She'd purchased a quality bedroom set, which she still owned. A Seth Thomas clock above the fireplace had been a wedding present, as was an artist's sketch of Dancing Falls in winter. A wedding picture of her and Paul sat on the end table.

She'd readily accepted donations of furniture when she was setting up the apartment, thinking herself frugal and clever. Now, with Liam in her living quarters, the term *stubborn* came to mind. Her sisters had offered to update the apartment at different times, but Jude had always turned them down, insisting, "I don't need anything. Wesley and I are fine." She ended by suggesting instead that they donate to the Paul O'Leary Foundation.

She handed Liam a glass of tea and hoped that maybe he wouldn't notice the eclectic jumble of objects that made up her life. Maybe her space was cluttered, but underneath all the minutiae of her and Wesley's existence, her world was polished and waxed.

Liam took his tea and pulled a chair from underneath the dining table. He sat down and gave serious attention to the items Wesley had spread out in front of him.

"My project is about constellations," Wesley said, sliding over the four-syllable word with ease. "I'm making a chart to show what constellations look like and what they're called." He looked into Liam's eyes as their guest nodded slowly, showing what had to be exaggerated interest.

"Did you know the constellations have names that look like things?" Wesley asked. "There's one that's called the Big Dipper. One is called the Great Dog, and another the Swan." As he recited the names, Wesley placed a matching picture cutout on the poster board. Soon the white cardboard became a microcosm of the night sky with streaks of white against a dark blue background.

"Some constellations you can only see some times of the year," Wesley said. "Like Andy Meade."

Liam smiled. "Andy Meade?"

"I think that's what it's called."

"Aren't you thinking of Andromeda?" Liam offered.

Jude stood at the entrance to the kitchen, her hand on her hip. So the accountant knew a bit about astronomy. Maybe his interest in Wesley's project was genuine. "Tell Liam when he can see that one," she said.

"Only in November and December," Wesley said. He grinned. "That's now! The stars will be really bright around Christmas."

"I'll definitely have to take a look," Liam promised.

Jude glanced out the window. "Johnny Ray is here, Wesley. No more stalling. You have to go down and help him with the goat herd."

"Aw, Mom, do I have to? Liam and I are just getting started." He looked at Liam. "You really like constellations, too, don't you?"

"I do."

"Maybe we can persuade Liam to stay until you finish with the goats," Jude said.

Wesley looked to Liam for confirmation. Liam nodded. "My pleasure."

"Now go on," Jude said. "There are three of you to help. You, Mutt and Johnny Ray. You'll have the goats in their pen in a few minutes."

Obviously understanding his part in the process, Mutt stood at the front screen door, his paw scratching the metal frame, his tail wagging.

"Okay." Wesley grabbed the jacket he'd hung on a hook and trudged to the door to open it for Mutt. "I'll be right back, Liam."

"I'll be here."

Jude waited for the sound of Wesley's footsteps to fade before she turned to Liam and said, "Thanks for being so attentive to Wesley."

"It's no problem," Liam said. "I've been interested in astronomy since I was his age."

"Before you got interested in numbers and finance?" she said.

"Way before. When I was a kid studying the stars, I probably never pictured myself as a bean counter. But now I find financial highs and lows fascinating."

Jude carried his glass to the sink. "I don't know what Wesley will choose to be when he grows up. He flits from one thing to another. Now it's astronomy."

"How does he handle himself around the goats?" Liam asked. "He's so young for such responsibility."

Jude tried to detect a note of disapproval in Liam's voice. Finding none, she said, "I train him carefully for everything he does around the farm. And besides, goats have a herd instinct. All Wes has to do is basically open the gate and they all go through. And Johnny Ray is there if anything goes wrong. It's an easy job but gives Wes a feeling of accomplishment."

Liam nodded, leaned back in his chair. "Why don't we use this time to talk about some of your foundation issues?" he said.

"What do you mean by 'issues'?" she asked.

Liam frowned. "I didn't mean bad issues," he said. "It's just a figure of speech."

"Okay. Where should we start?" She brought a ledger to the table and sat next to Liam. When she realized their shoulders nearly touched, she scooted her chair to provide extra room. Liam smiled at her, making her feel just a bit foolish. He couldn't have thought she was flirting by sitting so close, and yet she'd behaved self-consciously. Well, why not? It had been a long time since she'd had any practice at male/female relationships.

"Why don't you show me a list of the charities you fund?" Liam said.

That was easy. Jude was proud of the people she helped in the county. All of the charities that benefitted from the Paul O'Leary Foundation were in Geauga County. That was what Paul would have wanted. He'd been a proud country boy, and a well-liked Bees Creek Township native.

Jude showed Liam the names of veterans' kids who'd received scholarships to the junior college. She also explained how monetary gifts were awarded to wounded warriors. "It's not much, but the families need a lot of help, so we do what we can," she said. "Families of soldiers who don't make it home get a onetime death benefit check from the government, but very little is done for wounded vets."

"So you received a death benefit when Paul died?"

"Of course, but I didn't want it for myself. Besides, I'm very lucky. I've lived here on my father's property since I was born, and I had no plans to move away."

"So you're saying you didn't keep the money?"

"I'm saying it was a moral issue for me. Morally I didn't think I should accept that money because I have other means. I know many survivors need it, but I didn't."

Liam's eyes widened. "So, what did you do with the money? You didn't turn it down, did you?"

"No, of course not, but I wanted to use it as a tribute to my husband. I used my hundred thousand to start the foundation."

"The whole thing?" Liam seemed surprised.

"Most of it. I kept some out for the expenses of Paul's memorial service." She cleared her throat as an image of that bleak, rainy day invaded her consciousness. "I figured the bulk of the money would do more good as a legacy to Paul than just sitting in my checking account."

"What about Wesley's education? Did you start a savings account for him?" Liam asked. "I'm sure that's the kind of usage the Veterans Administration has in mind when they issue checks to widows."

Jude wasn't sure she appreciated the inference in Liam's question, as if she were a negligent mother. "Wesley will be just fine," she said. "Who knows if he'll even want to go to college. Not everyone is born to achieve higher education. I was forced to go and stuck it out for three semesters until I quit." She gave Liam a lingering stare. "Are you questioning my decision about the money, Liam?"

A SLOW BURN crept into Liam's face. He was not off to a good start here, but it was part of his job to ask people about how they spent their money, to get them to reexamine their priorities. Jude didn't know that, though, nor would she care. She didn't seem to care about money, other than for what it could do to help others. She was absolutely confident that her decision to fund the foundation was the correct one.

Still, Jude's attitude about Wesley's future seemed at odds with her obvious mothering nature. Liam barely knew her kid, but even he sensed a strong mind and eagerness to learn. If ever there was a six-year-old on a premature road to higher education, it was Wesley O'Leary. Couldn't the boy's own mother see that?

He wisely remained silent, tapping a pencil eraser against Jude's ledger.

"I have the feeling there is something you want to say to me," she said.

"No, not really. I'm just surprised that you would use your benefit this way. The VA gives the money so families will have a head start on making their way without the breadwinner."

"I told you. I'm sure most veterans' families need the funds, but I didn't." She glanced around her apartment as if taking stock of her material possessions, which were modest in Liam's opinion. Liam's gaze locked on the photo of a man in uniform and Jude in her wedding dress. A modest shrine to the dead soldier, he decided.

"What do you think when you see the way I live?" she said.

"It's fine. I don't know what you want me to say."

"I know it's not fancy. But Wesley and I have everything we need or want. We have plenty to eat, decent clothes, Wes has friends and playdates, toys like other kids. We have a dynamite dog and a purpose for getting up every morning. Why should I use government money to amass more stuff?"

"I wasn't suggesting you do that. But opening a savings account is another way of using the money to ensure your family's well-being."

"Like opening an account for my son, you mean?"

There was no denying Liam had made a mistake the moment he implied that Jude wasn't preparing for her son's future, just like he almost had when suggesting that the foundation had "issues." These blunders might cost him her trust. What right did he have to question Jude's plans for her son? No right, but definitely an obligation—to Dr. Foster.

She leaned back and practically glared at him. "Does Wesley look like he's suffering to you? He's six years old, Liam. He wouldn't know if he had a savings account or not. I'm sure my father opened one for him. He did for my sister's daughter, so he was probably as generous with Wes. Right now, if Wesley knew he had money, he'd be just like every other kid and want to buy a new video game."

Liam was definitely crossing a line. He hadn't come here to interfere in family dynamics, and that was just what he was doing by intimating that Jude had misused her widow's fund. He would do well to remember he needed to make an ally of Jude.

He placed his hands flat on the table. "I'm sorry, Jude. I misspoke. Wesley is obviously a happy, well-adjusted kid, along with a bright one. It says a lot about your skills as a single parent."

She relaxed in her chair, but the resolute look on her face told him he'd better be careful. He flipped a few pages of ledger paper and changed the topic. "I haven't seen this two-column bookkeeping system in quite a while," he said. "Don't you have a computer?"

"Sure I do." She nodded toward a desk under her living room window, where he saw a laptop model. "I use it every day to send and receive messages about the foundation, to do research. I just don't use the computer to keep track of the money. I'm still a simple calculator girl when it comes to adding and subtracting."

"Well, that's okay. Why don't you show me the foundation's assets?"

"Prepare to not be impressed." She leaned forward and thumbed through some entries. Locating the page in question, she ran her index finger down the list of contributors and investments. "This is the initial investment from the VA. My father donated fifty thousand. A few people in the community, friends of my dad's, gave a total of about twenty-five thousand."

"What about Paul's friends and family?" Liam asked.

"He wasn't well off," Jude said. "He was raised on a farm. His parents barely made ends meet. But Paul served his country proudly, and I always envisioned the foundation as a legacy to him without expecting money from his family." She gave him an earnest stare. "I'm sure you'll agree that his family gave enough."

"Of course." Liam returned his attention to the books. "And what about these treasury bonds?"

"My father's accountant said I should have solid investments, so I bought a few bonds. I don't touch the principle, just the little interest I get. I probably should check how they're performing."

Liam scratched the back of his neck. A lot of money had come in to start the foundation and this simple bookkeeping system, with its erasures and write-overs would be difficult to follow even for him. He turned the pages to find the expenses section and noticed one item missing right away.

"Jude, where is your salary? Even a non-profit organization has to pay the employees. I don't see any record of you getting a regular paycheck."

"I take money when I need it, when it's available. Usually about a thousand a month. But I don't have many personal expenses."

Liam released a deep sigh. She took money when she needed it? How did she budget, plan? "I've only just scratched the surface here, Jude, but I've come to a conclusion already."

"What's that?"

"You're not protecting yourself financially, which could lead to big problems down the road. And, maybe more importantly, this foundation is losing money. You're spending more than you're bringing in. At this rate, the foundation will be broke before the new year!"

"That's ridiculous," she said. "I realize I'm not the best bookkeeper, but we can't be broke. Too many people depend on us."

He held back a cynical chuckle. "Jude, come on. That's like saying you can't be out of money because you still have credit cards."

"Okay, maybe I'm naive. But by the first of the year? I don't believe that."

"I may have exaggerated, but you should trust me when I tell you you're heading for bankruptcy. You need to make some changes, and you need to make them now."

Her eyes widened and her jaw dropped. "Trust you? You're practically a stranger." She obviously intended to say more, but the door whooshed open and Wesley came bar-reling inside. "We're done, Mom. Can I show Liam more of my constellations?"

The look on Jude's face made him wonder if he was violating Dr. Foster's primary warning. *Don't bully her, Liam.*

"No, Wes," Jude said. "It's nearly supper time, and I believe Liam was just leaving."

As HE WAS driving home, Liam kept thinking about what he could have done differently. His conclusion was, almost everything. He'd been a hit with the kid, but that was all. With Jude, he'd been too blunt, too matter-of-fact, too much the cocky expert. He made the mistake of trying to reason with Jude the same way he approached wealthy clients who came to his office for advice. Over the years, he'd learned that money was personal to everyone, but maybe more so to Jude. Every dollar she worked with was intimately connected to her dead husband, and he should have been more in tune to her personal feelings. But Liam wasn't a personal feelings kind of guy. Money brought problems into peoples' lives, and problems had solutions.

He'd never forget the look on her face when he walked out the door, and that was a shame, because earlier he'd decided that Jude O'Leary had a beautiful face. Not perfect, too suntanned, marked with a few worry lines, but it was a good, strong, naturally glowing face that appealed to Liam.

But now that he'd told her the foundation was nearing ruin, he would probably never again see the face he was imagining now. If she let him in her house one more time, he figured he would instead see the firm set of her lips, the furrowed brow, the crinkles around her memorable blue eyes. That was the face that had watched him slink toward the door, say a quick goodbye to Wesley and quietly escape.

"Now you've done it, Manning," Liam said aloud. He felt a bit like he'd made a deal with the devil the day of the wedding, though no one who knew Dr. Foster would make the comparison. Naturally Martin wanted to know why foundation bills kept coming to his mailbox. Of course he wanted to stop the flow of good money after bad. Of course it was worth two hundred bucks an hour for him to pay a financial whiz like Liam to evaluate the foundation's leaky books.

Some whiz. Liam had earned six hundred

dollars this afternoon. He'd discovered major flaws in Jude's bookkeeping system, weaknesses in her ability to make sound decisions. But he'd also succeeded in making the hardworking CEO so angry at him, she didn't even say goodbye. No, Martin Foster wasn't the devil. No one was. This was a situation where everyone was doing good things—maybe in a sloppy manner—but still good. The doctor was helping his daughter. Liam was helping the doctor. And Jude was determined to help everyone.

He couldn't leave his relationship with Jude in shambles. He'd told Martin he'd make repeat visits to Dancing Falls before he summarized his conclusions and presented the beleaguered doctor with his bill. And Liam Manning was a man of his word—a blunt, unfeeling, interfering man of his word apparently—but nevertheless, more visits were in order.

The problem was, he liked Jude. She was no nonsense, practical and determined. She didn't mind getting her hands dirty. In fact, compared to his own hands, Jude's were practically a germ minefield. He liked the way the wind tended to wreak havoc with her hair. And he liked the way she smelled. A mix of flowers and leather, as calming as it was rich. He was steel and concrete of downtown Cleveland, and Jude was Mother Earth of Dancing Falls.

And now she hated him.

Well, he just couldn't have her hating him. That emotion benefitted no one. Today was Monday. He'd give her a day to cool off and then he'd reappear on Wednesday, apologize, offer helpful sound advice and use his skill to set the Paul O'Leary Foundation on its feet again.

Paul O'Leary, the husband, the obvious legend about whom no smudge must be allowed to tarnish his image. Liam recalled his father telling him not to get romantically involved with Jude. Ha. Nothing to worry about, Dad. How could any man compete with a dead hero? Liam's background was silver spoon all the way, so how could he square off against a guy who'd grown up poor and proud in Bees Creek Township and gone off to serve his country? Jude was in love with a saint, and even though the guy didn't warm her bed at night and never would again, competition didn't get any more unfair than that.

He rolled down his window an inch to let in a cool blast of air, turned up his radio and hoped his mind would wander to more logical arenas. But the funny thing was, all he could think about was Wednesday morning.

CHAPTER SIX

ON TUESDAY EVENING, Jude and Wesley came to the big house for Rosie's enchiladas. The housekeeper always served the Mexican dish on Tuesdays, and her talent at putting it together was legendary.

Martin wanted to know how Jude's meeting with Liam had gone, but since he wasn't supposed to know anything about it, he couldn't figure out a way to question his daughter. Between bites, he said, "So, Jude, anything new with the foundation?" That question was harmless enough.

"Not really. I got a few miniscule donations in the mail in response to sending out preprinted address labels to neighbors, but ironically, not enough to cover the cost of mailing the labels."

That figures, Martin thought.

"And I got an interesting proposal in my email today from a fifteen-year-old Bees

Creek Township girl. She asked the foundation to fund her trip to Columbus for the statewide 4-H convention. Her father's a veteran, and the girl wants to study horticulture. I'd like to help her."

"How much does she need?" Martin asked.

"Five hundred should do it. I might be able to scrape that much together."

Martin disagreed with this use of fund money. He figured many of the parents of these so-called hard-luck kids could afford to finance their children's trips, but instead of arguing with Jude, he switched his attention to Wesley. "And what about you, kiddo? Anything interesting in your life the last couple of days?"

"Yeah," Wesley said with more than his usual enthusiasm. "Mom and I had a visitor yesterday, this really neat guy who was at Aunt Alex's wedding."

Now they were getting somewhere. "Oh? What was his name?"

"Liam, and he looked at my science project and told me some stuff about constellations."

Martin nodded enthusiastically and waited for Jude to say something. When she didn't, he prompted, "Who is this guy, Jude? Is Wes talking about Liam Manning, Lawrence Manning's son?"

"That's him," she said with a coy smile. "The same Liam Manning you coerced into dancing with me at the wedding."

Martin felt his face flush with heat. "He told you that?"

"He did, but don't worry, Daddy, I've already forgiven you for pawning me off on Liam."

Martin made a disgruntled sound in his throat. "You're a beautiful girl, Jude. I don't have to pawn you off on anyone. And anyway, I saw you talking to him before dinner. He seems like a nice fellow. So he dropped by to see you, did he? Looks like my little plan to have him dance with you at the wedding worked." Martin winked at Wesley, who giggled.

She fixed such a hard stare on her father that Martin actually thought she could see the lies inside his head. "When we talked at the wedding, he asked what I did," she said. "Then he said he would come to the barn on Monday and see about making a donation. Only he got sidetracked and started giving me advice."

"Oh, he did?"

"Yes, but I didn't pay much attention. He doesn't understand how the foundation works and what we're trying to do."

Martin put his elbows on the table and gave Jude an intense stare. "You know, Jude, I understand that Liam is pretty good with numbers. Maybe you should let him take a look at the books…"

"Everybody is good at something, Daddy. It doesn't mean they have a heart." She pushed an enchilada around on her plate. "For your information, though, I did let him have a look, and that quickly reinforced my previous opinion. The Paul O'Leary Foundation isn't just about columns in a ledger. It's about helping the community."

Feeling chastised, Martin remained silent.

"And he played with Mutt," Wesley said, as if the intervening conversation hadn't happened. "I don't think he liked the goats too much. He's like me. He thinks they stink."

Martin chuckled. "I think they stink, too."

Deciding not to press the issue of Liam further, Martin folded his napkin and stood from the table. "Thanks for coming to dinner," he said, bending to plant a kiss on Wesley's head. "I'm going up to say good-night to Grandma. You stay as long as you like."

"We'll leave soon. I'm going to drive Wesley by Aurora's house. Have you seen it? She already has Christmas lights up, and it's only the first of December."

"I saw her struggling with the lights when I went by yesterday. I stopped and helped her for a few minutes. Aurora definitely has the Christmas spirit."

"Oh yeah," Wesley said. "It's almost Christmas. Mom, can we get a big tree this year? One with lots of ornaments and lights?"

Jude smiled. "We'll see, but we don't have room for a big, tall tree. Maybe we can compromise with a slightly larger one than we had last year. Besides, Grandpa will have a big tree here, and Santa will easily see all the lights from the sky so he can leave your presents underneath."

"As I recall," Martin said, "Santa found the tree last year with no trouble."

Wesley crossed his arms and fixed a disgruntled look on his face. "I want our own tree! A big, giant one like at the mall."

Jude shook her head. "No matter what we

decide," she said, "we're not going to have that big a tree."

Martin chuckled and headed for the stairs. On the way up, he thought about the conversation he'd had with Aurora yesterday when he helped her with the lights. The woman had an amazing way of clarifying issues that Martin appreciated.

She knew a bit about his plan to get Jude on the right track financially, and he'd told her that Liam Manning was going to help him.

Martin had said, "I may have misjudged the situation, I hope this young man understands Jude's purpose behind the foundation."

Aurora's attention had remained fixed on her task, but strangely she said, "Does anyone? I wonder."

"What do you mean by that?" Martin asked her. "Jude is trying to do good things for the community, specifically Bees Creek Township, where her husband grew up."

"Nothing wrong with doing good things," Aurora said. "But if you think that's all she's attempting to do, you haven't been paying much attention to that girl's grieving the past years."

Martin had managed to tamp his irritation. How could Aurora, or anyone, suggest he wasn't in tune with Jude's grief? Aurora had only known Jude a few months. Martin saw Jude's sadness in her eyes, heard it in her voice and personally agonized over it. "I know she's been lonely," he'd said. "She won't date, doesn't socialize much. She's not over Paul, and I know the foundation is a way to fill her time while honoring her husband's memory."

"Yes, she's filling her time," Aurora agreed. "But even more significantly, the foundation is filling a void."

Martin had stared at Aurora for a few moments, letting her words sink in. "You're saying Jude is compensating for the loss of her husband with the foundation?"

Aurora met his gaze. "I might even go so far as to say the foundation has *become* her husband. She nurtures it, spends valuable hours growing it. She's closer to that foundation than she is to any friend."

"Jude could have friends," Martin argued.

"Of course she could, Marty, but she doesn't want any. She has the foundation. Paul O'Leary still lives today because his name is on every document that crosses Jude's desk."

Martin had wanted to disagree with Aurora, but his common sense told him that her psychoanalysis was probably on the mark. It was time for Jude to let go. "If you're right," he said, "that's just not healthy."

"*You* should be talking to her, Marty, not some stranger. Maybe this young man can help plug some holes. And maybe he can help Jude in ways you never thought of. But a discussion of the money problem should come from you."

Martin knew he was a good doctor, and in many ways a good father, but he had one major fault in the parenting arena. "I'm not good at criticizing my girls, Aurora," he told her. "They've all been through so much. And now their mother... It was always Maggie who counseled our daughters when they needed it. She dealt the disciplinary blows. I just loved them, maybe too much."

Aurora had put her hand on Martin's shoulder, a gesture of the solid friendship that had grown between the two in the months since she had moved in next door. "I wouldn't worry about having too much love in that house," she said. "But I might add a pinch of practicality. I just don't see how you can justify letting Jude continue down this path by claiming that you're not up to the task of criticizing her. It's not good for her mental well-being in the long run and it's causing you unneeded stress." She smiled. "Talk to her, Marty. She's a clever girl. I think she'll understand your concerns, financial and otherwise."

Martin had been forced to agree. "You're right, Aurora, I know that," he said. "I just don't want Jude to feel like I'm pulling a rug out from under her by withdrawing my support."

"There are lots of ways to show support, Marty."

He nodded. "I'll talk to her before the end of the week."

Liam called his office on Wednesday morning and told his assistant, Connie, he wouldn't be in until after lunch.

"You only have two appointments," she'd told him. "I can easily rearrange those for this afternoon.

"Thanks, Connie." Then he chose sensible, casual clothes—a pair of Dockers, a button-down shirt and a suede sports coat to ward off the morning chill. He thought about dressing again in the attire Jude suggested, but abandoned the idea. Most of the jeans Liam owned were made for going out, not tending animals, and wearing them to Jude's the other day had only made him feel more like a city boy than ever.

He drove from his condo in Cleveland to Fox Creek, rehearsing his apology on the way. He wanted Jude to know he was sorry if he had minimized the importance of the foundation, but he wasn't about to apologize for trying to help her, and her father, save money. It was what he did, why he was Wharton trained. He saved people money and he made people money. There was no shame in that.

He arrived at the barn around eight thirty. The goats were in their pen next to the barn. A few chickens wandered about, free-range-style, nibbling at whatever Jude had left on the ground for them. One horse was in the paddock, the giant bay named Titan. Liam walked close to the fence but maintained a safe distance. He remembered Jude's warning about not getting too close to the grumpy animal. Even so, Titan eyed him sharply, seeming to take in every move Liam made. The animal snorted loudly, a reaction Liam attributed to displeasure. Or maybe he was issuing a strong warning of his own.

"It's okay, big guy," Liam said. "I'm just here to see the lady of the house."

He went up the stairs and knocked on the door. No answer. Wesley would be at school, and a quick perusal of the empty barnyard convinced Liam that Jude had gone somewhere in her old pickup truck.

"Great, just great," he muttered to himself. Why hadn't he considered that Jude might be away from the farm? He'd hoped to catch her when she wasn't expecting him, thinking his apology would be more readily accepted if she didn't have a chance to come up with a way to refute him.

Deciding not to give up, especially since he'd stolen a few prime hours from his firm, he got back in his car and headed to the main house he could see from the barn. All was quiet at Dancing Falls, as well, but Liam decided to try the front door.

Tucking a strand of dark hair behind her ear, the woman who'd driven the Toyota the other day answered. "Can I help you?" she asked.

"I'm looking for Mrs. O'Leary," Liam said. "Jude."

"She lives a quarter mile away, above the barn," the woman said, her clear eyes seeming to take in his pressed trousers and tailored coat.

"I know that," Liam said. "I'm a friend of hers, and I've already checked there. I thought she might be here, since her truck isn't at her living quarters."

"It wouldn't be, would it?" the woman said. "It's Wednesday."

Obviously that explanation was logical to anyone who kept tabs on the Foster family, but it meant nothing to Liam. He waited, hoping the housekeeper would give him more info. When she didn't, he improvised. "Oh, I remember now. Wednesday, right? How long ago did she leave?

"She's supposed to be at the radio station by eight thirty. And since it's all the way in Bees Creek Township, she probably left by eight."

Liam had all the information he needed. He remembered Martin telling him that the foundation supported a local radio station. How many could there be in Bees Creek Township? He thanked the housekeeper and returned to his car. Taking out his smartphone, he began researching. He found one small-band station, WOIH, located on a two-lane road in the mostly-farming community.

Thank goodness for GPS. Twenty-five minutes later, Liam pulled into a gravel lot in front of a small, wood-sided cabin. A sign out front identified the structure as home to WOIH the Voice of Bees Creek Township. Liam parked next to Jude's pickup truck and went inside.

The cabin served two functions—personal and professional. The "lobby" or business reception room, had an overstuffed sofa, a couple of comfortable chairs, solid tables and a big-screen TV. A small kitchen area occupied the back of the room and was partially hidden by a wicker screen. From the aroma, Liam surmised that someone had recently cooked bacon behind that screen. This space was cozy and welcoming.

What should have been the kitchen, a room to the right, had a large glass window separating it from the living room. All signs of cooking functionality were gone, having been replaced with a central U-shaped counter with rudimentary broadcasting equipment on its surface. A sign above the window indicated in glowing red letters that WOIH was on the air.

In the center of the counter sat Jude, a set of headphones over her ears. She leaned into a microphone and spoke in a low, and disturbingly pleasant gritty kind of voice. Liam felt a quiver in the pit of his stomach.

"We'll get to the calendar in a few minutes, folks," she said. "But next on the schedule is the Dog Gone Bulletin Board brought to you by locally produced Pooches Pleasure, high-quality dog food in both dry and canned varieties. Please listen carefully. One of these lost pooches could be your neighbor's."

Jude began her public service announcement with a detailed description of a five-year-old beagle named Maisie who was last seen chasing a goose on Bees Creek. Maisie's mother was frantic and was offering a twenty-dollar reward for the return of her beloved canine. Two more dogs were on the most-missing list, and Jude gave each of them equal airtime. She ended by saying that all of the doggies on last week's list had been returned home. Canned applause accompanied the joyous announcement.

Liam listened to the local-color broadcast with a mixture of amusement and admiration. He doubted that any news of the Middle East or Pacific Cyclone now ravaging the islands would be forthcoming. This radio station was strictly for the people of northeast Ohio, the ones who could pick up the limited signal that probably only reached fifty miles or so.

Finished with the dogs, Jude went right into the calendar of coming events, which was relevant to the locals of Bees Creek Township. Stan's Used Cars was having a sale this Saturday and Stan himself would be grilling hot dogs. The Red Barn Theater was showing *Barefoot in the Park* with two of the local favorites as the stars. The Methodist church was having a bazaar and food drive… And so it went until the week's activities were concluded.

It was at that same time that Jude abandoned her script and glanced out the window to the living room. When she saw Liam, her brow immediately furrowed along with the tug of a serious frown on her lips. She turned the programming over to a white-haired man who spun a country favorite on the turntable. She rose and came to the door separating the two rooms.

"What are you doing here?" she said as she came into the room where Liam waited.

"I came to see you."

"Why?"

"I didn't like the way we left things on Monday. I'm not really accustomed to being thrown out of places."

"Do you want me to apologize for hurting your feelings?"

"No, I'm not that fragile, but I'd like a chance to start over with you."

The frown stayed in place. "Start over how? Are you going to continue sending me into a panic about my life's mission?"

"No. I'm sorry about that. I really did come to Dancing Falls to learn about your charities, and I wasn't kidding when I said I could probably help you sort out some of the financial problems you're having. And I was serious when I warned you about a shaky future. Where I overstepped was when I failed to fully appreciate your involvement in the foundation and your influence in the community. Obviously you are helping a lot of people."

Appeased, at least for now, she said, "Well, thanks for that."

Another elderly gentleman came from the back of the house and walked up to Liam and Jude. "Is everything okay, here, Judie?" he asked.

"Yes, Harvey." She introduced the older man to Liam. "Harvey McGinty, this is Liam Manning. Liam, Harvey McGinty. Harvey and his brother Gary, who's in the control room now, run this radio station. Their voices are well known to the people of Bees Creek Township. The McGintys were original settlers of this area in the late 1700s."

Liam shook Harvey's hand. "Impressive. So you're sort of an expert on broadcasting and this radio station?"

Harvey nodded. "Inside out and upside down."

"Would you mind if I asked you a few questions, Mr. McGinty?"

"I suppose not."

Liam looked to Jude for approval. Her nod was not really a vote of confidence, but she didn't deny his request. "I'll just stick around and listen," she said.

"How long has this radio station been operational?" Liam asked.

"'Bout three years, isn't that right, Jude? We couldn't have gone on the air if it hadn't been for the foundation. Jude has helped us out from day one. She gave us the start-up money to get WOIH running."

"How big a staff do you have?" Liam asked.

"Just me and my brother. We don't broadcast on the weekends, and Monday through Friday we're on air from seven in the morning until five in the afternoon."

The logistics of what he was hearing was enough to make Liam question the existence of the station. Even a radio broadcast this size must have considerable expenses. Licensing fees, connectivity and electrical charges, professional association fees. And that wasn't taking into account the salaries of the Mc-Gintys. Who knew what they were making?

Liam lightly took Jude's elbow. "Can I speak to you outside, Jude?"

"I guess." She didn't look happy with the prospect. Maybe she knew she couldn't defend the expenses required to keep Harvey and Gary in business. She led the way outside and stopped between her pickup and Liam's car.

"What's the matter now?" she asked.

"I'm not sure yet," Liam said. "But for some reason I'm determined to help you sort out the financial difficulties you're having with the foundation."

"I thought I made it clear that I don't need your help."

"You did. But you need help from someone, even if it's not me. Money is trickling out of your bank account at an alarming rate. Don't you want to be made aware of ways in which it may be misspent?"

Her face softened, as if she were considering the obvious logic of his question. But she didn't back down. "I suppose you're going to tell me that the radio station is a worthless drain on the foundation's budget." Her tone dared him to agree.

"I'd like to ask some questions," he said. "Like, for instance, what is the purpose of the station? What are Harvey, Gary and apparently you hoping to accomplish with your limited time on air? How many people exactly are affected by the broadcast?"

She crossed her arms over her chest. "I doubt you'll understand my answers to your questions, but I'll try. Bees Creek is a rural farming community, Liam. People work hard. They don't have time to watch the networks sunup to sundown to get information. Too many radio stations in this country today have become talking-head ego boosts or all-music venues.

"Besides that," she continued, "when's the last time any of the major AM stations gave news that mattered to the people of this area? For that matter, how many AM stations even exist any longer?"

Sure, her arguments had merit, but broadcasting had changed to adapt to the times and unfortunately made something like WOIH obsolete. "And why do you think that is, Jude? AM radio has outlived its usefulness. People don't need the Dog Gone Bulletin anymore."

Her face transformed, and he wished he'd used a different example. He reminded himself that everything about the foundation was intensely personal to Jude. "I'm not saying it's not helpful to be able to go on the air and assist folks find their lost pets, but there are more efficient ways to do that. The internet, for example."

"Listen to you, Liam. You seem to have forgotten that much of the population of this part of Ohio, and other rural areas in the nation, hasn't yet caught up to you executives in your chrome and glass downtown offices. The people of Bees Creek who own computers probably use them to keep in touch with family and to check corn and stock prices, which, by the way, is another service Harvey and Gary provide. Some of the farmers in Bees Creek wouldn't know when to take their corn to market if it weren't for WOIH."

"So, what does it cost to run the station? Are you making any money?"

"There it is again," she snapped. "Always about the bottom line."

"Is that so hard to accept? That's where I can help." He lowered his voice to what he hoped was a more soothing tone. "Are you making any money?"

"We will," she said. "It's only been three years. We've signed up three new advertisers this year."

"All of whom are local and got a great price from Harv or Gar, along with a promise of being lauded on the air," he said.

She didn't disagree.

"One more question," Liam said. "Whose

idea was WOIH? Who sent in the proposal to the foundation?"

She paused before answering. The toe of her boot kicked up a small whirl of dust. "Harvey and Gary," she finally said. "And I know you're going to read something into that."

"Jude…" He wanted to point out all the ways he'd investigate the station, but he knew this project was too close to her heart. After all, she came here every Wednesday just to read a calendar and talk about lost dogs. "I'm sure the guys do a service to some of the people who live around here."

"They do!"

"Okay, I get that. What did the brothers do for a living before starting the station?"

In the last couple of minutes, some of the fight had gone out of her features. "They were having employment problems," she said softly. "Neither one could get a good job."

"Ah." He waited, staring into eyes that were such a liquid, iridescent blue that looking into them, he wasn't sure he could organize his thoughts the way he wanted to. There was something about Jude O'Leary. Something that went beyond the tragedy of her life. She was tough. She was strong on the outside. But deep down she was also about the most fragile person he'd ever met. "I get it," he said softly. "You wanted to help them."

"It's not all about me helping them. Paul would have wanted me to. The McGinty brothers have known Paul's family for generations. They fell on hard times. The station seemed like a good idea. Gary used to be in broadcasting on a small scale." She blinked hard. "I know Paul would have wanted to give them a hand, and ultimately it's his foundation."

He nodded. "I know."

She smiled then, and the gloom of the last minutes seemed to vanish. "Maybe I do need help," she said. "Maybe you are just a nice guy who happened into my life to give the foundation a hand."

He touched her arm, a natural gesture that suddenly felt right. For that moment, she seemed so uncertain, confused, and he wanted more than anything to be the one to rescue her.

"Here's what I can offer you, Jude. I'm your man, financially speaking, if you'll have me. I promise to try to be more understanding. I really do know what I'm doing. All you have to do is…"

She appeared uncertain, like she was going to turn him down.

"…give me a chance," he finished anyway.

And then she completely surprised him. "I guess I could." She looked up into his eyes. "You really will try to understand, right?"

The question made her seem as if she'd trusted before, and her faith had disappointed her. A stab of guilt shot through him. He'd made a deal with her father, even though he hadn't been comfortable doing it. Liam didn't like keeping secrets. He didn't even like knowing any.

And yet here he was, working undercover for Dr. Foster. But why should he feel guilty? Foster was a famously well-intentioned father, and Liam was an expert with numbers. The foundation, and Jude, would benefit from his advice. He would help Jude. He would satisfy Dr. Foster. These weren't rationalizations. They were facts. And once the foundation was on more solid footing, just maybe this normally strong, determined woman would accept an invitation for dinner.

An unexpected breeze kicked up from the

woods behind the station. Strands of Jude's hair tickled Liam's nose. Where had the dinner idea come from? Most likely she wouldn't go out on a date with him. How could he forget that she loved another man?

"I'll stop by Friday night if that's okay," he said.

"Do you like stew?"

He smiled. "Probably not if it's made from goat meat."

Her laughter, soft and sweet, went straight to his heart.

CHAPTER SEVEN

FRIDAY SEEMED TO DRAG, even though Jude filled her hours with housecleaning, stew preparation and imagining Liam Manning in her living room. He would be the only man in five years who was even close to her age who would share this space with her. By three o'clock, she'd picked up her son at the bus stop and brought him into a home scented with beef and potatoes and an assortment of other veggies that she'd added to her Crock-Pot.

"What's going on, Mom?" he'd asked her as he sniffed the air. "Is it a holiday or something?"

Poor kid. She wasn't a great cook and much preferred taking her son to her father's house where the food was always carefully prepared by Rosie.

"No, not a holiday, but we are having company," she'd told him. "Liam is coming over."

"Oh, wow, that's great!"

Wesley had brought up Liam's name several times since Monday. When was he coming back? How did he know so much about constellations? It seemed the man had a way of working himself into both of the O'Learys's agendas.

Liam had called her that morning to say that he'd come directly to her house after he got off work at five. That gave her a little time to try and get the foundation's books in order. She didn't want to come across as unprepared in addition to incompetent.

She'd just begun that impossible chore when her cell phone rang. The digital readout said "Carrie." She put down her pencil and connected.

She discovered that Carrie had been sent to a lake near Ann Arbor where they'd been getting some troublesome data concerning the water at the shoreline affecting roots of the native birch trees. Carrie attributed the problem to runoff of insecticides left from the summer season. Jude listened patiently, though she was just pleased that Carrie was feeling well and healthy.

After talk of trees and Wesley, Carrie said, "Have you seen Liam Manning again?"

Jude swallowed at the unexpected question. "Why would you ask that? I told you he only paid attention to me so I wouldn't feel like a wallflower. And that was thanks to Dad."

"Just wishful thinking, maybe," Carrie said. "I remember how cute you looked dancing with him, and I haven't seen you dance with a guy since Burton Hollis had that hayride two years ago. And then there were those few minutes when both you and Liam were missing and no one knew where you were."

Jude sighed. "We'd been talking about the foundation, you know that. But to be totally honest, you're not completely off base with your wishful thinking."

"I knew it! Tell me. What's going on?"

"Now, don't read anything into this," Jude said, "but he tracked me down on Wednesday. Seems we've got past that argument we sort of had about my philosophy and his expertise."

"I remember," Carrie said. "Not a smooth move, sis, especially if I'm right that he wasn't interested in the foundation. Can't you recognize a ploy when you hear one? He was interested in you. I swear, Jude, you are the most clueless woman I've ever known."

"I'm not clueless! Not this time anyway. Liam is some hotshot financial whiz, and he truly was here to talk about ways to save money for the foundation."

Carrie chuckled. "So, just out of the blue, this gorgeous guy decides to come out to Dancing Falls and do his good deed for the day? I don't think so, honey. This guy has an ulterior motive, and I believe you're it."

Carrie's assessment made Jude wonder if this could be true. Not about her being his ulterior motive, but maybe he did have one. It certainly didn't make any sense for a man like Liam, a man who was busy and successful, to suddenly find time for a small foundation run by a grief-stricken widow. Just as Carrie Foster had always looked for ulterior motives, Jude had always been too trusting—lesson learned the hard way when Paul talked her into trusting *him*. But where Paul's foundation was concerned, she'd tried to be more careful. She had a lot to make up for because of the ungenerous thoughts she'd had when Paul joined the army.

Maybe she'd been blindsided by Liam, by his charm, his manners, the way he made promises and told her everything would be all right. *Heck, admit it, Jude, you were partly blindsided by his good looks.*

"All you need to do is show Liam a bit of encouragement, and who knows what can happen?" Carrie continued. "Maybe you'll end up putting on a dress and going out to dinner sometime."

Or maybe I'll discover that Liam Manning is a first-class con man who has enough knowledge of figures and spreadsheets to take advantage of an inexperienced country girl who is only trying to keep her husband's memory alive. Jude decided that Liam deserved close watching. He might very well be a card-carrying member of Carrie's ulterior motive crowd, and not in a good way.

"We'll see if any of your theories are correct," Jude said. "Liam is coming over tonight to talk foundation business."

"Wonderful. Will Wesley be home?"

"Naturally. He does live here."

"Okay, you can work around that. Oh, by the way, what does Liam think of Wesley? I can't imagine he doesn't adore the greatest nephew in the world."

Jude laughed. "We are all slightly prejudiced, but yes, I think Liam likes Wesley, and Wes is gaga over his new friend."

"Great. Put on something nice, and for heaven's sake, Jude, give Liam a break. He already took the first step. All you have to do is isolate whatever quality it is that makes goats, horses and chickens love you so much and apply it to a human male."

Jude started to protest, but Carrie didn't let her.

"You've been alone too long, Jude. Maybe Liam isn't the one for you, but you have to start somewhere. I've got to run, but I'll call you tomorrow."

"Okay. Stay well," Jude said.

"I'll stay well, and you try to be happy."

Jude disconnected and sank down into her comfy sofa. What was she going to do? She had to admit that she was looking forward to seeing Liam. Her mind kept replaying his kindness at the radio station. Now she wondered if she weren't being taken for a ride by a guy who preyed on hapless females, especially ones who had money at their disposal but didn't know how to use it wisely.

"You won't get away with it, Liam," she said aloud. She considered calling him and canceling, but decided against it. She might catch him in a mistake, and then he'd understand just how determined she could be when her world was threatened. Jude might be too trusting, but that was partly because she was nearly fearless. Her mother always told her that was a combustible combination. She wasn't afraid of unleashing some of that fiery Foster temper her father teased her about when it was deserved, and she wasn't afraid of Liam Manning.

LIAM ARRIVED AT 6:00 P.M., exactly when he'd said he would. Wesley had been waiting at the front door, his eyes peeled to the gravel lot below. "He's here," Wesley shouted when Liam's car pulled up. With unprecedented enthusiasm, he opened the door and waited for Liam to climb the stairs.

"Hi, Liam!"

"Hi there, Wes."

Jude had a sudden flashback to the wedding when Liam was wearing a three-piece black suit. He'd caught her eye that night and did so again in his work attire, a much simpler two-piece suit and white shirt with a gray-and-black tie, which he'd loosened at the collar. The man did fill out a suit admirably, she thought. He had a shopping bag from a local bookstore in his hand.

"What's that?" Wesley asked with a kid's curiosity about any mysterious bag.

"Something for you," Liam said. "Ask your mom if you can see what it is." He smiled at Jude, and a quick spurt of warmth spread to her abdomen.

"Can I take your coat?" she asked.

"Sure." He shrugged out of the jacket and she hung it on the hook by her front door. "I think I'll take off the tie, too."

He did more than that. He rolled up his sleeves as if he were preparing for something really important—a total rehab of Jude's books perhaps.

"Mom, the bag," Wesley said. "Can I look inside?"

"Yes, you may, but remember your manners."

"Thanks, Liam," Wes said, taking the bag and sitting on the sofa. He pulled out a large book with the word *astronomy* across the top and pictures of celestial properties splashed in glowing colors underneath.

"It's a book about constellations," Wes said. "This is so cool."

"It's about more than constellations," Liam said. "It's about galaxies and suns and all sorts of stuff."

Wesley spread the book across his lap. "Will you read it with me?"

"Absolutely. Just let me say hi to your mom."

He crossed to the entrance to the kitchen, put his hand on Jude's arm. "Something smells wonderful."

This wasn't the first time Jude had been touched by Liam, but each time left her a bit more breathless than the last. "Don't let your imagination run away with you," she said with as much nonchalance as she could muster. "I've been known to make dishes that smell like heaven and taste like much less. This could be one of them."

He leaned close to her ear. "Hope you don't mind about the gift for Wes. I couldn't resist. It says it's for a third grade level, but he's so smart, I figured he'd get something out of it at his age."

"I'm sure he will. Thank you."

"Liam, come on." Wesley was growing impatient.

"You can get started with him. I'll finish dinner," Jude said. "I don't have much in the way of alcohol here, but I can serve up a beer at least."

"That would be great." Liam sat next to Wes, and Jude twisted the cap off a Budweiser and brought it to him. He took a long swallow and settled back against the cushion. "Okay, Wes, let's start with the first page, all about the Milky Way."

Fifteen minutes later, Jude had supper on the table. Thick stew, hot biscuits and crisp salad. The simple meal exceeded even her expectations, and Liam wolfed down his portion as if stew were his favorite dish in the world. Halfway through, Wesley thanked Liam for coming over. "Mom hardly ever cooks," he said. "You'll have to come over every night."

Liam laughed. Jude felt her cheeks warm. "There's a reason I don't cook much, Wesley. And you know what it is."

"Yeah. She's not very good at it."

Jude ruffled his hair in pretended anger. "Whose cooking would you rather eat? Mine or Rosie's?"

Wesley pumped his fist in the air. "Rosie's!"

"Then don't complain, or you can do the dishes."

As expected, that suggestion was met with

round eyes and a shocked expression. "After I clean up, we can get started on the foundation's books," she said to Liam. "Wes…"

"Thanks again for the present, Liam." Wes smiled.

"That reminds me," Liam said. "I was able to pick up three tickets to the Shafran Planetarium for this Sunday. They are having a show geared to kids, and I thought you both would like to go."

"A real planetarium?" Wes said.

"Yes, indeed. With an auditorium and telescopes and people who can tell you all sorts of things about the sky."

Wesley looked up at Jude with pleading eyes that had always been able to convince her of almost anything. "We can go, can't we, Mom?"

The last thing Jude wanted was to disappoint Wesley, but she hadn't made up her mind about Liam yet. And even more significant was her growing desire for her instincts about Liam to be totally wrong. She was becoming more comfortable with him every minute. Could Carrie be right? Could Liam symbolize a new beginning for Jude? She was letting her imagination cloud her common sense. "I don't know for sure, honey. Let me—"

She never finished her evasive answer. A knock on the door interrupted her. "Who could that be?"

A call came from the stair landing. "Jude, it's Dad. Can I come in?"

"Grandpa!" Again Wesley rushed to open the door.

Martin came inside. "Whose car is that outside? I didn't recognize… Oh, it's you, Liam."

"Yes, Dr. Foster, it's me."

Did Jude sense a furtive glance pass between her father and Liam? Good grief, she hoped her father hadn't talked him into coming tonight. A simple dance was one thing, but coercing a guy into a romance was entirely another!

"I came up to have a talk with my daughter," Martin said.

"We were just about to go over the financial records for the foundation," Liam said. "Maybe you could come back later."

Whoa! Liam practically telling her father what to do. Strange. Jude sensed tenseness in the room. Why were her father and Liam giving each other suggestive glances?

"I think I'd like to get this over with, Liam," her father said. "I've waited too long as it is."

"What's so urgent?" Jude asked. "Should Liam leave?"

"No. This concerns him, too."

Jude looked at first one, then the other of the men. Liam avoided her gaze by staring at the floor. Her father's eyes were steely and determined. She didn't like the way this conversation was headed. And she definitely believed her father and Liam had a connection she didn't know about. If her father was trying to fix her up as if she were a hard-luck case, she was going to be mortified.

"Wesley, please take your book into your room and read it in there," she said.

He hugged the gift to his chest. "I don't want to."

"Do it anyway." When he'd left the room, Jude approached her father first. "What's this about, Dad?"

"You're a man of your word, Liam," Martin said. "You didn't tell her, and I appreciate that."

Jude shot a glance at Liam. "Didn't tell me what?" Suddenly she felt as if all her misgivings were coming true. Liam hadn't been straight with her, and her father was using him to offset the grief of the last five years.

"I wanted to," he answered. "I would have told you myself. I was about to…"

"Well, someone better tell me now."

Martin gestured toward the sofa. "Honey, sit down."

"No, thank you. I'll stand."

"Okay." Martin took a deep breath. "You know I love you, Jude. At times, you and I have seemed at opposite ends of important issues. And in some ways, your life has had more challenges than the other girls'."

"We're not going to talk about me dropping out of college again, are we, Dad?"

"No. I've made my peace with that. I just mean that you've always been a fighter. You believe what you believe and the rest of the world had better get out of your way. Sometimes I admit I didn't understand that fierceness in you."

"This overview of my personality still isn't making any sense." She looked to Liam for explanation. He nodded slowly but didn't speak.

"Here it is in a nutshell, Jude," Martin said. "Thanks to all the spending you've been doing for the foundation, I've been taking some serious hits to my bank balances lately. I hired Liam to straighten out this mess with the books. I thought he could sort through all the projects and eliminate the ones that are a drain to the bank account, my bank account especially."

Certain words stuck in Jude's head. "Hired. Eliminate."

"Drain to the bank account."

She backed away from her father and took a deep breath to fill her lungs for what she was about to say. "You hired him? A complete stranger is supposed to make decisions about a foundation that I started on my own years ago?"

"He's not a stranger," Martin said. "He's Lawrence Manning's son, and Lawrence has always been a good friend. Liam came very well recommended…"

"Great," Jude said. "Just not by me." Betrayal clawed at her stomach. "How could you do that, Dad? This foundation was the only thing that kept me going after Paul died."

"That's part of the problem, honey. You've allowed the foundation to occupy the emptiness in your life."

"That's ridiculous," she said.

"Is it? You're much stronger than you give yourself credit for, Jude. You had Wesley, and you've always been a good mother."

"I love Wesley, and I loved Paul. And I was doing something worthwhile. How can that be a bad thing? We've helped people, Dad. The community depends on us."

"I know that, but the spending has gotten out of hand. Besides you and the survivor money you put in, who was your biggest donor, Jude?" Martin asked. "Who gave you the start-up money to get the foundation off the ground?"

"You know the answer to that. You did. You said at the time that you were happy to help me."

"I was. I would have done anything to take away some of that grief that seemed to eat away more of your soul every day. Fifty thousand was a small price to pay to see you involved in something that took your mind off the loss. And you're right. A lot of good has come from your help to the community."

She shook her head. If her father truly believed what he was saying, then why did he hire an outsider to clean up what he obviously thought was her mess? Weren't they a family?

"And now you're sorry you funded me?" she said.

"No, now I'm sorry I keep funding you. The foundation was a great experiment at first, but it has grown beyond the ability to be funded by donations. There just aren't enough of them."

She tried to keep her mind clear, to concentrate on something other than her father's revelation. He'd just called her life's work an *experiment*, as if it could be tossed aside as a miserable failure. "Then why not talk to me? Why didn't you sit down with me and discuss the problems?"

"I tried, Jude. Remember last Christmas when I wanted you to turn in that wreck of a pickup truck and get a new vehicle? I pointed out that too much money was going for the wrong things, that you should pay yourself a decent salary." He nodded toward the front door. "In the parking lot right now is the same beat-up old truck. And a couple of months ago, I showed you the bills I received in my mailbox from the feed store. I asked you why the foundation hadn't paid them, and your answer was the same as always. 'We're a little short this month. I'll pay you back.'"

She dropped her forehead into her hand. The conversation was typical of many they'd had. And now that she really listened, she knew her father was keeping the foundation afloat. Unfortunately she'd come to depend on her father's help more than she realized.

"I didn't know a few hundred dollars was about to break you, Dad," she said as tears came to her eyes. She knew that was a snarky thing to say, but she couldn't help herself. She'd never heard her father complain to her sisters about money. But of course they weren't so indebted to him.

"That's not the point." He scowled. "And, believe me, it's a lot more than a few hundred. This is a pattern that's developing. It's been five years. This foundation should be viable by now. You should be meeting expenses and paying your bills." Martin sighed. "Bottom line, Jude, you should have learned how to control the money. You should have said no to a few of these projects."

Jude didn't care about money. She lived in a converted apartment. She kept personal spending to a minimum, all sensible ways to live, she'd believed. And she was grateful for her father's support, but she hadn't looked at her money management, or lack of it, from his point of view. "Maybe you're right," she admitted. "I have been taking advantage of your generosity, but that doesn't excuse you for hiring this…"

She had glanced at Liam a few times since her father had started talking, but now she really looked at him with narrowed eyes, tight lips. He met her gaze until some other part of the room seemed to draw his attention. Was he embarrassed? Did he feel guilty? She felt a little part of her heart break knowing that the thoughts she'd had about him earlier were proving true. He wasn't just the nice guy she'd hoped he was. And Carrie had been completely wrong. He wasn't interested in her, and this wasn't a new beginning.

"…This Wharton School graduate," she finished as if Liam had been educated at the university from hell. The words that came from her lips were bitter. "He's not family, Dad. His father may be a friend of yours, but Liam isn't. As far as the foundation goes, he's nobody. And yet you somehow convinced him to work his way into my affairs, into my house, into my son's life…"

"That's not true, Jude," Liam said. Finally he'd spoken up.

She shut him down with a simple warning. "I'll talk to you later."

"I know I should have talked to you, Jude," Martin said. "But you and I have never talked easily, not like…" He stopped, looked down.

"Not like you've always been able to talk to Alex, right, Dad? Alex, who brought home awards and listened to every word you said."

"Alex had her problems, too, but you're two different people, even though I love you both the same."

Jude exhaled. She didn't question that her father loved her.

Martin continued. "I knew you wouldn't appreciate anyone trying to take the reins just as I knew you probably wouldn't take my criticism with an open mind. I just wanted Liam to find ways to put the foundation back on track, to save some money. I wanted him to earn your trust and then make suggestions."

A bitter laugh came from her throat. There was that word—trust. Next to love, trust was the most important quality in a good marriage. Trust was the basis of all good friendships, business relationships. Trust was everything, and Jude, who had lived the last five years determined never to be taken in by it again, had almost faltered with Liam. "Well, good news, Dad. He almost did."

Wesley returned at that moment. "Everyone sounds mad," he said. "Can I come out now?"

Jude looked out the window. "It's still light. You can go down and fill the horses' water buckets and make sure there's water in the goats' trough."

"But Johnny Ray isn't here to help."

"Grandpa will help you." She fixed a stern stare at her father, daring him to refuse.

After a moment, he took Wesley's jacket from the hook and handed it to him. He'd never removed his own. "Put this on, Wes. We've got work to do."

When just she and Liam were in the room, Jude took several deep breaths while she gathered her thoughts. Then she turned to face him.

CHAPTER EIGHT

LIAM HADN'T MOVED. He'd stood by the dining table when Martin came in, and he stood there still. Jude didn't know what to make of him. With his tie off and his sleeves rolled up, he looked less like perfection. In fact, he looked drained, defeated. And Jude had no sympathy for him.

She hated herself for nearly succumbing to the same mistake she'd made so often in her life. Her trust issues had begun with the boy who'd talked her into jumping from a tree house into pine needles because "the needles would cushion her fall." A broken arm had taught her a valuable lesson. Or the "friend" who convinced her the day she got her driver's license that the police never clocked cars on Route 21. "Open her up," he'd told Jude. Her father had made her work off the entire two-hundred-and-fifty-dollar speeding ticket.

Her mother was right. Being too trusting

along with being fearless was a bad combination.

She moved toward Liam. "How much is he paying you?" she asked.

"Jude…"

"How much?"

"Two hundred dollars an hour."

"Impressive. Let's see how that works out. You were here about three hours on Monday. With drive time to the radio station on Wednesday, that's another two hours." She stopped, stared at him. "Do you charge extra for convincing your subject that you will be fair and unbiased?"

"Jude, come on…"

"Wait, I'm not done with my calculations. I have trouble with numbers, remember?" She began pacing in a small circle. "Then there's tonight. Another two hours. Wow, Liam, you've racked up a whopping fourteen hundred dollars so far."

He exhaled. "I'm not billing your father for tonight or Wednesday. Those visits were my idea."

"How nice. So, tell me, how did this little charade get started in the first place?"

"The first I heard about it was at the wedding. My father asked me to listen to what your father needed. I was more or less pressured into helping your dad because of the long friendship between the two. But I didn't mind taking a look at your books because getting people out of financial messes is what I do, and I'm darn good at it."

"So you've told me a number of times. And you agreed to the secrecy, the whole thing?"

"I was against the deception from the start. I told your father that, but he convinced me that you wouldn't listen to him, and anyway he wasn't comfortable taking this role with you. He felt you would benefit from professional, not fatherly, advice."

"Advice like 'Watch out, Jude, or your foundation will go belly-up by the new year.'"

He grimaced. "I already admitted that was an exaggeration, but if your dad withdraws his support, and nothing changes, your days of keeping the foundation afloat are numbered. That's the truth."

"My father wouldn't withdraw his support. Now that I know how he feels, I'll pinch a few more pennies, work harder at paying the foundation's bills."

"Jude, that's fine, a good start, but you need

someone with a financial background to step in. We're talking about a substantial sum of money here."

She tapped her finger against her bottom lip. "Here's how I see it, Liam. My father believes you're a financial genius, and maybe you are. But I believe you're just a fancy hatchet man who will take it upon himself to see which projects the foundation continues to support and which ones will be left out in the cold."

"I don't appreciate the terminology, but yes, I will make suggestions. Just with the little time I've spent looking at your books, I've uncovered some serious trouble spots. You've got too many projects going on. Caring for that menagerie in the barnyard is eating away ridiculous amounts of money. If you don't curb the spending, those goats will never make it to Central America."

Jude thought of Paul and her eyes burned. She felt them fill with unshed tears again, but not from missing him. This time she wanted to cry because she'd disappointed him—and herself. For five years, she had carried the burden of trying to make things right with her dead husband. She'd almost hated him for deserting her, for dying on her after begging her to trust him. What kind of wife had those feelings? The foundation had become a way to redeem herself.

Liam closed the distance between them, his footsteps soft and sure. When he reached her, he touched her elbow. "I'm sorry you're upset, and I don't blame you. I'd like to start over. Let's try again."

The same pleasant tingle spread to her wrist, made her heart leap. But this was not the time for emotions. "You think I'm going to listen to you now?"

"I hope so. I regret the deception. All I can say is it wasn't my idea. Even so I wish I hadn't agreed to it."

She sniffed, rubbed a veil of moisture from under her eyes and looked deeply into his face for the truth. "I guess I believe you. I know my father can be persuasive about some things. But I can't operate the foundation the way you want to," she said. "I know that you don't believe in what we're accomplishing."

"I don't believe in the *way* you're accomplishing things, but I do believe in you, Jude." He spoke slowly, deliberately. "I believe in you."

She didn't detect any deception in those words. In fact, his blatant honesty shot straight to her heart. He believed in her, the girl who always took the wrong advice, the girl who accepted every dare, the girl who got arrested for her beliefs. Almost no one had ever believed in her before.

Still she couldn't give in. There was too much at stake, her past, her future, her path to forgiveness from a man who was long dead. "Your belief in me won't pay the bills."

He chuckled. "That's true, but together we'll look at all the charities you fund and decide which ones can seek support elsewhere, and which ones can't."

Her gaze remained locked with Liam's. Her world was unraveling at the same time her heart was expanding, and the feelings frightened her. The two emotions were so strong, so confusing. Could the same woman who'd vowed never to trust anyone again trust Liam? Or did one secret always lead to another? Deep down, she didn't want to trust him. She'd trusted Paul with her life, her heart, and he'd left her. She didn't want to start over with the trust factor. She didn't want to feel this overwhelming guilt ever again. She'd kept the foundation going for so long. The foundation had done the same for her. To withdraw support of people who depended on her would seem like she was abandoning everything she believed in.

"I don't think so," she finally said.

"What?" His eyes rounded. "Jude, I won't take any salary from your father. Consider my help a donation. Let's just do this, make it work."

"Thanks, but no. I'll find a way to keep going."

"But you won't, not without help."

She cleared her throat, stepped away from him. "You barely know me, Liam. You don't know what I'm capable of. I think you'd better go."

"You're throwing me out a second time?"

She nodded. Her eyes burned with tears that threatened to spill onto her cheeks. Were they tears for Paul? For herself? For the good folks of Bees Creek she would have to disappoint if she aligned with Liam?

He grasped both her arms. "You're an impossible woman, Jude, and yet I don't want to go."

She tried to look away from him but couldn't. "You don't have a reason to stay," she said.

His fingers tightened on her arms. "Maybe this will give me a reason."

He leaned down and brushed his lips over hers. It was a featherlight touch, sweet and honest. And it was the first kiss Jude had experienced in more than five years. When he drew back, he brushed her hair away from her forehead and left a kiss there, too. Then he retrieved his coat from the hook by the door and slipped it on.

"I'll see you Sunday, Jude," he said. "I'll pick you and Wesley up around noon and we'll go to the planetarium."

She started to protest, but her lips, so soon kissed, wouldn't form the words.

"We don't want to disappoint him, do we?" Liam said. "He's a kid. He wouldn't understand what went on here tonight. And I promise you, no business. Just pleasure. You do believe in pleasure, don't you?"

If he'd asked that question five minutes ago, she might have said pleasure was for people who didn't have a purpose in life. But since the kiss, with her lips still warm, she wasn't so sure.

LIAM REACHED THE bottom step leading from Jude's home, just as Wesley ran out of the barn.

"Hey, Liam! Are you done talking to my mom?"

"Yeah, Wes, I think I am."

"Great! Grandpa and I have been waiting for you guys to quit talking."

Liam cast a quick glance at Martin, who had followed Wesley into the open. Martin's face showed no sign of emotion. Maybe he was still processing what had happened. Maybe he was acting for his grandson's sake.

"The good news is, it's Friday," Wesley said. "I don't have to go to bed until nine thirty, so you can come back upstairs and we can look at the book."

"I'd really like to do that, Wesley, but I'm afraid I have to go somewhere. Maybe next time."

"Aw, shoot! You promised!"

"I promised I would look at the book for a while with you, kiddo, and I did that."

"You're coming back Sunday, though, right? You're taking us to the planetarium?"

"I'm planning to," Liam said.

"You run along," Martin said. "Tell your mom we finished our chores."

"Okay. See ya on Sunday, Liam."

After Wesley had gone inside, Martin fixed a guilty stare on Liam. "Guess I might have left you with an awkward situation in there," he said. "I'm sorry about that, but you wanted Jude to know the truth. How do you think she took the news?"

"Frankly I don't think either one of us scored any points with our delivery. You may have to find yourself another adviser, or talk to your daughter yourself."

"Don't give up on her, Liam," Martin said. "This is typical Jude. She gets angry, hurt and disappointed. You'd think her world was caving in on her. But she just needs time to think things through. I'm sure you two can work this out."

Liam opened his car door. He was suddenly tired and didn't want to discuss this problem any longer. He'd failed. Martin had failed. Now all Liam could think about was making things right with Jude the woman, not the foundation CEO. He admired her, respected her. He… His thoughts stopped churning in his head. Heck, he wasn't sure how he felt about her, but he hadn't been able to stop thinking about her, and he didn't want to quit trying to reach her, not the obstinate widow who was determined to keep her husband's memory alive, but the warm, caring woman who existed under all that crust and thunder.

"You come back on Sunday like you planned," Martin said. "Jude can surprise you. And she won't let Wesley down. She'd never do that."

Liam got in his car. "Good night, Dr. Foster."

Watching in the rearview mirror as Martin slowly returned to his daughter's living quarters, Liam sped down the drive to the road. This was not a happy night for any of them. And then he thought of the kiss and decided maybe he was judging too quickly. She'd responded to the kiss. She'd kissed him back. He hadn't imagined the pure emotion in the sweet press of her lips against his. It was a start. Relationships had been built on less.

His cell phone rang and he activated his car speaker. His dash screen identified his mother. He wasn't prepared to talk to his mother, who always seemed to have an agenda, but he connected anyway. "Hi, Mom," he said.

Alicia Manning-Cooper had hyphenated her maiden name onto her married name soon after her divorce. Liam always assumed she didn't want anyone to forget her status as wife of the area's top dermatologist, but she wanted to regain her independence at the same time. All in all, as far as Liam was concerned, calling her Mrs. Manning-Cooper was a mouthful.

"Hello, sweetheart." Her voice was breathless but chipper, typical of the way she opened all conversations, as if she really wanted to talk to you but didn't truly have the time. "What are you doing now?"

"I'm driving, Mom. On my way home."

"Oh dear. You don't have plans tonight?"

"I have to catch up on some work. I've been a bit preoccupied recently."

"Well, that's all right. I have good news that should cheer you up."

What had he said that made his mother think he needed cheering up? He was always careful to present an emotional vacuum where she was concerned. The last thing he wanted her to believe was that he was desperate or gloomy and needed her help. His mother's methods of cheering could really depress a guy.

"I want you to meet me at the Cloak Room in Chardon for brunch on Sunday, say noon-ish."

"I can't, Mom. I have plans for Sunday."

"When I give you details, you'll want to break your plans."

He doubted that.

"I've invited the most delightful young woman and her mother to join us."

"Mom, how many times—"

"The daughter's name is Valerie. She's a graduate of Georgetown, and she's currently managing the Cleveland Historical Museum."

"She sounds quite accomplished," Liam said, "but I still have plans for Sunday. And I still don't appreciate you trying to fix me up."

Alicia chuckled. "That's fine to say, darling, but if I leave you to accomplish the job yourself, I will never see any grandchildren."

"That may be something you'll have to live with," he said. "I'm sorry, but Sunday is out."

"What are you doing that's so important?"

"I'm taking a client and her son to the planetarium."

"Who's the client?"

Not that his mother had any right to know, but Liam wasn't going to hide Jude's identity. "Jude O'Leary, formerly Jude Foster, Dr. Foster's daughter."

There was a pause during which Liam recalled his father telling him that Alicia had never liked Jude Foster, thought her wild and undisciplined. He suddenly wished he hadn't said her name and given his mother a target.

"Isn't she the middle daughter?" Alicia said, her voice tight.

"Yes, she is." Liam prepared for the criticism he knew would follow.

"Oh, sweetheart, you don't want to date her. She's not appropriate at all."

"I'm not dating her, Mom. I'm taking her and her son to the Shafran because the kid has an enthusiastic interest in astronomy. He's a lot like me in that regard. That's all there is to it."

"Yes, you were interested in the stars, weren't you, honey? But don't get involved with Jude, Liam. The stories I've heard. She has always been trouble for her parents. She quit school, lives in a barn of all places. She's even been arrested. Martin's other two daughters are sweet and charming, but the middle one… Something happened with her."

"Mom, this conversation is unnecessary and out of line. Who I see is none of your concern."

"That is unkind, Liam. I only care about your welfare."

"You don't need to care so much, Mom.

I'm fine. It's just a visit to a planetarium." *If she'll even go*, Liam thought.

"All right, then," Alicia said. "I'll cancel plans for Sunday, but please tell me when you're free. I'm certain you'll like Valerie. You two will have so much in common."

Doubt it.

"Right," Liam agreed. He was anxious to disconnect. "Have a good weekend, Mom." He cut off his speaker and watched the asphalt stream in his headlights. What if he hadn't gone to that wedding? What if he'd ignored his dad and refused to tackle Jude's problems with the foundation? Getting close to Jude was like hugging a porcupine, and he didn't know if he should have gotten involved.

But then he smiled, thinking of how her hair was always in disarray, how she didn't like to cook, how she looked in a pair of worn denims. And how her lips felt when he kissed her. What was so great about meeting a woman with whom you had a lot in common? he wondered. Where was the fun in that?

CHAPTER NINE

ON SUNDAY MORNING, as the sun came up over Dancing Falls, Jude sipped her first cup of coffee and mentally made a list of all she had to do. Three new proposals had come in for foundation consideration. WOIH was having a remote broadcast from the local feed and grain store beginning at ten o'clock, and she'd promised to support Harvey and Gary by attending.

Her father wanted to talk to her—again. He probably wanted to make certain things were okay between them, which of course they were. Jude could never stay angry with her father, and besides, he had made a very good point. She needed to make the foundation less reliant on his support. How? That was the big question.

And then there was the planetarium, the Sunday plan that Wesley hadn't stopped talking about for two days. He went to bed at night telling her what he thought the sky would look like in the auditorium. He got up each morning asking her how many hours until Liam picked them up. In spite of everything that had happened, she enjoyed watching her son's enthusiasm. And as far as trust allowed, she didn't doubt that Liam would keep his promise to Wes.

She sighed. So much for reviewing proposals. If she was going to at least make a showing at the remote broadcast, she had to rearrange a tight schedule. She left her mug half-full on the table and grabbed her jacket from the hook by the front door. She definitely couldn't put off feeding, any more than she could cancel plans for the planetarium. She could make her schedule work by texting Liam and asking him to pick her and Wesley up at the remote location.

LIAM ARRIVED AT NOON. Concerned that he'd been stood up when he didn't see Jude's truck, he checked his text messages. There was one from Jude, left almost an hour ago. Liam, it read. Wesley and I are at the Feed Box in Bees Creek. If it's not too much trouble, can you pick us up there?

Not too much trouble? Bees Creek Township was a good fifteen miles away. But at least it was in the general direction of the planetarium. With luck, they might still make the presentation. He got back in his car, though he had no idea where this Feed Box place was. Thank goodness his Google search did.

"A feed store?" he said aloud when the address popped up. "Couldn't she have saved her animal errands for another day?" Feeling slightly miffed, he nevertheless took off toward Bees Creek. Maybe Jude was being inconsiderate, but he owed this planetarium trip to Wesley. He'd take the kid himself if he had to…if Jude was too busy picking out pellets and hay bales.

He arrived twenty minutes later and pulled behind Jude's truck, which was parked in the back of the store. When he headed toward the entrance, he heard a good deal of commotion. A country band was playing and the scent of hamburgers on the grill wafted through the air, reminding Liam he was hungry. He'd planned to stop for a late breakfast with Jude and Wes if they'd kept to the original schedule. Now there wouldn't be time.

In the front parking lot, dozens of people

were milling about. Some were waiting for their hamburgers. Others were foot-stomping to what seemed a local and very popular band. And then there was Jude. She stood on a make-shift platform near the front door. She asked for the band to pause a moment, and she spoke into a microphone with that same husky, kind of disturbing voice he remembered from his visit to the radio station. That voice captured his attention with a series of mellow vibrations that seemed to reach his toes. He had to try hard to pay attention to her words.

"This holiday food drive is so important to the people of Bees Creek," she said. "Harvey, Gary and I appreciate all your donations, but we still need more." She nodded to a building across the street. "The Save and Pick Mart is open today just for this event. If you haven't already put your donation in the barrel here…" Yes, there was a giant barrel in front of her "…there's still time to run over to the market and purchase a few nonperishables. We want this holiday season to be scented with good cooking for all our Bees Creek families."

"Liam, you're here!"

Liam turned when he heard Wesley's voice.

Part of a crowd of youngsters running out of what was left of a fall corn maze, the kid barreled up to Liam and skidded to a stop.

"What's going on here?" Liam asked.

"The radio station likes to raise money and get free stuff," Wesley said. "Everybody helps the people who might not have enough food. Mom and I have a dozen frozen turkeys in our cooler in the truck."

Jude was just finishing an extra push for donations. Harvey and Gary mounted the platform to stand on either side of her. "This sounds like a good idea," Liam said to Wes. "But I wonder what you guys would have done if it had been snowing or freezing."

"We woulda had free hot chocolate instead of free Cokes," Wesley said. "And everyone gets a free hamburger, even you if you put something in the barrel."

Jude thanked her friends and neighbors and left the podium to a nice round of applause. Gary took the microphone. "Thanks again, Judie, for a wonderful event. WOIH couldn't do this without you." He signaled for the band to start up again, and the foot-stomping and line dancing resumed.

She came over to Liam and her son. "Hi. I see you got my text."

"I did," Liam said. He couldn't seem to take his gaze from her face. The cold air had put a glow in her cheeks and a sparkle in her eyes. She wore a stocking cap pulled over her ears, and a pair of copper earrings twinkled from her earlobes. Her hair, tamed a bit more than usual, still stuck out from the knitted cap and framed her face in curls. She was enchanting and Liam had to remind himself that he was still angry because he'd missed breakfast.

"You didn't mind, did you?" she asked. "I had this commitment, and this wasn't so much out of the way."

He swallowed the truth. "No, hardly out of the way at all, but we'd better get going."

"Mom, I'm hungry," Wesley said. "Can I get my burger and Coke?"

She looked at Liam. "It's okay with you if he eats a burger in the car?"

Liam strictly forbade eating in his meticulously kept automobile. The most he consumed in the BMW was a bottled water on his way home from his gym. And a kid eating a burger? He didn't have kids. He was rarely around them, but he knew they were messy eaters. "Sure, it's fine," he heard himself say.

Wesley headed toward the huge grill.

"Wes, wait a minute," Liam called. "As long as you're there, pick up three burgers."

Wesley gave him a thumbs-up sign.

"And a bunch of napkins," Liam added. And then he walked over and tossed a twenty-dollar bill into the barrel.

WHEN SHE SAW Liam in the crowd at the feed store, Jude almost forgot why she had the microphone in her hand. In jeans, a red button-down shirt and a bomber-style jacket, open in the front, he looked as casual as she'd ever seen him and yet, mixed in with the feed and grain crowd, he appeared as an eagle would look with a nest of barn swallows. She wanted a moment to gather her thoughts, though since the kiss she'd been doing a lot of thought-gathering. But Harvey had called up from the parking lot beside her, "Go ahead, Judie. The mic is on."

She'd been watching for Liam's car, wondering if he would just turn around and go home once she'd made it so difficult to meet up. Was it a test? Maybe in a way it was, but Jude wasn't ready to admit to that. Just in case he showed up, Jude had taken her sister Carrie's advice and chosen a cotton blend skirt with a blue background and tiny cornflowers adorning layers of circular stitching. She'd added a lemon-yellow peasant blouse and low boots and wound her hair into a topknot at her crown.

Topping off her outfit, she picked a waist-length winter jacket and a colorful knitted hat. She didn't look anything like Alexis, with her designer exclusives, or Carrie, who bought preppy clothes from LL Bean, but for Jude, she looked pretty good.

Waiting for Wesley to return with the burgers, Jude caught a whiff of Liam's cologne, subtle, yet just woodsy enough to make her think of the forests of New England. Believing an explanation for her behavior was owed, she said, "This is WOIH's biggest food drive of the year. I had to come. You understand, right?"

"Sure, but we'd better hurry if we want to be at the Shafran for the start of the program."

Swinging a brown paper bag, Wesley ran toward them. Jude noticed grease already seeping through the sack. "Be careful with that, Wesley. You don't want to get grease in Liam's nice car."

Liam was smiling, but it looked forced. Maybe the hamburgers weren't such a good idea. She gave him a questioning look.

"It's okay. Let's go."

"I've never been to the Shafran," Jude said. "How far is it?"

"About an hour."

She could do an hour sitting next to Liam. She'd keep the conversation light and harmless. No foundation talk. No mention of the kiss. Or she could let Wesley do the talking for both of them.

An hour later, Liam pulled into the parking lot of the Shafran Planetarium. They walked toward the building, which seemed to shine in the sunlight. Jude's gait was typical of everything she did—fast and determined. Ordinarily she expected Wesley to keep up with her, often turning and urging him to hurry. Liam did not do that. He adjusted his gait to coordinate with Wes's. He slowed so Wes could set the pace.

"Wow," Wesley said when they approached the building. "It looks like it has stars all over it."

"Those are fiber-optic lights," Liam explained. "The building is made of stainless steel and a metal called titanium, and the lights shining out of the metal are supposed to resemble stars. At night the angled roof helps visitors locate the North Star."

Wesley nodded. "You mean Polaris."

Jude felt a sudden burst of pride. She'd never told Wesley the real name of the North Star. The book Liam gave him was definitely having an impact.

"That's right," Liam said.

They entered the auditorium and headed for the theater-style seats. Liam waited for Jude to choose, let Wesley sit between them before he sat. In a few minutes, the show began.

Wesley seemed spellbound by the virtual trips through the universe and beyond. Astronomical bodies drew trails across the darkened ceiling. Planets zoomed in and out with three-dimensional precision. At intervals, an astronomer's voice explained the celestial phenomena taking place through the projector.

"Look, there's Saturn," Wesley exclaimed. "That's my favorite planet."

"You understand that what you're seeing now is done with the aid of a very technological projector," Liam said. "When you're older, you can see the actual stars and planets through a high-powered telescope at the Mueller Observatory."

"That will be so cool."

Though Jude enjoyed the show, she felt left out of the animated conversation going on in whispered tones beside her. Wesley wasn't only spellbound by the show, he was totally immersed in Liam's explanations. They were both like a couple of kids, each one pointing and making exclamations of awe as if nearly thirty years didn't separate them in age. Halfway through the presentation, she glanced over at her son just as he slipped his small hand into Liam's. Liam looked at the boy's hand and let the tiny fingers entwine with his.

Jude's heart clenched, not with jealousy, although she wished she were the one holding the small hand. Regret, strong enough to make her heart ache, brought tears to her eyes. Paul should have been holding Wesley's hand. He should have been here today to introduce their son to the universe. But Paul was gone, and Jude wasn't sure he could have taken the time to bring their son here anyway. She stared at Liam's face. He looked at her and shrugged, one of those "what could

I do?" looks that told her he hadn't expected her son to make such a gesture.

She sighed and settled back in her seat. Wesley had positive male influences in his life. Johnny Ray teased him. His grandfather played with him and listened to him. But this was different. What was happening between her son and Liam was intimate and personal and made Jude long for a relationship in Wesley's life that would be lasting, positive and nurturing. She could do without a love again, she'd always told herself, but maybe her son needed a father. She just prayed he wasn't pinning his hopes on Liam Manning.

If he was, Jude was going to have to work extra hard with her own relationship with Wesley. Yes, she was a good mother, but she was busy, often distracted, and her son needed a full-time parent who was always available. She could have planned a trip to the planetarium but in fact hadn't even thought of it. Life was just too demanding, her responsibilities too great. Her heart too heavy.

Before she even sorted through the emotions battling inside her, the tears that had been gathering on her eyelids rolled down her cheeks. She quickly wiped them away. Were the tears for Wesley, for Paul, for herself? She didn't even know anymore. Her grief, her longing, her guilt were all wrapped up in an emotional chaos that never seemed to get any better.

When the presentation was over, Liam treated Jude and Wesley to snacks in the planetarium cafeteria. Wesley was a bundle of questions, and Liam answered each one with authority. When he didn't know an answer or wasn't certain, he admitted his lack of knowledge with the same confidence as he gave the answers he knew. And he always promised to look up the correct response.

While Jude marveled at his patience, she couldn't ignore her increasing concern about Liam's influence over her son. Managing a few dozen questions from a six-year-old wasn't difficult if someone wasn't with the child day in and day out. How would Liam react if he were around Wesley twenty-four hours a day? Would he become impatient or cross with Wesley? What if Wesley's questions centered on a topic Liam wasn't interested in? Would he be so accommodating then? Or would he say just enough to satisfy him and get back to work?

And would she have reacted exactly that way if Wesley had asked her all sorts of questions about astronomy? Oddly he hadn't asked her even one question. Maybe he just assumed she wouldn't care, and that was sad. Other than watching him cut and paste images for his school project, she hadn't known the subject interested him. What else didn't she know about her son?

During the ride back to the feed and grain store, Wesley fell asleep in the backseat of Liam's car.

"I think all that accumulation of knowledge tuckered him out," Liam said.

"Looks like it. He'll have a lot to tell his friends in school tomorrow."

Liam gave her a warm smile. "How about you, Jude? Will you tell your friends about the visit today?"

Her friends? Did she even have friends? Sure, Harvey and Gary, and the guy at the feed store. She was friendly with one of the clerks at Winnie's Western Wear, and she knew the waitress at the Bees Creek Diner and the checker at Kroger's. Carrie always told her she should make new friends, younger ones near her own age. Jude supposed she was right because tell-all, laugh-a-lot gal pals had somehow escaped Jude in the last five years. Alex and Carrie were her closest confidantes, and she wondered now if they even liked her or if they were forced to give her attention because they were connected by blood.

What was happening to her? Of course her sisters loved her just as she loved them. They were a tight group, the Foster girls, and the fact that she would question their loyalty and care was evidence of a general lack of confidence she was experiencing lately.

"What kind of music do you like?" she asked suddenly.

"Most anything," Liam said. "But we started this day with a country band so why change now?"

"That would be great." And certainly much better than continuing to ponder the path her life had taken lately, her path as a mother, a sister, a social being.

He chose a station and she tapped her hand on her thigh to the laments of down-and-out cowboys suffering from broken hearts. She liked country music. In many cases, the words reflected a life even more solitary than she now realized hers had become.

As the miles registered on the odometer of the shiny BMW, Jude became more and more aware of Liam beside her. Sometimes he sang along with the lyrics, his voice raspy and low, the voice she thought about even when he wasn't around. Just like she so often thought of the man himself. He was a puzzle to her, one whose pieces often kept her awake at night.

When they reached the store, the parking lot was empty. The fund-raiser had ended in the early afternoon, and there was no one left to give Jude the final tallies. She could call Harvey at the station for the report. "I'll wake up Wesley," she said. "Thanks, Liam, for a nice day."

"Let him sleep," Liam suggested. "I'll follow you home. It will be dark in a few minutes, and I wouldn't feel right not seeing you safely home."

"We'll be fine," she told him. "I drive these roads all the time."

"Jude, please, let me do this. Don't you know that men like to feel helpful and needed?"

She laughed softly. "I thought all men hated to be asked to do things for women."

"Some things, yeah," he said. "But not the

ones they specifically suggest. Now get in your truck and let me follow you home."

The evening had grown chilly, but the concern in Liam's voice seemed to warm her to her toes. It was nice being the one watched over for a change. "Okay, Liam," she said. "But I hope that fancy automobile of yours can keep up."

The estate was dark when they reached Dancing Falls. Jude opened the backseat of Liam's car and jiggled her son awake.

"Are we home?" he asked groggily.

"Sure are. You skipped dinner, Wes. Are you hungry?"

Wesley stumbled out of the car. "No, just sleepy."

"You should get ready for bed, then. Don't you have anything to say to Liam before you go up?"

"Oh yeah. Thanks, Liam. This was the best day ever."

She remained at the bottom of the steps until Wesley was inside. "Thank you, Liam. This day was a special treat for Wesley, and I know he'll never forget it."

"And you?" Liam said. "Will you forget it as soon as you've gone upstairs?"

"What does that mean?" she asked, automatically climbing a couple of steps.

"It means I want you to remember it, too." He grasped her elbow, preventing her from going higher, and said, "Have you thought about the kiss?"

His question, so blunt, so direct, made her feel off-kilter. Perhaps he'd been waiting for an opportunity to ask this question.

"Because I have," he added. "I like you, Jude. You don't make it easy all the time, but I can't help myself. And I liked kissing you." He came up one step to be eye to eye with her. When his hands came to rest on each side of her face, she felt a strange flutter in her stomach, one she hadn't felt in a long time. When his lips came down to taste hers, the flutter became a thrumming in her head.

Oh goodness, the man could kiss.

She leaned into him, melting against the strength of his chest, appreciating the protectiveness of his surprisingly strong arms. Before she could think to stop herself, she was kissing him back.

Blissful seconds ticked by. He kissed her for a long time, longer than a six-year-old boy might take to get his pajamas on. A vision of

Wesley interrupting them flooded her mind and she stepped back.

"What are we doing?" Her voice was breathless.

He smiled down at her. "I think we're both testing to see if a second kiss would be as satisfying as the first. My vote is yes. A third time would be even better."

"We can't be doing this," she said. "And besides, I'm still supposed to be mad at you," she added. "For not telling me you were working for my father." Her lips warm, her gaze on Liam's face and the highlights the moon created in his soft sandy hair, she almost couldn't remember that anger.

"I know. Anything else?"

"Well, yes, but this is a good thing. I appreciate all your attention to Wesley."

"I like him. He's a great kid."

Yes, and he's vulnerable and impressionable, and probably already too attached to you. Unable to express these thoughts, Jude chewed on her bottom lip.

"What's going on, Jude? Are you wanting to say something else to me?"

Oh, heck, just say it. "I'm not sure how I feel about his feelings for you, Liam. We have a certain life here. It's a good life and Wesley has always seemed satisfied with it. I want him to take over the foundation eventually…if he wants to, I mean. What will happen once you…"

A glimmer of skepticism crossed Liam's face.

"What is that look for?" she asked. "You don't think he likes living on the farm, caring for the animals? He's never said anything about that."

"I don't know him well enough to comment," Liam said with carefully measured words. He glanced in the door window. "But now probably isn't a good time to discuss it."

Wesley came out the door. "I'm ready for bed, Mom. Are you coming in?"

She climbed the rest of the stairs and ruffled his hair. "Right away, honey. You're a good boy, Wes." *But maybe not the cowboy I'd always hoped you would be.*

When Wesley went back inside, Jude called down to Liam, "Drive safely and good night."

"One more thing, Jude… How does Wesley feel about babysitters?" Liam asked.

"He's never had one. I always drop him at Dad's house if I need to be away."

"Why don't you try to do that Wednesday

night? Let's go out, just the two of us. A nice dinner, a walk."

"A date, you mean?"

He smiled. "I didn't think I'd have to explain it in those terms exactly, but okay, a date. And you don't have to say the word as if it were a summons for jury duty. Besides, we're already at the kissing stage, so I would think a date is an overdue step."

She wanted to say yes. Her body had responded to his kiss. Inside, her stomach was fighting a swarm of butterflies. But could she do this?

"It's just dinner, Jude. And a chance to see where this is headed. I told you, I like you. Too much maybe, considering you might not feel the same about me."

She took a step back. *Like you?* Her mind spun. Oh yes, she liked him. "A real date, huh?" She smiled. "I'll think about it, but right now I'd say you can consider yourself busy Wednesday night."

CHAPTER TEN

LATER, AS JUDE tucked Wesley into his bed, she noticed a concerned look on his face. "What's wrong? Something you want to talk about?"

He frowned. His little eyes, so like Paul's, crinkled in the corners. "Why can't Liam stay with us?"

"He has his own home, honey. He likes it there, I suppose, just like we feel about our home."

"I wish he lived here."

Jude picked up the little hand that lay on the horse comforter. "I know you like Liam," she said. "But we really don't have room for another person in this apartment. We only have two bedrooms. Where would Liam sleep?"

He thought a moment, then propped himself up on his elbow. "Mark's parents are married, and they sleep in the same room. You could marry Liam and then he would be here all the time!"

"Oh, honey, people don't get married just to solve a space problem. You understand that, don't you?"

"I guess. They have to like each other a lot, too."

"They have to love each other, like Grandpa loves Grandma, like Aunt Alex loves Daniel, like I loved your daddy."

"And you don't like Liam enough to love him." Wesley nodded slowly as if the full impact of the realization saddened him.

Jude fluffed Wesley's pillow. "I like lots of people, sweetie. I like Liam. But love is a different thing. Many people only love one person enough to get married once in their lives."

"So we'll never have a daddy in our family?"

She felt tears well again for the second time that day. She had long expected this question and should have prepared for it. She laid her palm on Wesley's chest. "I don't know, Wes, but you have Grandpa…and if your daddy hadn't died, you would have had a wonderful father. I don't want you to forget that, ever. Just like I don't want you to forget that I love you very much."

She leaned over and kissed his forehead. "Now get to sleep."

His eyelids fluttered. It had been a busy day for all of them. "Okay."

Jude turned off his bedside lamp and switched on the cowboy night-light by his closet. Maybe she should think about changing his room decorations from cowboy stuff to astronomy things. As she left his room, she thought about his request to give Liam a bigger place in their lives. How easy to be a child and come up with perfect solutions to problems. How difficult to be a parent and have to tell the child that perfect solutions don't exist often in the real world. That the kind of love she'd felt for Paul only happened once in a lifetime.

Parents often disappoint their children without wanting to. Children often disappoint their parents. It's all part of a family cycle, which helps people grow and teaches patience and tolerance. Jude had learned that lesson years ago.

Eight years earlier

"WHAT DO YOU mean you're dropping out of school?" her father asked. Jude had requested that she and her parents meet in the living room to discuss an important matter.

She started by being logical. "You know I'm not the student in the family. That would be Alexis. She makes you proud every day."

Maggie leaned forward. "You make us proud, too, Jude. Don't ever think otherwise."

"Yeah, I know. I can ride and rope and train even the most stubborn animals, but I'm not a scholar. I never will be one. I'm miserable taking those hygiene classes."

"But you need a skill beyond your roping and riding abilities," Martin said. "How will you support yourself in life?"

She took a deep breath. "That's another thing I wanted to talk to you about."

They waited, expectant looks on their faces.

"You know I've been dating Paul O'Leary," she said.

"Of course," Maggie said. "He's a nice boy."

Jude nodded. "I suppose I might as well come out and say it. Mom, Daddy… I love Paul. From the first day I met him, I felt we were born to be together."

"How can you know that so soon?" Martin asked. "You've only dated him a few weeks."

Jude smiled. "You said you knew you loved Mom after only a few dates."

"That's different…" Maggie covered his hand with hers. He calmed.

"Paul and I want to get married," Jude said. "As soon as possible. We want to start our lives together."

Martin stared at a spot over her shoulder. Maggie leaned forward. "Oh, honey, what's the rush?" Her eyes widened. "You're not…"

"Pregnant? No, Mom, I'm not pregnant." Her parents had already coped with that problem with their eldest daughter. Jude always used protection. "Paul and I want children, but not now, not for a while."

A stillness settled over the room as if no one knew quite how to respond. Finally Maggie said, "How soon, Jude? Have you discussed a date?"

"Two weeks from Saturday," Jude said. "Paul and I have visited Pastor Windham, and he can perform the ceremony that day."

"Two weeks?" Maggie's eyes misted. "But that doesn't give us enough time. There's so much to do…"

"We don't want a big wedding, Mom. Just our two families. You'll really like the O'Learys.

We'll all meet at the church. It will be simple. If you want to have a brunch afterward here at the house, something small, that would be fine."

Maggie blinked. "I had so hoped for big weddings for you girls," she said. "Alex married Teddy in a rush. Now you're telling me you don't want all the fuss…"

Jude smiled. "Mom, you've known for years that I'm not the fussy type. This really isn't a surprise."

"Well, it's a surprise to me!" Martin barked. "This whole thing—you're in love, you're getting married. It's all a surprise."

"I love him, Daddy. I know he's the man for me."

"Where will you live?" Maggie asked. "Will you move in with the O'Learys? With us? How can you and Paul afford a house?"

Jude carefully managed her words. "We thought, we hoped, that maybe we could fix up the apartment over the barn. We don't have a live-in groom anymore. There's only my horse. And I can take care of her. It won't cost you anything. Paul and I will do all the work."

Maggie looked at her husband, who was still trying to process all this information. "It's not what I envisioned for you, sweetheart," Maggie said. "But if you're determined... If this is what you really want."

"It is, Mom."

"You'll at least get a new dress for the ceremony?"

Jude laughed. "Yes, I'll get a new dress."

Maggie rose from the sofa and came over to give her daughter a hug. "I suppose it's time we met the O'Learys," she said.

Jude walked away from the window where she'd been thinking about that night. Yes, children disappointed their parents. It seemed to be a natural evolutionary event when a child reached for independence. And last week, her father had disappointed her when he hired Liam to "help" her. But people get over these incidents. They have to because nothing is more important than family. When she realized the tears had started again, Jude went into the kitchen to get a paper towel to wipe her eyes.

Nothing more important than family. Then why did she still carry such ungenerous thoughts about Paul in her heart?

CHAPTER ELEVEN

AFTER WESLEY WAS ASLEEP, Jude attempted to do what she'd promised Liam. She began to "think about" accepting his date for Wednesday night. But as soon as she envisioned just the two of them together, eating dinner, driving, perhaps taking a walk in the moonlight, a panic encompassed her.

She wasn't actually frightened at having a date. While she wasn't certain that Liam would handle her foundation the way she desired, she did trust him to be a gentleman. He would be considerate of her feelings, allow her to set a pace that would be comfortable. No one would say that Liam wasn't a considerate, respectful companion. She could have one little date and then decide if she wanted to see him again.

A good plan, but what frightened Jude was the possible results of one date. She already liked Liam. She appreciated what he did for

Wesley and the qualities that would eventually make him a good father—for some lucky kid.

So what was the problem? Well, if she enjoyed the date, if she accepted another and another, she would eventually have to reveal the most personal aspects of her life—the emotions of loss and guilt that still haunted her. With Jude, everything came down to the issue of trust. Where relationships were concerned, trust was not something that could be applied in half measure. You either trusted the person you were letting into the most intimate aspects of your life, or you didn't let him in. There was no leaving the door half open.

The question was, could she let Liam into her life? Could she admit the failings that kept her from leading a fulfilling existence?

Trust meant different things to different people. Jude trusted Nick at the feed store to sell her the correct mixtures of grain and oats. But would she trust him to take Wesley on an overnight camping trip? Certainly not. Would she trust Liam? Without a doubt. Jude thought about the times in her life she'd trusted the wrong people, and the results had been devastating.

And then she'd met Paul, the most honorable man she'd ever known with the exception of her father. And when he didn't consider her feelings about leaving her to serve in the army, and her with an infant, the result had been more than simply devastating. She felt she'd lost everything.

Carrie would tell her to take a risk, give this dating thing a try. Risks were fine for Carrie. She took them almost daily. But maybe it was time for Jude to take a note from her sister's playbook. Sitting on the sofa, Jude glanced over at the picture of her and Paul. He was so handsome in his uniform. She was smiling, though now that she recalled her feelings when the photo had been taken, she knew the smile had been false because she'd been sitting next to a man who would soon leave her. What she had truly felt was fear and betrayal because the man she loved had chosen to volunteer, to put distance between them.

Seven years earlier

PAUL ARRIVED HOME, hung his coat on the hook by the door and crossed to the kitchen where she was making dinner. Placing his hand on her rounded belly, he said, "How's my little mama tonight?"

She laughed as he nuzzled her neck. "You stink," she said. "How many cow patties did you step in today?"

"Only a few. I'll leave my boots outside and take a shower."

Later, when they'd eaten, Paul asked her to sit beside him on the sofa. His face was serious, his mannerisms guarded. "I need to talk to you, Judie," he said.

She sat next to him, their thighs touching, her hand over his. "What's up?"

"I made a decision today, and it concerns you almost as much as it does me."

She experienced the first tingle of panic across her shoulders. Paul had never approached a subject with such a dire tone in his voice. "What's wrong? Did something happen?"

"Nothing's wrong," he said. "I went to the recruitment office today. Now stay calm, honey. I've decided to enlist in the full-time army."

Her heart pounded. Her brain buzzed with alarm. She must not have heard him correctly. He'd been in the National Guard for two years, but he'd never mentioned wanting to join the regular army. In fact, they'd always been grateful that his unit hadn't been called up.

She sat a moment, her hand over her belly as if protecting her unborn child. "No," she finally said.

"I know this isn't what you want to hear, Jude, but it's what I want to do, what I feel I have to do."

"Why, Paul? I don't understand. You have a good heart, but you can't save the world, you know?"

He shook his head. "It's not that, although there is some truth in what you said. There are many reasons why this is a good idea."

She tried to draw in slow breaths to ease the burning in her throat. "We have plans, Paul. We fixed up this apartment, we have a baby coming…"

"I'll still be here in two months when the baby is born," he said. "It's a provision I made with the enlistment officer."

"But you can't leave us then. We'll have another mouth to feed. What will I do? How will we get by?"

"You'll stay right here, close to your family.

Or move back into the big house, whatever you like. And as for money, I'll make more in the army, considering health benefits and other perks, than I'm making at the farm." He looked sad but resolute when he added, "The farm just isn't cutting it, Jude. My brother just had a baby. We have one on the way. The farm can't support three families anymore."

"Then you'll get another job!" Her voice rose with her anger and resentment.

"Where, Jude? What kind of job? I'm not college educated. I've been a farmer all my life. That and my National Guard training is all I know."

"My dad will hire you. He needs someone to manage his property." She'd known when she said it that Paul would never agree to what he would view as Foster charity.

"No, he doesn't," Paul said. "He has a gardener, a groundskeeper and a housekeeper. He doesn't need a manager."

"Well, I need a husband! What about that? What about our vows when we promised to be together until death parts us?" Her voice broke when she said the last words. "You could die, Paul. Because of your experience in the Guard, they'll probably send you overseas to a war zone."

"They might," he said, breaking her heart. "But I'm well trained, Jude."

He picked up her hand. "I won't get killed, Jude. The number of casualties are minor compared to the number of soldiers on active duty. The statistics are heavily weighted on my side. I'll be fine."

"Paul, I trust you more than anyone I've ever known. I can't believe you're doing this, risking everything we have."

"Your trust means everything to me, honey," he said. "So I'm asking you one more time. Trust me on this. I'll email you every day. We'll talk often." He stared at her tear-streaked face, and ran his thumb down her cheek. "I'll be back all in one piece, with all my parts working. I won't take any unnecessary risks. I'm not a hero, Jude. I just want to do my part, provide for my family. I've thought about this for a long time. Trust me, baby. I'll come home to you."

After that night, their marriage changed. For the first time in their life together, Jude did not understand her husband. Why would

he give up everything they had to volunteer—
volunteer!—to put his life in jeopardy.

Jude didn't believe that his decision was
about the money. Her husband could have
brought home a paycheck many ways. Perhaps it was wanderlust, a desire to get away
from Bees Creek and see the world. He'd
never been anywhere farther away than Canada for a fishing trip. Maybe it was the challenge of facing down an enemy. Or maybe it
was a sense of honor, like he said, for Paul
had always been an honorable man. At least
Jude had believed that. Once he made a decision that seemed to exclude his family, once
he'd chosen to leave her, she wasn't sure what
honor was any more.

Meanwhile, Paul kept working at the farm,
waiting for the birth of their baby. But now
their nights were quiet as though Jude and the
man she adored couldn't find any common
ground to support a conversation. The relationship was strained, though the love somehow persisted.

After two months, their son, Wesley Martin O'Leary, was born. Paul was a wonderful,
caring father for the month he knew his son.
And he was a helpful, understanding husband

as far as his wife's new role as mother was concerned.

He continued to promise that he would come home. "I have no desire to be the bravest guy out there," he told her over and over. "You have to trust me, Jude. Once you start getting those paychecks, once you start reading daily emails proving that I'm fine, you'll see that this was the right decision for us. I can build a future for my family in the army."

AND THE EMAILS CAME. For five months after Paul left for Afghanistan, he religiously wrote Jude. Until the day an email didn't come. Jude worried through an entire night until the next morning when her father came to the apartment and told her she had a visitor at the house, a chaplain of the US Army.

She knew, of course. There was no other explanation for a chaplain to visit. As she rode with her father and her young son to the house, her body trembled, her head ached until she thought it might explode. She was consumed with anger and shock. She wanted to scream at Paul, as she should have when he made that decision. She wanted to grab his shoulders and shake him, and then to wrap her arms around him and hold on.

Her mother met her at the door as she came in, took the baby and embraced her with tears on her face. And the words Maggie had often said came back to haunt Jude. "You are too trusting, sweetheart. You need to think about what people tell you. You must learn to rely on yourself."

Those words came true that day. From the moment she heard the chaplain pronounce the end of the life she'd always hoped for, Jude learned to rely on herself. Part of her never forgave Paul. All of her grieved for him. Paul had died a hero, saving two fellow soldiers who had been riding in a truck with him when their convoy was hit by an IED.

Jude accepted her neighbors' condolences and even an award recognizing Paul's bravery. She stared at the medal, trying to imagine the act that took her husband. Could he have saved himself if he hadn't risked his life for two other men? Sadly, as the days passed, Jude became consumed by a guilt so profound it nearly crippled her. She resented the act of a hero.

In the end, she had a medal, an infant son

and bitter feelings that she believed would never go away. During one of her darkest days, the idea of the Paul O'Leary Foundation was born, and perhaps the birth of the foundation saved her. She suddenly had an outlet for her grief and her guilt. She would honor the hero, though she never quite forgave the man.

But Liam was different. He was solid, reasonable, a man who valued his job and his family. Would he feel the need to leave everything behind and cross an ocean for a principle? Some men would, honorable men like Paul perhaps, but there were different types of honor. Liam didn't take risks. If he gave his word, he kept it. Though it was late, Jude called Liam's number.

"Hello, Jude. Is everything okay?"

"Yes. I just called to tell you I would like to go out with you Wednesday night."

"Great. I'm so glad. I'll pick you up at seven."

She had just taken a cue from Carrie. Accepting a date with Liam was a small risk, but Jude felt empowered. And perhaps just a little ready to trust again.

CHAPTER TWELVE

ON WEDNESDAY MORNING, once she'd finished her on-air time at WOIH, Jude called her sister to tell her about the date.

"I think you should get your hair cut," Carrie had said almost immediately.

"What?" Jude had never considered altering her appearance. "I haven't had my hair cut in five years."

"My point exactly," Carrie said. "That long hair ages you, hon. Go to a salon and get a more contemporary style. You won't believe the difference. And neither will Liam. You'll wow him, Jude, I know it."

"I don't even know where to go anymore," Jude said. "The last beauty shop I went to closed down. And if I go alone, I'll probably chicken out."

"Call Aurora. She'll go with you."

"Aurora?" It wasn't a bad idea. Jude liked Aurora. "I guess I could."

"Great. Now hang up with me and call her. It's almost ten o'clock. You want to have your new look by the time Wesley gets out of school."

Jude disconnected. A new look at the age of thirty-two. She wasn't too old to consider a makeover, she knew that. She took her phone back out of her pocket and called Aurora.

"Feel like going to the beauty parlor with me?" she said when Aurora answered.

"Sure. I'm not doing anything. I could use a trim and gray touch-up myself. Your salon or mine?"

"Ah... I don't really have one."

"No problem. I'll call mine and make two appointments. Pick me up in a half hour unless I call you back."

"Sounds good."

That kind of quick decision-making, lack of chitchat, was one thing that endeared Aurora to Jude. Their entire day had just been planned out in under a minute. Jude hopped in her truck and headed toward Fox Creek.

"I WANT THE braid to go to Locks of Love," Jude said to a stylist an hour later. "Someone who has had chemo can use it."

"That's a nice thing to do," the young man said. "I'll see that it's donated." He finished unbraiding Jude's hair and ran his fingers through the mass of twists and curls. "Oh my, this is some head of hair."

"What do you think?" Jude didn't want a short cut, but she'd made up her mind to listen to the stylist—within reason.

"Some layering," he said. "Shoulder length at the sides to accentuate those gorgeous cheekbones, longer in back. That way you can still put it up if you want to."

She took a deep breath, closed her eyes as if she were sitting in a theater watching a horror movie. "Okay, let's do it. Cut."

He wound the long strands into a loose gather, wrapped a piece of tape around the top and bottom and cut. Jude's hair fell into his hands in one flowing bundle. "It's done," he said, putting the ponytail in a plastic bag. "I'll bet they get two or three wigs out of this."

Jude had expected to experience remorse, at least regret at saying goodbye to something that had been a part of her for so long. Oddly she felt only a lightness, a freedom.

"Now we style," the man said.

Aurora, sitting next to Jude with color

product on her roots, smiled. "It's only hair, Jude. How many times in my life have I had to say something similar to calm my own nerves? 'It's only money, Aurora.' I've used that one too many times to remember."

Jude smiled.

A half hour later, Jude's cut was nearly complete. A stylist was beginning on Aurora. "Take a little off the top," Aurora said. "And the sides, and the crown and the back." She hooted, looked at Jude who was getting ready for a blow-dry. "I never know how far I'll go until I sit in one of these chairs," she said. They left the salon poorer but happy. Jude's hair swung about her shoulders in a breezy, easy way. Aurora's curls had been temporarily tamed into a sleeker style, which she hoped would last at least a couple of days.

"We won't look like this for long," Jude said. "The first shampoo will see to that, but for now, I think we've earned a late lunch and some good English tea."

"I WANT TO GO, TOO," Wesley said. "I haven't had supper, and Liam is my friend more than he is yours."

"I know he's your friend, honey," Jude responded. "But you don't want to go tonight. We're going to talk business. You'd be totally bored. And Rosie is having hot dogs, which you love."

Wesley thought a moment, seemed to appraise his mother from top to bottom, taking in her low-cut boots, simple black dress slacks and short-sleeved red-and-black sweater. "Is that why you got your hair cut? To talk business with Liam?"

Smart little guy. Wesley didn't miss much. Talking business had nothing to do with it, but she would never admit to that. "I got my hair cut because I wanted to." She touched the stylish barrette that held one side of hair back from her face. The stylist had talked her into the indulgence. "And you haven't said anything about it. Do you like the haircut?"

"Yeah. You look pretty."

Jude smiled. One male down. One to go.

When a knock sounded on the door, Wes ran to open it. "Hi, Liam," he said when his good friend came in the door in tan chinos, a brown sweater and a tan jacket. "I got an A on my arithmetic test today."

Liam held up the flat of his hand. "High five, buddy. That's super."

"And we had a dentist come to school and talk to all the first graders about how to brush our teeth. And gums are important, too. Let me see yours."

Liam glanced at Jude. His gaze held for a warm, appreciative moment before he drew back his lips.

"They look good," Wesley said. "Pink like they're supposed to be."

"Good to know." He returned his attention to Jude. "Wow, you look fabulous. Is it a cliché to say, 'I like what you've done with your hair'?"

"Even if it is, I'll take the compliment. First real haircut in five years." She wished she could take back the comment as soon as she said it. Liam knew that five years was a reference to when Paul died, when a big part of her life had stopped.

As of this moment, no more of those references for the rest of the night. Jude felt feminine and pretty and modern. She felt warm as the object of Liam's gaze, and she would enjoy this feeling for as long as she could.

"We need coats," Liam said. "It's chilly out there."

Once they'd bundled up, Liam leaned close

to Jude and said, "If our date had anything to do with the haircut, I'm surprised, flattered and blown away."

She thought about saying she'd been contemplating a haircut for a long time, but why lie? So she said, "Maybe a little."

Wesley, several steps ahead of them, turned around. "You're taking me to Grandpa's. We're having hot dogs. I bet your supper won't be as good."

"Probably not," Liam conceded. "Be sure to bring your mom a doggy bag."

Wesley laughed, hopped in Liam's car, and they took off for the main house.

MARTIN OPENED THE door when they arrived. "Could this stunning woman be my daughter? Honey, you look great."

She laughed and thanked him.

Martin enjoyed seeing his daughter this happy. Admitting that he might have been wrong about not approving of a romance between Jude and Liam, and that Aurora might have been right, he hoped this date would be the start of something important for Jude. "Let Wesley stay here tonight," Martin said.

"That way you don't have to rush back. We could use some sleepover time."

"There's school tomorrow, Daddy."

"I know. I'll make sure he's in bed by nine. You can bring a change of clothes in the morning and take him to school."

For some odd reason, she looked to Liam.

"Sounds like a good plan to me," he said.

"You two have fun," Martin said, and announced that their hot dogs were ready.

Fifteen minutes later, Wes had wolfed down three frankfurters and a healthy helping of fries.

"What'll we do now, Grandpa?" Wesley asked. "Do you want to play checkers?"

Martin had already come up with an idea. "Why don't we go out for ice cream?" he suggested. "How does that sound?"

"Super."

A few minutes later, after Martin had given instructions to Maggie's nurse, he and Wesley were passing the path of white Christmas lights that led to the bed-and-breakfast.

"It's like a fairyland," Wesley said.

"Sure is. Aurora loves Christmas." He noticed a car blinker on the vehicle approaching them. The car slowed and a window buzzed down. It was Aurora. "Where are you two headed?" she asked.

"We're going for ice cream," Wes hollered. "You can come, too."

"Thanks, hon, but I've got to watch my waistline."

Martin wasn't usually an impulsive man, but an easy invitation just seemed to slip from his lips. "Why don't you come, Aurora? It's not like I don't owe you for a few dozen baked goods you've sent over to the house."

She smiled. "Well, okay. I don't have anything on my schedule tonight. No guests." She pulled up to her front porch, parked and slid into the backseat of Martin's car. To Martin, she looked like a little snow bunny with her fur collar and earmuffs. Martin noticed her hair right away.

"What's with you ladies today?" he said. "This must have been beautifying day."

"Jude and I went to the salon together. Nothing like a little moral support." She removed her earmuffs, displaying the hair that hadn't yet had a chance to return to her normal riot of curls. "You like?"

"I definitely do," Martin said. "Wes, doesn't Aurora look pretty?"

Wesley slowly nodded and dragged out the single syllable, "Yeah…"

Aurora laughed, a sound that had become comforting to Martin over the past months. He did enjoy her cinnamon rolls, but there was an inner strength to Aurora that he'd come to appreciate, as well. She seemed to understand the responsibilities he faced at home. And she'd been right on about Jude when she advised him to talk to her. "Okay, folks, start thinking about which of the twenty-four flavors you want."

AN HOUR LATER, Wesley was still licking his fingers.

Aurora dug around in her large pocketbook and withdrew a package of moistened wipes. Taking one out, she passed it to the backseat. "Here, clean off your fingers, honey."

"I remember my wife always having a supply of those," Martin said.

"It's a mom thing," she said. "Wipes are as important to the contents of a purse as a driver's license or house keys."

That was the first time Martin had heard Aurora mention family in a long time. He wondered. How many children did she have? She'd only mentioned one son.

Before he could ask, Aurora began singing along with the radio. Martin tabled his question.

When they drove up her lit lane, Aurora said, "Thanks so much for this, Marty. It was a treat and a good end to my day."

"I'm glad you could come with us."

When her house came into view, a strange automobile, an older-model Honda, was parked in front. As they got closer, Aurora leaned forward and squinted out the windshield toward the dim porch light she'd left on. A lone figure was perched on the bottom step. "Who could that be?"

Martin's alert system took over. "You said you didn't have any guests tonight. Did you forget about a reservation?"

"No. I don't have anybody coming until the weekend."

"I'll check it out," he said. "You and Wesley stay in the car." In a softer voice he added, "Wouldn't hurt to keep the doors locked." He parked and opened his car door. "Do you have your cell phone handy, Aurora?"

She started to answer but instead put her

hand on Martin's arm. "It's okay, Marty. You can get back in the car. I'll handle this."

"Like heck you will."

"No, really, it's okay. I recognize the person now that we're closer."

"Who is he?"

She stared out the window and took a deep breath. "That's my son, William."

"Your son? You didn't know he was coming?"

She shook her head. "He's always had a rather erratic schedule. I never know when he'll show up."

"Well, fine. Maybe he'll stay through Christmas. I'd like to meet him."

"Not tonight, Marty, if you don't mind."

He gave her a hard stare. She was in control, didn't seem upset or anxious about this unannounced visit. Still, he couldn't ignore his suspicious nature. "Are you sure? Maybe I can be of some help."

"I don't need help, but thanks. I'll be in touch with you soon." She looked over the front seat. "I'm glad I got to see you tonight, Wesley. It was fun."

She opened her door, and the man on the step stood. He was average height, slim, with a knitted stocking cap on his longish, dark hair. He remained where he was, his hands in his jeans pockets. Next to him sat a large duffel bag. Martin figured he'd come to stay awhile.

Martin couldn't explain his misgivings, but they were strong. "I'll expect you to call, Aurora. If you don't, I'll call you."

She leaned into the car window for a few seconds. "He's my son, Marty. I'll be fine."

He watched her approach the steps where William still waited. The two spoke. Aurora put her hand on her son's arm. There was no embrace, no sign of true affection, strange for a woman like Aurora who didn't mind showing her emotions. Strange, really, for any parent.

Martin backed up, turned and headed down the drive. In his mirror he saw Aurora enter her house with her son following. Then the lights in the living room came on.

AFTER TURNING ON the lights, Aurora moved quickly to the kitchen. "I'll put coffee on."

William followed. "Thanks. I could use a cup. It was pretty cold out there."

Thank goodness she'd made thousands of

pots of coffee in her lifetime, and didn't have to think about what she was doing. She could perform the simple task without worrying about what had brought her son to Ohio, or how he'd discovered where she lived.

"I see you have a car," she said while the coffee brewed.

"Picked it up a week ago. It's not much, but it got me here."

She hated herself for thinking the worst. Had William stolen the car?

"Where did you come from?"

"Idaho. I've been staying with some friends there."

She nodded.

"You could have told me you moved," he said. "You knew I was going into the rehab place. I stayed there for three months. You could have reached me."

She carried the sugar bowl to the table. "I suppose I could have."

"I found out from Aunt Agnes where you were. She didn't have the address, though. She just said you were opening a bed-and-breakfast. I found this place on the internet in the library."

Aurora wasn't close to her ex husband's

sister, but she had told Agnes a bit about her plans just in case there was a true emergency. Aurora had lived so long expecting to hear about emergencies related to Phil or William that she couldn't let go completely.

William looked around the cozy kitchen. "This is nice. You buy it outright?"

She frowned. It hadn't taken William ten minutes to turn the conversation to money.

Without answering, she brought a mug of coffee to the table and set a spoon beside it. "Did you have a job in Idaho?"

"This and that. Saved up enough to buy the junker out there."

"How long do you plan on staying?" she asked.

"Depends. Are you even a little glad to see me?"

His words were more a challenge than a logical question. She couldn't tell him the truth—that just seeing him reminded her of the strength she'd finally found to remain separate from him physically and emotionally. With a mother's passion, a mother's memories of long-ago years, she wanted to take him in her arms and comfort him. But experience had taught her to not show a moment of weakness. She answered evasively. "You're my son."

He took off his cap, ran his fingers through his long hair. "I'm clean," he said.

She sat on the other side of the table, stirred her coffee. "Glad to hear it." Out of a force of habit, she stared into his eyes. Pupils small and clear. He seemed to be telling the truth— for now.

"Dad's living in Oregon," he said. "Some little town near the coast. He's got a pretty decent mobile home."

"Good."

"I told him I was going to look you up. He sends his regards."

She took a sip of coffee. So alike, the two men who had once been the center of her life. They each could work her over until the sympathy just oozed out of her pores, and the money trickled out of her bank account. But she'd learned. The lesson had been hard and heartbreaking, but she'd finally learned. If she hadn't made a clean break, she would never have been done helping the two addictive men in her family. She could never give enough.

Gambling, alcohol and, most horribly for William, drugs. It was all the same disease, and it afflicted both her men. Their problems had paved a road to ruin. Thank goodness, after trying for years to change them, she'd decided not to take another step with them.

"He's okay, Dad is," William said, though Aurora hadn't asked. "Working part-time at a restaurant. He gets by."

Aurora did a quick mental survey of her refrigerator. "Are you hungry, William? I could scratch up something."

"No, not hungry."

Of course not. He hadn't been hungry in years. That was one of the effects of the heroin. She thought about telling him he was too thin, but didn't.

"Can I stay here tonight?" he asked. "Maybe a couple of days? The last rehab was pretty tough, and I haven't had a proper bed to sleep on in weeks. I need a rest."

"Yes, you can stay tonight." Before she let her past affection and her gullibility get the best of her, she established limits. "You can stay a week, but I don't know how much rest you'll get. The downstairs bathroom and the sunroom need coats of paint. The basement needs cleaning out. My truck could use an oil change and a tire rotation. I'll pay you fifty dollars a day as long as you're working. A week from tomorrow, you plan on taking your salary and going wherever it is you've planned to go next."

He nodded. His hand shook as he drained his coffee mug. "Thanks, Mom."

"Don't lie to me, William. Don't steal from me. If you do, this will be the shortest week you'll ever remember."

"I won't, I promise."

She stood and walked away from him to the sink, not wanting him to interpret any emotion in her face. How sad, a thirty-six-year-old man making a promise to his mother that sounded like it might have come from a five-year-old.

CHAPTER THIRTEEN

THE BOTTLE OF local vintage Kelly's Island Red was almost empty. Liam poured the rest into Jude's glass. "I'm driving," he said. "You finish it. Then we'll have coffee and dessert. This place is famous for their crème brûlée.

"I'm stuffed," Jude said. "But I might have a taste of yours."

The waiter removed the remains of Jude's shrimp dinner and Liam's steak. Liam gave him the coffee and dessert order. When he'd walked off, Liam stared at Jude's face. "You look so pretty in this light," he said. "But that didn't really come out the way I meant. You always look pretty no matter what the light is like."

"Come on, Liam, you don't have to flatter me. I know you've got something to tell me."

"Why would you think I have an ulterior motive?" he asked.

She smiled. "Well, don't you?"

"Okay, I sort of have one, but still, what I said is true. You look pretty."

She didn't argue again. The truth was, she felt pretty. And she was especially happy that she looked pretty to Liam. Maybe the couple of glasses of wine had contributed to her sense of well-being. Or maybe it was the haircut or the red-and-black sweater. Her sisters always told her she looked good in red.

And she'd had a good time. She and Liam talked about everything from their childhoods to her failed attempt at college and his successful completion of his education at Wharton. He'd made some great friends at school, he told her. Many of them he was still in contact with. A couple of times, when he was making a point, he reached across the table and stroked her hand. The gesture tingled all the way up her arm and settled as a comforting warmth in her chest.

What was happening to her? She hadn't considered dating for so long she'd definitely gotten out of practice. And she certainly wouldn't have expected to enjoy it so much. She'd sighed with contentment about halfway through the meal when she realized the date had been easy. She hadn't struggled to make conversation. She hadn't worried about what she would say or do. How was it possible that in this five-star restaurant with a man she'd only recently been furious with, she could feel so at home?

She took a sip of the wine and smiled at him. "Okay, you might as well hit me with whatever you want to say. I'm assuming you want to talk to me about the foundation."

"I do. Have I plied you with enough alcohol?"

She laughed, though her senses warned her that this smooth-sailing date might be ready to hit a sand bar. "I don't think there's enough in this restaurant, but go ahead."

"I've been thinking about the groups who benefit from your charity, the ones that aren't a great financial burden and the ones that are. I don't believe you'll have much trouble supporting the scholarships for veterans' kids, although maybe you should cut back. Many organizations give scholarships of only five hundred or a thousand dollars, enough for the student to buy books at least. And the kid has to reapply each year. Plus, you should demand a financial statement from the parents to justify the gift."

"You're saying I'm giving money to applicants who might not really need it?"

"It's possible. Anyone who's applying for one of your scholarships should be willing to show financial need."

That made sense. "Okay. I can do that. And you'll help me interpret the financial statements?"

"Sure."

He seemed so cool and confident that Jude wondered if she was making this too easy on him. "What's next?"

"Get rid of the goats."

Even for a guy who didn't like goats, that was a pretty blatant suggestion. "Now, wait a minute. I told you that takes time. I want to first make sure that the goats are well enough to withstand a sea voyage to Central America."

"Do you have a destination point in mind?"

"No, not yet." Perhaps she should have been researching this more diligently.

"I'm sorry, Jude, but that herd is probably the biggest drain on your day-to-day operation. I'll admit I'm not a goat expert, but I didn't see a one that wasn't fit to go on a little cruise."

She remained silent a moment. He was right. The goats were fine. Her vet hadn't treated one for a problem in weeks. Their weight was ideal, and there was no reason she shouldn't let them go to the homes where they could do some good. "Okay, but not Eloise. I'm going to keep her."

He smiled. "Okay, not Eloise. You've got to keep one so Mutt will have something to do."

"Tomorrow I'll make some calls and get estimates on getting the animals to Central America. I'm hoping I can find a charitable organization that might be willing to chip in on shipping costs if the goats will help their local population."

"That's a great idea," Liam said. He cleared his throat. "There is one last thing."

He'd saved the worst for last. "What?"

"The radio station," he said.

"I knew it!"

"Jude, in just the little time I had to look at your books, I immediately determined that WOIH is your biggest expense, next to the animals' care."

"Maybe so, but I won't pull the station. It's too important to the people of Bees Creek."

Liam gave her an earnest stare. "All five thousand of them?"

"That may not seem like a lot to you—"

"Jude, that's not a lot of people to anyone. WOIH is a minimum-wattage station whose broadcasts only reach fifty miles or so. Even if you enlarged the listenership, which wouldn't make sense because you'll be encroaching on major markets, the expenses will keep eating up your budget."

"But I have plans for the station I haven't even put into effect yet. A recipe program, a show where we talk about the best prices on goods and services, a neighbors-helping-neighbors feature... And then there's Harvey and Gary—"

"Who each take a salary," he finished for her. "I know how you feel about them, but you can't keep supporting these guys because they're friends or original settlers. Both those men can find jobs, even if it's not in the radio business."

She straightened her spine. The radio station was her personal favorite of all her charities. WOIH's building was located in Bees Creek, where Paul had been raised. The men who ran it had known Paul since he was a child. She herself contributed by broadcasting information that was important to the people, Paul's people. She leaned forward and spoke in a low, but harsh whisper. "You're going too far, Liam. I won't dismantle the station, I just won't."

He expelled a long breath. "Jude, I'm not saying you should. In fact, I've got a plan so you won't have to."

She tried to relax, though she doubted if his idea would appeal to her. But she would listen. "Go ahead."

"I've done some research, made a couple of contacts. There's a new company in northeast Ohio called Northern Ohio Media. They're buying up local stations like WOIH, modernizing them with new formats, making them more accessible to greater numbers of people."

"What sort of new formats? All national news? All rock music?"

"No. They incorporate the best of what the station currently broadcasts and add some newer, modern features."

"So they would keep broadcasting local info that the farmers need?"

"It might be arranged, yes. It's all about the contract of sale."

"Fine, but they'd fire Harvey and Gary, and I can't let that happen."

"It's possible," Liam said. "I talked to the director today, and told him about WOIH. I said the listenership is small but loyal, thanks to the two guys running the station now, men who would be essential to the future success of WOIH. I might have convinced him that to get WOIH to sell to Northern Ohio Media, he'd have to promise a fair and impartial audition to Harvey and Gary." Obviously sensing her reluctance, he added, "They're grown men, Jude. They know that very little is handed to them on a silver platter. They'll go along with this."

"But they at least agreed to give them an audition?"

"Yes. Besides, everything is negotiable now. We can make it a priority in any contract."

The waiter brought coffee and Liam's dessert.

"I appreciate that, Liam," Jude said. "I would definitely consider those terms."

"It's a win for the foundation," Liam said,

stirring a teaspoon of sugar into his coffee. "The foundation will experience a boost to its bottom line from the sale. And your boys will probably still have a job doing what they love, as long as they can accept that they're not their own bosses anymore."

"They'll be okay with that," she said. "And maybe I can pay Dad back for some of his expenses." She couldn't keep a smile from spreading across her face. "Paul would be so pleased about Harvey and Gary..."

She paused, looked down a moment. Why did she have to bring Paul into this now? "What I meant was..."

He held a spoon close to her lips. "Don't worry about it. Try the crème brûlée."

She let the flavors melt on her tongue. Sweet and smooth, like most of this night had been. How strange that after all the years of denying herself pleasure and passion, she could find herself in this restaurant, with a man so completely unlike herself, and feel so comfortable.

They had discussed important topics tonight. They'd compromised and listened to each other, and Jude now understood why Liam Manning commanded such a high salary. He was a man of his word, honorable in his own right without betraying those closest to him. He was steadfast, trustworthy, *here for the future*.

Now, where did that notion come from? Jude rarely thought about a future. She was so consumed with the responsibilities of living each day. And yet suddenly a future of happiness and contentment, and maybe even romance, didn't seem like it was for everyone else, but not her. She didn't know how Liam felt about her, but she now knew that if she could ever fall for another man like she'd fallen for Paul, Liam might be the one.

WITH HER ARM tucked in his, Jude and Liam took a brisk walk along the lakefront in Cleveland. In spite of the temperature, she felt warm, protected. At one point they stopped, she leaned her head against his shoulder and they stood quietly, just looking out at the waves. Any rancor that might have sprung up between them at dinner seemed to have faded in the soothing cool evening air. Later, on the drive to Dancing Falls, Jude made a list of projects for the next day. She planned to take each of Liam's ideas seriously and make a dent in the foundation's debt.

After several miles, Liam spoke in an obviously feigned grumpy voice. "I was hoping you might sit a little closer to me on the way," he said. "I didn't know you'd have your nose buried in your homework."

She slid the paper into her purse and scooted over on her bucket seat until their shoulders touched. "You're right. There are more important things than making lists, even if I am implementing your ideas."

He settled his hand on her thigh. "Oh, well, in that case, don't let me interrupt you."

"Too late," she said. "You have ruined the list-making mood."

He smiled at her. She settled close and just watched the miles slide by. There was no urgency to talk in the peaceful environment of his car. Enveloped in darkness, she felt like the interior of this car was the only place that existed. Maybe she even felt, almost...trusting.

"Are you happy with me now?" he asked when they pulled into the drive of Dancing Falls. "You don't think I'm the horrible hatchet man anymore?"

"We'll have to see about that. I fully expect you to take this small victory tonight and spoil it with many more cutbacks."

He chuckled.

"But for now, right this minute…" She sighed and spoke a few simple words she never thought she'd say. "I am sublimely happy with you."

He pulled in front of the barn, cut the engine and lifted her face to his. The first kiss was different. Needy, expressive, saying with the press of his mouth and invasion of his tongue what words didn't have to.

I am falling in love with this man, she thought. It can't be happening this fast. But, oh, how she felt about him. If this wasn't love, then it was the next closest thing, and she didn't want to let go.

She stopped a sigh in her throat, blinked. "Liam…"

Just a moment ago she had been lost in the feel of him, the wonder of him, the wonder of herself…but it all changed when she was suddenly faced with this life-altering decision. Could she commit to this man? When she'd married Paul, the memories of every other boy ceased to exist as she said her vows. And she couldn't so easily forget those vows now. She would be giving too much too soon.

She sat back, hugged her arms to her chest.

He cupped his hand on the back of her head and stared into her eyes. "Whatever it is, Jude, don't worry about it, okay? It's all right. How about I come by on Sunday and pick up you and the kiddo and bring you both to my place for dinner? I'm cooking. How does that sound?"

"Perfect. But just give me the address. I'll drive."

"You sure?"

"Yes. You've driven out here so often. It's more than my turn."

"Okay, then. I'll call you tomorrow." He got out of the car and walked her to the door for one last kiss.

CHAPTER FOURTEEN

"HOW MUCH LONGER till we get there, Mom?"

Jude told herself to exercise patience. Yes, this was about the hundredth time Wesley had asked this question. Yes, she was driving in afternoon rush hour, and yes, this was Cleveland. She should have agreed with Liam's plan to pick them up, but no, she had been in Super Woman mode and convinced him she'd drive herself.

"We're almost there, Wes," she said, glancing quickly to consult her GPS. "We only have two more miles, less than the distance to your school. I need to call Liam now to tell him we're close. Can you dial the number for me?"

Wesley was happy to oblige. Like most kids his age, he knew the basics of cell phone operation. He found the list of Jude's contacts and zeroed in on Liam. He was grinning as he held the phone to his ear. "Hi, Liam. It's Wesley."

"Yeah, we're coming. Mom says we're about two miles away." There was a moment of silence. "Okay, I'll tell her. Bye."

"What did he say?" Jude asked, stopping at yet another red light.

"He'll be outside his apartment building watching for us."

"That's good. He'll be able to tell us where to park."

Ten minutes later, they were on Lakeshore Drive, passing an endless stream of modern high-rise buildings. One of these elegant structures was Liam's, and each one was about as different from an apartment above a tack room as any place could be. Jude patted the dashboard of her truck. "It's okay, baby. Don't feel embarrassed. You run as well as any of these fancy cars."

Wesley giggled. "Yeah, our truck looks pretty bad next to some of these other cars."

They rounded a graceful bend in the road and saw Liam standing in a parking lot waving his arms. Jude navigated to a stop next to him while he motioned her into an underground parking garage. She followed his instructions and slid into a narrow spot labeled "Guest."

"You made it," Liam said when Jude and Wesley got out of the truck. He high-fived Wesley and planted a chaste kiss on Jude's temple. "I'm so glad you're here."

"Nothing to it," Jude said, grateful to be out of her truck.

"I'm anxious for you to see my place. Thank goodness the cleaning lady was here yesterday, so things are pretty tidy."

Wesley was spellbound as they entered the brass and mirrored elevator and rode to the eighteenth floor of the Wave Crest Building.

"Wow, this is high up," Wesley said.

"Yeah, it's pretty high," Liam confirmed.

They stepped into a wide entrance hallway with four doors leading to apartments on this level.

"You only have three neighbors?" Jude asked, looking around at extravagant silk flower arrangements under low lighting.

"That's right. There are larger apartments on floors above me with only two units each and the top floor is for the penthouse."

Impressive. Jude was anxious to experience

what lay beyond the double door to Liam's apartment.

He proceeded to the door marked with a *B* and slipped his key into the lock. "After you," he said, swinging the door wide.

LIAM TRIED TO see his living quarters as Jude might see them. More than anything, he wanted her to feel comfortable being here so she would want to come back again. But would she? Jude, with her gently used furniture and minimal space, might view his apartment as a tribute to excess. Or she might see it as a testament to a young man's success after years of study and deprivation. Liam had made his own way through graduate school, and as far as he was concerned, this condominium was a result of his accomplishments.

Wesley charged ahead of them, but Jude walked slowly through the foyer and into the open great room, which had a coveted view of the lake. Stopping to rub her palm along his tan suede sectional sofa, she stared at lights blinking on in the city below. "This is beautiful, Liam. I could look at this view for hours."

He sighed with relief. "I didn't have anything to do with the view. That was all Mother Nature. And I hired a decorator for the rest, so I don't deserve a whole lot of credit for any of it."

She smiled, focusing her attention on Wesley, who stood with his palms against the floor-to-ceiling glass. "What do you think, Wesley? Pretty nice, huh?"

"It's great," he said. "I'm gonna live in a place like this when I grow up."

"You'd better start saving your allowance, then," Jude said.

Liam indicated that Jude should sit on the sofa. She did, and stretched her legs out toward the glass coffee table. "These are my best 'going out' jeans," she said. "Yet I still feel underdressed."

"You look beautiful," he said. "That sweater is a knockout."

She raked her fingers along the soft arm of the garment. "It's cashmere, not all that practical for a country girl. My father got it for me for Christmas."

"He has good taste," Liam said. "Can I get you guys a soda or some iced tea?" Liam asked. "We're having spaghetti. I hope that's all right. I'm not really much of a cook."

"I love spaghetti," Wesley said, finally walking away from the window. "Don't cut mine. I like to spin it around on my fork."

"No problem," Liam promised. "Sodas?"

"That would be great," Jude said.

"Before I get them, I have a surprise for Wesley."

"A surprise for me?" He grabbed Liam's hand. "What is it?"

"Come with me," Liam said. "I want to show you something in my office." He turned to Jude. "You can come with us if you want, Jude, or wait here and just relax after that drive."

She didn't budge. "Relaxing sounds good."

Liam returned a few minutes later with her drink and sat next to her on the sofa.

"What's Wesley doing?" she asked.

"I set up a telescope for him," Liam said. "I aimed it at the sky from the office window and told him what to look for."

"That was nice of you," she said.

"No praise necessary. I wanted us to have some time together, just the two of us. I hope that's okay."

She angled her body nearer to his and he

slipped his arm around her shoulders. "It's perfect."

Liam fought his desire to kiss her. Jude looked so unique, so stunning—a mysterious combination of natural beauty and feminine innocence. She was clever, strong, nurturing, and as each minute passed, and their conversation wandered toward more personal, intimate topics, Liam felt even more invested.

But he wouldn't rush her. She had only recently forgiven him for his deception with her father. She had resented his interference in the foundation's running with his unwanted advice and financial common sense. But they were on the same page now, and he didn't want anything to disrupt the relationship they were building toward what he hoped would be a happy ending.

"Hey, Liam, come here!"

Wesley's voice came from Liam's home office. With a mother's natural instinct, Jude stood up suddenly. "We'd better go check."

They rushed into the room that held the telescope, computer equipment and mementoes of Liam's professional life. The decorator he'd hired when he bought the condo had made sense of his files and records with tasteful built-in cabinets. A contemporary walnut desk occupied nearly one entire wall. Above the desk was a collection of photos of which Liam was especially fond.

"What's wrong, Wesley?" Liam asked when both he and Jude had determined there was no real emergency.

Wesley pointed to one of the photos. "Is that you?" he asked.

Jude went immediately to the bank of pictures. She briefly studied each one. "You're in every one of these!" she said before drawing in a sharp breath. She pointed to one taken a few summers ago when Liam and his friends covered two hundred miles of the Appalachian Trail. In the photo, he had on camouflage pants, a windbreaker and a bandanna around his head. He especially remembered that trip because it was the longest time he'd ever gone without a shower.

"Yeah, that's me all right," he said. "That backpack must have weighed thirty pounds, and I lost about ten." He walked up beside her and pointed to the other men in the photo. "These are my three best friends from college. That's Don, Lenny and George. We met as freshmen, joined the same fraternity, and have stayed close ever since."

She scanned the other pictures, her features seeming to grow more alarmed by the second. "For heaven's sake, Liam, you four guys have actually done all these things?"

"Look at this one, Mom," Wesley said. "Liam jumped from an airplane!"

"We sure did." Liam smiled at the picture of the four of them free-falling from a small plane, hands joined, huge smiles on their faces. "I must admit I was scared nearly out of my mind that day, but it was a thrill I'll never forget."

She turned slowly to face him. Her bafflement seemed to have transformed into terror. "But why would you do such a thing?"

He stood a little taller, hoping she recognized the pure guts it took to make the jump. "We had to. Our senior year we made a pact to do one adventurous thing each summer. We called ourselves the Bucket Club, you know, after the term Bucket List." He chuckled. "I must admit that not all these things were on my personal bucket list, but once a majority of us agreed to an adventure, then the testosterone kicked in, and we all went along."

He gestured toward a picture of a boat on calm waters. Four men were on the deck. "This was the summer we went to Australia, donned scuba gear and went down over the Great Barrier Reef in a shark cage. I came within several yards of a great white. Took my breath away."

She indicated a photo of the four men standing next to donkeys. "And this one?"

"Grand Canyon. We went to the bottom. Lenny insisted we learn the terrain ourselves and go down without a guide. It wasn't as hard as it sounds, since the burros pretty much knew the way. The nights were tough. You don't want to sleepwalk when you're perched on sheer rock cliffs."

Wesley seemed unable to tear his gaze from the photos. "Isn't Liam the coolest guy ever, Mom?" He looked up at Liam, his eyes bright with excitement. "I want to do all these things. Will you take me with you next time, Liam?"

"No, Wesley, not the next time. You have to be quite a bit older to—"

Jude interrupted him. "Of course not, Wesley. Don't be silly. You're never going to do such crazy things." She then turned to Liam and gave him a sharp stare. "I hope this is all history?" she said. "You're through with these *adventures*?"

"Not hardly," he said. "This summer we're climbing Mount Dunwoody in Utah. It's not the highest peak, but it's pretty challenging. This one is my idea, so I'm really looking forward to it."

Her eyes grew wide. "I can't believe you would do this," she said, cloaking her words in a guttural whisper. "Besides setting a terrible example for Wesley, it's foolhardy. It's dangerous."

"It's also life-affirming and requires great team-building skills, and excuse me, Jude, but why is it my job to set a good example for your son?"

"If you're going to be around him, then it is," she said. "I only want positive role models in Wesley's life."

"And you don't think I'm a positive role model?"

Wesley tugged on Jude's sweater. "Mom, what's going on? Why are you guys mad?"

"We're not mad," she said, but Liam knew

better. Jude was furious. Her anger was misdirected, based on an irrational fear of what she didn't understand. What he viewed as the indulgences of friends testing their skills she judged as death-defying absurdity. He touched her arm. "Are you okay? You need to take a couple of deep breaths."

She leaned down and spoke to her son. "Finish looking out the telescope, Wes. I need to speak to Liam."

She marched out of the office and stood near the windows in his living room.

Liam came up behind her. "Talk to me, Jude. Tell me why you're so upset."

"You don't know?" she replied as if he were the densest man on earth.

"I think I do. You believe I'm a bad example for your son, but there's obviously more to it than that."

"You're right," she began. "I just can't imagine why these adventures are so important to you. What if there were an accident? What if something went wrong?"

"First of all, we've been doing these things for years and nothing has gone wrong—nothing that we didn't anticipate and prepare for anyway—a few failed batteries, a sudden change of weather, that type of thing."

"What about your parents? Surely they don't approve of these trips."

"They do worry sometimes, sure. But as my parents they've never stood in the way of doing something that was important to me," he said. "Besides, we're grown men, Jude. We don't need to ask our mommies for permission." Obviously his answer only served to add fire to her fury, so he tried again. "We don't take these trips without proper training, careful planning. By the time we're set to participate, we're ready, physically and mentally. And frankly, Jude, we have a great time.

"As for why it's important to us…look at me. Five days a week in a suit and tie, stuck behind a desk working with numbers, analyzing stocks, writing perspectives. And my buddies are just like me. The summers are our chance to unwind, get a little wild, face the challenges of nature, test our stamina."

She scowled at him. "Pardon me for saying so, but that's a bunch of nonsense…" She clamped her lips together and drew in a breath through her nose. "You're going to continue doing these things?"

"Until we're too old, too feeble or run out of ideas, yes."

She stared out the window, at what, Liam didn't know.

"Why does this bother you so much?" he asked.

"Because…" She seemed to be gathering her thoughts. "I thought I knew you. I had no idea there was this side to you. It seems so foolish to take such risks when you have a good job, a bright future…"

He smiled at her, trying to avoid an argument that made no sense to him. "Hey, come on, Jude, it's just a couple of weeks out of our lives each summer. And the risk is minimal. Trust me, I don't have a death wish."

"Trust you?" The words were harsh, her voice raspy and cold. "How can I trust anyone who would jeopardize everything he's worked for to have so-called adventures that are, to my way of thinking, ridiculous, unnecessary and stu…!" She bit her lip.

"Jude, you're overreacting. Everyone has to have the opportunity to blow off steam."

"But you're adults! As you, yourself just pointed out, you're grown men with jobs and responsibilities and people who depend on you. This isn't normal blowing off steam, Liam."

"Look, how can I explain? When the guys and I do these things, we all feel alive…"

"By facing death?"

He waited, hoping she would calm down and see that her misgivings were unnecessary and irrational. Or at least understand that what he did in the summers was none of her concern. He struggled to tamp his own anger before finally saying, "Jude, this doesn't have anything to do with you, with us."

She took a long breath. "You know, Liam? You're right. It doesn't. You can take two weeks of every summer and do any dangerous thing you want to." She picked up her coat from a nearby chair. "It's your life. And I can do what I want with my life."

He spoke in a mellow voice. "Put your coat down, Jude, please. We haven't even had dinner. And frankly I don't know why you're so upset. You put yourself at risk every time you go near that firebrand of a horse you keep locked up in the barn. I wouldn't go near that beast. He terrifies me, but you feed him apples."

"That's different. I relate to animals."

"Yes, I know that," he admitted. "And when I was at your barn and asked about Wesley's participation with the goats, you told me you taught him or trained him for that. What's different from what I do? I train for my summer exploits in ways you refuse to take into consideration."

"I'll tell you what I did take into consideration," she said. "My son's reaction to the foolhardy things you do. Jumping out of an airplane is a far reach from herding goats into a pen. He's impressed by you. He wants to be like you, and I'll keep him home with me until he's a senior citizen before I let him follow in your footsteps!"

Now she'd gone too far. "Fine. Wrap him up in a cocoon if you want to. You're his mother. I'm nothing to him, and I certainly never asked to be anything more than a stargazing buddy." That wasn't the total truth. Liam had connected to Wesley from the moment he'd met him. But right now, he just felt sorry for the kid and he didn't want to face any blame for Wesley doing things his mother didn't approve of. He hadn't signed on for any type of parenting.

Jude glared at him. "I'd like to go home now," she said. "I'll get Wesley."

This was not the way he'd pictured this night ending. And he had a mountain of spaghetti sauce simmering on his stove. "At least stay for spaghetti," he said. "It's all ready. I'm sure Wesley is hungry. You can leave right after."

After several long, uncomfortable moments, she nodded. And Liam figured he'd have a powerful case of indigestion to take to bed with him that night.

CHAPTER FIFTEEN

"DIDN'T YOU LIKE your spaghetti, Mom?"

Jude had hardly spoken during the twenty miles they'd so far traveled toward Dancing Falls. Her hands gripped the steering wheel, as she recalled the last few hours. During dinner, Liam had tried to keep the atmosphere light, engaging both her and Wesley in small talk. But Jude had endured the longest meal of her life.

"Not so much," she answered. "I think my tummy is a bit upset."

Apparently thinking he'd broach only safe topics, Liam had discussed his suggestions for the foundation. She'd answered briefly and unenthusiastically. What was there to talk about? She'd already decided to follow his recommendations for Paul's foundation, and she would do that, but their personal relationship had been altered dramatically.

Just hours ago, Jude believed she might be

falling in love with Liam—at least falling for the man he'd presented himself to be. Hard-working, bright, steadfast. But those were the qualities of the man he was for most of the year, the one whose life and career could be ruined, ended, because of what he did for two weeks every summer.

Why did he have to behave like an overgrown frat boy? At least Paul's life-threatening decision had been for a nobler purpose. Liam? Well, his actions were simply recklessness without redemption, the decisions of a thrill seeker. And she didn't need a thrill seeker in her life. And she certainly didn't need one in her son's.

She swallowed, tamping her bitter disappointment. She was driving on twisting, curving country roads now. She could hardly give in to tears. But the bottom line was obvious. Jude couldn't go through it again. She couldn't watch someone she loved take risks that were unnecessary. If she couldn't accept that a man who said he loved her would leave her for a principle, how in the world could she accept that Liam would leave her for a mere lark? He should believe in her—in them—more. And she certainly couldn't justify saying goodbye to a man who was leaving her for a bucket list daredevil act with old college buddies. Couldn't they just get together and play poker or watch sports?

The closer she got to Dancing Falls, the more her nerves remained on edge. She suggested turning on the radio. She found a station, turned the volume high and watched the dark landscape of Ohio out of her windows. When they pulled in front of the barn, she got out of the car quickly. Wesley got out his side and raced for the stairs, probably thankful he got to be away from her.

And then her phone rang. Liam. "Go on inside, Wes," she said. "I'll just be a minute." She connected. "Hello."

"Did you get home all right? I was concerned."

"You needn't have been. Driving is actually an activity with an acceptable amount of risk. If you keep your eye on the road, it's pretty safe." Yes, she was being childish, but he had pulled the safety net she'd been searching for over five years out from under her tonight.

"Jude, this isn't making any sense to me."

"I suppose not," she said. "We've already established that I'm acting irrationally."

"Yes, I believe you are. At the very least, you're putting importance on something that doesn't really merit it. I was beginning to think that you and I had something special going on. Isn't that what's important?"

She paused, considering her answer through. "The foundation is what's important, has been from the start. I appreciate your help with it. We can continue a relationship in that capacity, but you needn't come out here so often. Phone calls will suffice."

He breathed deeply into the phone. "So that's it? You're blowing me off because of what I do on my vacations? That's ridiculous."

"Maybe so, but I can't go through it again."

"Go through what? I was hoping we'd make our relationship permanent. Are you assuming I could leave you a widow a second time?"

"No, I'm not assuming that. I doubt many husbands choose to leave their wives widows."

"Then what are you talking about?"

Her throat started to burn. This conversation could only end badly. Liam could decide that she simply wasn't worth the trouble, and maybe she wasn't. She had issues with men who took chances, and they'd only gotten worse in the last five years. "You wouldn't understand. I need to hang up now, Liam. I have to change clothes and check the horses. Thanks for dinner. Wesley said it was really good."

She didn't need to check the horses. A few minutes later, when she had gotten Wesley to bed, she sat on her old sofa and picked up the nearest photo of Paul.

Clutching the picture to her chest, she said, "I loved you from the first day I laid eyes on you, Paul. You were everything to me. You were all I wanted. But you left. I begged you not to go. You told me to trust you, that you would come home. And I did that, as much as I hated your decision, I made myself believe in you. But your promises were as flimsy as the paper this picture is printed on. I could rip up this photo as easily as you ripped apart my heart."

She held the picture so she could stare into the warm brown eyes of the man she'd put her trust in. A strange smile came to her lips. "Mom was right. I am too trusting. I trusted you and you let me down. I hated you for that, Paul. And I hated myself for hating you. Everyone who knew you said you were a hero. But to me, the hero would have been the man who stayed with his family and faced the tough times ahead. Simple, hardworking men can be heroes, too. That's all I wanted from you.

"And tonight, Liam said the same words you did. 'Trust me, Jude,' only now I know better. I won't be twice a fool." She ran a finger down the face in the photo. "I could have loved him as much as I loved you, and that's the really sad part. But I'm wiser now. I don't want to love someone if it means there is so much to lose. I won't lose half of myself again."

She set the picture on the end table, leaned her head back and closed her eyes. She recalled her mother's words again. *"You're too trusting, Jude. And you're fearless. Those two are a very bad combination."*

"You may have been right about me once, Mom, but tonight you're not even half right. I can't trust anymore, and I'm suddenly afraid of many things. I'm afraid for Liam, and I'm afraid for myself if something happened to him." Her next words came out on a sob. "I don't think I could be fixed the next time. I'm afraid to love him. Loneliness and loss change a person, Mom. I've become a skeptic, filled with what Liam would call my irrational behavior Maybe that's what you were always trying to warn me about. Now I'm listening."

THE NEXT EVENING MARTIN, Jude and Wesley had dinner at the big house. Martin tried to get a conversation going, but it seemed every attempt was met with clipped responses or glum expressions. He didn't know what was going on. Jude had recently gotten her hair cut, a physical step out of her doldrums. Martin believed she was completely over her anger at Liam. They'd been seeing more of each other, going on dates, all of which made Martin very happy. Yet tonight she seemed to have regressed into a state of depression. Her hair was bound in the single braid again, though a much shorter one. She wore her standard attire of jeans and a plaid blouse. She was Jude again, his troubled middle child.

"Mom, when is Liam coming over again?" Wesley asked.

Martin stopped chewing so he could hear her answer.

"He's busy, Wes. He may not have time to come over for a while."

"Then can I call him? I have a couple of things I need to tell him."

"You'll have to wait until you see him. Like I said, he's busy and probably doesn't have time to accept phone calls from children."

"He'll take a phone call from me," Wes insisted. "He's my friend."

Jude rubbed her forehead, sighed. "Just finish your dinner, okay? You were up late last night and tonight you're going to bed early."

So that's it, Martin thought. The date with Liam hadn't gone well. Martin was surprised, considering Jude had come to the house tonight talking about ideas for the foundation and ways to save money. She credited Liam with coming up with the suggestions, and he'd assumed their relationship had taken a turn toward the personal. Maybe it had, for a while, but something had definitely gone wrong.

Again Martin wished Maggie were able to talk to their daughter. She had always been so much better at getting to the bottom of problems. They'd been a good team, he and Maggie. She discovered what was wrong, and he made it right. Now he was forced to try and make his daughter's life right without knowing what was wrong. Impossible. He had to get to the bottom of whatever was troubling Jude.

He cleared his throat. "Uh, Jude, do you think you could spare me a few minutes after dinner? I'd like to talk to you."

Her expression was wary, not unusual for Jude when faced with a father-daughter talk. "Wes, you watch the TV in Grandma's room and visit with her until Grandpa and I are done."

Wesley always appeared comfortable with his grandmother. He knew she was ill and couldn't react to what he said or did, but he was too young to fully realize that she was never going to get better. So he'd sit beside her and tell her what was happening with a particular television show or read her a book. Sometimes when Wesley picked up Maggie's hand, Martin envied his sweet innocence. Maggie was his grandma, someone he knew was supposed to love him without reservation, and despite her condition, he loved her back.

"Okay. Can I pick the show? I'll pick something Grandma will like."

"Sure."

The phone rang, and Rosie came into the dining room. "Mr. Martin, the phone is for you. It's Miss Aurora. Should I tell her you'll call her back?"

Aurora had been on Martin's mind much of the day. The incident with her son showing up unexpectedly had him puzzled. Aurora had definitely not seemed pleased. He'd waited for her call, but five days had passed since William showed up. He decided that he would call her this evening if she hadn't reached him.

He stood. "No, Rosie, I'll speak to Aurora in my den." Nodding to Jude and Wesley, he said, "Excuse me."

He sat behind his desk and picked up the phone. "Aurora, how are things over there?"

"Fine, Marty. I'm calling because I promised I would."

"So everything is all right with your son?"

"Oh, sure. This isn't the first time William has shown up unannounced. He's kind of a wandering soul, and sometimes he wanders toward me."

"That must make you happy."

"You'd certainly think so, wouldn't you?"

A strange response. Martin wanted to question her meaning but decided to keep the conversation on another, less invasive level. "How long is he staying?"

"Only another day or two. I gave him a week, and it will be over soon. He's doing some odd jobs around the place. I can use his help."

Martin lined up the pencils on his desk in a neat row while he thought about what to say. "Aurora, just curious, I guess, but why haven't you ever talked about this son in much detail? I can only recall you mentioning him one time, and that was really a reference to his father."

"There wasn't much to say," she answered. "William and I aren't close. Certainly we're nothing like you and your daughters. His father, my ex-husband, and I divorced years ago, and William truly had more in common with Phil than he did with me. Over the years, I didn't see much of William. It's just one of those things."

"All families are different, I guess," he

said. "But it's hard for me to accept that you have an estranged relationship with your son. You're so good with my girls, with Wesley."

"It's easier with them," she said.

"I don't know about that. I've had my issues through the years. And William is your son, so what is the problem?"

"Let's just leave it, okay? Some stories are long and complicated, and this is one of them."

"I'd like to meet William. Can I come over while he's here?"

"I'd rather you didn't. I'm sorry if that sounds cold, Marty, but it's better if you stay away. William and I just seem to lock horns over the silliest things, and you don't need to be in the middle of the tension. I'll call you when he's gone. We'll talk then."

Martin didn't like the false confidence he heard in Aurora's voice. He'd come to know her well since she'd moved in next door. Right now she seemed uncertain, almost frightened. By her own son?

"You will call me if you need anything," he said.

"Of course. And the same goes for you."

They disconnected and he went back to the dining room. Wesley had already gone upstairs, so Martin prepared for his next difficult conversation.

"WHAT DID YOU want to talk to me about, Daddy?" Jude asked when they were seated in the living room. "What'd I do?"

Martin chuckled, but it seemed forced. "Nothing. Why do you always think I'm going to reprimand you for something?"

"I don't know. History, tradition. It's not like I wasn't the most troublesome of your three daughters."

"That's not true, Jude," he insisted. "Yes, you got into a number of scrapes, but that was only because of your big heart."

She smiled. "That's not what you said when you came down to the Fox Creek Police Station and talked to the officer who brought me in after I protested against animal abuse. And certainly not what you said to me." She lowered her voice, trying to impersonate a father's deep disappointment. "How could you, Jude? Picketing outside a laboratory, threatening to release all the animals.'"

"Turns out you were right," Martin said.

"There was animal abuse going on in that lab, and you were within your moral rights to picket."

"Was I right when I started the campaign to keep women from buying cosmetic products that had been tested on animals? I put together a small army of activists outside the drugstore. As I recall that was another bad night for the Fosters and their middle child."

"That's all water under the bridge, sweetheart," Martin said. "It's the past. I'm worried about the present."

"In what way, Daddy?"

"Do you want to tell me what's wrong? I can see that something's bothering you. In the past, I would have had your mother bring this up, but, well…"

"No, nothing's wrong."

"Did you have a fight with Liam?"

"Not exactly."

He smiled. "I'm not sure what that means, but I'll assume that something happened when you went to Cleveland last night. I have to tell you, Jude, I like Liam. He's a good man, a hard worker, a kind person."

She nodded. "He's all that. The problem we have isn't with him specifically. It's mostly with me. He doesn't fit into what I'm looking for in a man, a relationship. And he's not the sort of man I would want influencing Wesley."

"I'm surprised to hear you say this," Martin said. "I had feared you were never going to consider any man for a relationship, and then I guess my hopes were raised when you started going out with Liam."

Her shoulders slouched, just enough so her father would know he'd hit a nerve. "Sorry to disappoint, Daddy."

"I admire your ideals, Jude. They are responsible for making you the strong woman you are. From the day you were born, you were independent, less reliant on your mother and me. Alex needed our approval and praise all the time. You just went your own way and did your own thing."

"Like quit college," she said. *And besides, Alex got all the attention. What other choice did I have but to stumble along making mistakes?*

"Yes. I wasn't happy about that, but you were the self-sufficient child. Alex was the overachiever. Carrie the baby. I wanted you to go to college, but you had other ideas. From the time you were in elementary school, you were motivated by one social cause after another. First it was bullying, then donation jars to collect for someone's operation, then animal rights. You were determined to make the world a better place." He leaned forward, placed his hand over hers on her lap. "And you still are. I'm proud of you, Jude, and it's high time I told you that." He cleared his throat. "Now that I look back, I feel that you were always struggling to be heard, and no one would listen."

"Don't blame yourself for my quirks," she said. "You and Mom were great parents. I just didn't fit any particular mold."

"And you shouldn't have. Your mother never did. I only bring that up because I always felt Alex was more like me—struggling to achieve at the expense of a personal life. You were like your mother. Strong, independent, confident."

Jude sighed. "Maybe not so much anymore, Daddy."

"We all have our moments, honey. You'll come back stronger than ever." He paused, picked up a picture of his three girls and showed it to Jude. "Look at this carefully, Jude."

She did. "Okay."

"Do you know what's great about being the middle child?"

"Uh, no, not really."

"Where are you in this picture?"

She didn't know where he was going with the demonstration, but she played along. "The middle."

"That's right. And in nearly every picture we have of you three girls together, you're in the middle, the heart of the picture."

"Daddy, that's true, but—"

"My point is that you are special, Jude, to me, to all of us. You are so much like your mother that sometimes my heart hurts just hearing your voice, seeing your smile. I love you, kiddo. I want you to be happy."

Jude knew one thing for certain. She didn't want her father to feel responsible for her unhappiness. She didn't want him to assume any of the blame for the choices she made. "I am happy, Daddy. I'm fine."

"I'm not much good at giving advice, Jude, but I'm going to give it a try tonight. I want you to set some goals, sweetheart. Personal ones, not goals about helping the community or raising a kid. I want you to set a goal to stop grieving. Can you do that? Can you accept that there's a limit to grief? I'm not saying you should forget, but you might want to stop the heartache. You need to live, Jude, and to do that you have to let the bad feelings go."

"I'll try, Daddy."

He gave her a smirk. "I know you're just saying that, trying to keep the peace. But I'm going to take you at your word."

She stood. "Is that it, Daddy?"

"Almost. One thing you said disturbs me. Why don't you believe that Liam would be a good influence on Wes?"

"I don't understand some of Liam's choices. Let's just leave it at that. And besides, Liam hasn't indicated any interest in being part of Wesley's life." She sighed. "He enjoys the independence of not being responsible for a child."

She started to leave, but Martin stopped her. "Jude…"

She turned around. "Yes?"

"I'm here, honey. I'm not much good at girl stuff, but I'm always willing to listen.

Sometimes that's all a person needs, someone to listen."

She walked back to the sofa where he was sitting, leaned over and kissed his cheek. "I know you are. I love you."

CHAPTER SIXTEEN

Two DAYS LATER, on Wednesday, Jude had taken Wesley for pizza and now they were home at a very respectable seven o'clock with the night ahead of them.

"Are you sure you remembered to put fresh water in the horses' buckets, Wes?" she asked her son.

"Yes, Mom. I told you I did."

She almost wished he'd forgotten. She needed to get out of the small apartment for a few minutes. She felt restless, lonely, like the last three weeks had been only a dream, one she hadn't deserved, as if a second chance at happiness was for other people, not her. She would be okay in a couple of days, she thought. She'd get over Liam. Getting over him was certainly easier than watching him take off for his adventures every year.

"I'm going to check on Titan," she said.

"I'm not sure I gave him enough feed, and you know how cranky he can be."

"Okay."

Jude went to the door, and Mutt followed. They went down the stairs and into the barn. Jude turned on the light inside the door and checked the feed buckets hanging inside all the stalls. Before she got to Titan, she stopped at the vegetable bin nearby and took out a couple of carrots. She cautiously placed them palm up under Titan's nose. "Here you go, Mr. Troublemaker. Munch on these, and if you take off a finger, we've got a problem."

The Thoroughbred chomped through the treat and whinnied for more. When she didn't get more carrots, he pawed the ground insistently.

"One of these days I'm going to ride you, you grumpy old man. Maybe this spring, when the snow melts." She stroked his muzzle and drew her hand back when he attempted to nip at her. "That's all right, Titan. I see a beautiful friendship for us one day."

The irony of what she was feeling suddenly struck her. She'd been working for months to get Titan healthy, just as she'd been trying to get the animal to trust her. The horse was just like her in one very sad way. He'd put his trust in the wrong people. He'd given his all to a cause, a purpose, and his spirit had been broken.

She spoke softly. "You have a home here for as long as we can stand each other, Titan. I'm hoping we become friends. Whatever is wrong, we'll work through it—this spring, when the snow melts."

The cold air revived her, and she felt better when she went back up the stairs. Maybe she and Wes would play a game. Then after he went to bed, she'd watch a movie, call her sister. Her life would get back on track again. She would be fine.

It was almost Christmas. Soon, certainly by the weekend, she would put up a tree for her and Wesley. She wouldn't use the small one that fit in the center of her dining table. She'd buy a slightly bigger one, since Wes wanted it. Maybe a four-footer where she could put a few wrapped presents.

Pasting a smile on her face, she went in the door—and immediately noticed that Wesley was on her cell phone. He looked over at her, his eyes wide, as if he'd been caught doing something he shouldn't.

"Who are you talking to?" she asked.

"Liam."

"Liam?" Her heart hitched as she pronounced his name. "Did he call for me?"

"No. I called him."

She marched over to the kitchen where Wesley was standing. "I specifically told you not…" She stopped, knowing Liam could hear. "Give me the phone. Now. Go to your room, Wesley. I'll talk to you later."

She took the phone, breathed deeply and said, "Hello, Liam. I've very sorry that Wesley bothered you. I realize you are probably busy with—"

"Don't apologize, Jude. I was going to call you. Besides, I wasn't doing anything." He paused before adding, "Well, that's not exactly true. I had an early dinner with a lawyer friend of mine. We discussed the sale of the radio station, and he's drawing up a contract we can present to Howard Crocker of Northern Ohio Media."

"How long will it take to get the contract ready?"

"A day. That's all. My friend will send it to me tomorrow, and I can bring it out to show you on Friday…if that's all right."

Friday. Two days. He was coming so soon. She swallowed. It would be okay. This was business. She'd told him their relationship concerning the foundation could continue. "That would be fine. What time do you want to come?"

"I'm meeting clients in the morning, but I'm free in the afternoon. How about two o'clock?"

"That will work. Wesley will be so glad to see you."

There was a moment's silence on the other end of the connection. "Listen, Jude," Liam said, "don't be angry with Wes. I love hearing from him."

"You've been very generous with your time, Liam, but I completely understand your wanting to maintain distance between the two of you."

"Jude, that's not what I said…"

"Besides, he should have asked permission."

"That's up to you, of course. But as far as I'm concerned, he can call anytime. I miss both of you, you know."

Suddenly she felt as tightly wound as an overtuned guitar. One wrong stroke of the strings of her heart, and she'd snap. "Liam, don't…"

"I won't put pressure on you, but you know how I feel about you. Maybe we can find some time to be alone on Friday to talk."

"I doubt that'll be possible. I like to spend time with Wesley, since it's the beginning of the weekend."

"Sure."

Did he sound terribly disappointed? Was it wrong of her to hope that he was? "I'll make time to go over the contract," she said in her most professional voice, the one that hid all traces of emotion. "And, Liam?"

"Yes?"

"Well, considering the circumstances now, it would be totally appropriate for you to accept payment from my father for your efforts. I know at one time I might have insinuated that you shouldn't…"

He chuckled. "Insinuated? Jude, you blasted me with your fiery temper and made me feel like a schmuck. And you were right."

"That's all in the past," she said. "I've forgiven you for deceiving me with my father, and I hope you've forgiven me for my fiery temper."

His voice lowered. "Jude, it's not a stretch of the imagination to assume that I'd forgive you for almost anything."

Apart from a further blasting for his so-called recreational activities? "That's good, then." She hated to end the conversation, but she couldn't think of anything more to add. She wasn't about to apologize for anything. She felt how she felt. She'd lived the loss, and had decided that she was protecting herself, and her son, from ever losing Liam in the first place. A bit of misery now was better than a lifetime of misery and worry to come.

"I'll see you on Friday," she said.

"Good night, Jude."

She disconnected and went into Wesley's room.

He looked up from a book. "Are you mad at me, Mommy?"

"I'm not happy with you," she said. "But no, I'm not mad. Just please ask permission before you use my cell phone to make calls, okay?"

He nodded. "But if you're not mad at me, who are you mad at?"

She frowned. "No one, honey."

"But your face looks mad. Are you mad at Liam?"

She concentrated on finding the smile she'd brought into the house just a few minutes ago. "No, I'm not mad at Liam." The words were true. And she wasn't mad at Wesley. That only left one person as the target of her anger. What could she do about being angry with herself?

ON FRIDAY, WHEN THE chores were done, Jude showered and settled on a pair of brown denims and a gold sweater. Finding an old headband in a drawer that matched the gold of the sweater, she smoothed back her hair, letting a few wispy strands curl around her face. She went into the living room to wait for Liam and answered her ringing phone.

Alex. Jude had spoken to her newlywed sister a few times since the wedding, but only once since the honeymoon. She connected. "Allie Belle, how are you? Where are you?"

"Daniel and I just got back from a visit with Lizzie at OSU," her sister said. "Now we're at his apartment."

"How is my favorite niece?" Jude asked, recalling all the trials and arguments Alex and Lizzie had gone through before Lizzie got her wish to enroll in the theater department at Ohio State. Thank goodness Alex had made her peace with that decision.

"She's fine," Alex said. "Flourishing really. And you know how it kills me to admit that."

Alex had planned on her daughter pursuing a career in literature at an Ivy League school, and she'd been terribly hurt when Lizzie had other ideas. Alex was certain that if Lizzie followed her dreams of acting, she would end up waiting tables at some dive in Los Angeles, a far distance from the hallowed halls of a professorship at a major university.

Jude smiled. Kids. They could knock you right off your feet with some of their decisions, but it was all part of growing up. She and her sisters had certainly put their parents through a lot. And they were still testing their father's patience.

"You're a good mother, sis," Jude said. "Don't ever believe otherwise. And how's the dream husband?"

"He's busy being a senator and a candidate." Alex sighed with what could only be pleasure. "But he still finds time for us. I've taken a part-time job with the Columbus Art

Museum. Not as much responsibility as I had at the Chicago Museum, but I'm happy."

Jude laughed. "Gee, I couldn't tell. So the honeymoon bliss hasn't worn off yet?"

Another long, languorous sigh. "If I only give you one piece of advice in your lifetime—"

"Allie Belle, you've already given me hundreds of pieces of advice."

"Okay, true, but I really mean this. If you ever get a chance to go on a honeymoon, take it. Don't let your practical nature deprive you of one of the most satisfying—in many ways—experiences of a lifetime. Don't worry about how much it costs. Get someone to feed the animals and just go!"

"Okay, I'll go." The promise was an easy one to make. Jude knew her chances of having a honeymoon were slim.

"Any prospects on the horizon?" Alex asked.

"I had a brief flicker of contentment with a guy I met, but it's not working out."

"Do you mean Liam Manning? I heard you'd been seeing him."

Carrie. Of course. "We've had a few dates."

"What happened?"

"Well, we have different visions for the future." *Like I want to stay home, safe and sound, and he wants to traipse off to danger-ous locales.*

Alex laughed. "Look, I'm supposed to be the brains of this threesome, and I don't even know what that means, but maybe you can alter your visions a bit."

"Not about this, Allie Belle. It's a deal breaker."

"You want to talk about it?"

Since Jude wasn't craving advice from any-one, she elected to end the discussion. Her sisters would probably tell her she was being too cautious. Easy for them to say. They hadn't lost the loves of their lives. Even Alex, whose much older husband had died, hadn't known the kind of love with Teddy that Jude enjoyed every day with Paul. Until…

"Thanks, but no. Not at this point anyway. Tell me about your new job, Daniel's run for national office, Lizzie's studies at Ohio State."

Alex sighed. "Okay, I'll take the floor, but don't think I won't bring this up again at some time."

Jude smiled. That threat was a certainty.

LIAM ARRIVED IN the afternoon. Jude didn't hear the car pull up because of Wesley's video game, but she clearly heard the knock on the door.

"He's here!" Wesley called from his bedroom. His footsteps echoed through the tiny house as he ran for the door.

Jude came out of her room to see Wesley wrap his arms around Liam's hips. The gesture brought on a new twinge of sadness.

"Good to see you, buddy," Liam said, lightly stroking Wesley's hair.

"You, too. I've got so much to tell you."

Jude cleared her throat. "I'm sure Liam will have some time for you later, Wes," she said. "But remember what I told you. He's here today on business."

"I know," Wesley said, looking up at Liam with an imploring gaze. "How long will business take?" he asked.

"About an hour, I think," Liam answered. "And then I'm all yours…" He transferred a tender look at Jude. "If I don't have any other claims on my time."

She felt her face flush. So he hadn't given up on her—on them—yet. Did that mean he was ready to accept her point of view on his dangerous activities? She thought not.

"Why don't you go into your room and finish your game?" she said to Wesley. "I'll let you know when we're through."

He trudged toward his room. "Mom got me an action figure yesterday," he called over his shoulder. "You'll think it's really cool, Liam."

"I'm sure I will," Liam said, his eyes only on Jude. "You look very nice today."

The compliment rippled through her like warm chocolate. She hadn't really tried to look good, had she? He set a folder on the table and pulled out a chair for her. "I've brought the contract—delivered but not yet signed and sealed. I'll explain all the particulars to you."

She sat, hoping Liam would take a chair across the table. He didn't. He slid a seat around the corner of the table and sat next to her, their shoulders almost touching. Sort of like the first time he'd been to her house and they'd studied the foundation's finances. Then she'd been nervous, anticipating something she wasn't ready for because she hadn't experienced it in many years. Now she was more nervous. Now she knew his kisses, his embraces, his many kindnesses. Now he was trouble.

A half hour later Liam flipped the pages of the contract back to the blue cover sheet. "So that's it, Jude. Northern Ohio Media will pay fifty thousand dollars to the foundation for ownership of WOIH. I know in this day of big deals and corporate conglomerates, it may not seem like a lot, but for a radio station this size, it's a darn good deal. Harvey and Gary are guaranteed a fair audition, and the foundation will get an influx of cash to pay bills and maybe even fund a new project or two."

She had to agree. When she first funded the station, she saw it as an opportunity to connect with the people of Bees Creek. Harvey and Gary had done that. Several local businesses had benefitted from remote broadcasts, weather and farming forecasts were kept up to date, and many pets had been found and returned to their owners. She no longer would be part of the programming, but that was okay. The boys could take over her simple jobs.

"It looks good," she said. "I've spoken to my board members, Dad and Carrie, and they agree that this is a promising step. Harvey and Gary are in agreement that this is a good move. In fact, when Northern Ohio Media brings in a new disk jockey for the afternoon, they will have more free time. And the increased wattage will reach more customers, always a good thing."

He handed her a pen. "Sign your name and I'll present it to the Northern Ohio Media rep tomorrow. You can be there, but it's not necessary."

She signed, almost regretting that he hadn't insisted she be present for the meeting. Not because she didn't trust Liam on this matter, but because she would have another chance to see him.

What was wrong with her? *See him? Don't see him! Enjoy his company while you can! Don't let his risky endeavors drive you over another edge!* She'd made up her mind about Liam, but now that he was here, sitting so close, being so helpful, which was his way, she was questioning her resolve.

She stood. "I'll let Wesley know we're done. Thank you for giving him some time."

"No problem," he said. "Get him, but first I have something to bring up from my car."

"What are you talking about? You didn't bring Wesley another gift, did you?"

"Sort of." He smiled. "I hope you won't be angry, but when Wes called me the other day, he mentioned something he'd always wanted.

I wanted to get it for him, for you, too. It's a little gesture, that's all."

She questioned his description of "little" when, a few minutes later, he struggled through her door dragging a live, seven-foot Douglas fir Christmas tree!

CHAPTER SEVENTEEN

JUDE STRUGGLED TO catch her breath. "For heaven's sake, Liam, what have you done?"

Managing to get the evergreen upright in its pot, Liam grinned. "I got you guys a Christmas tree. It's a Douglas fir."

She shook her head. "I know it's a Douglas fir. I've lived in northern Ohio my whole life."

"Oh, this tree isn't from Ohio. It was shipped from North Carolina two days ago. It's so fresh it probably won't lose any needles between now and the holiday."

Already doubting that because of the trail of green Liam had left on her wood floors, Jude could only imagine sweeping up daily. Not to mention the size of the tree. Its top barely fit under her ceiling. Its width was half the size of its height. Already she couldn't see her desk, an end table, and part of the sofa. Realizing her mouth was gaping open, she snapped it shut.

"You're surprised, I can see that," Liam said.

"I'm surprised, yes. And Wes will be thrilled. It's just that…well, it's a bit big."

Liam squared his shoulders. "I know. It's great, isn't it?"

"Oh, it's great, in the literal sense. But I don't have decorations or lights…"

At that moment, Wesley came out of his room. "Are you guys done with business?" He skidded to a stop several feet from the tree. "Oh, wow, you got us a tree! You did it, Liam. A real, live tree!" Wesley gave his hero another hug. "It's the most beautifulest thing I've ever seen."

Jude released a long, slow sigh. By the time she was finished, she'd calmed enough to make peace with a huge evergreen in her home. And she delighted in the look of rapture on her son's face.

Wesley took a couple of steps back to admire the tree. Then he looked at his mother. "Isn't it the greatest tree you've ever seen, Mom? Now we won't have to use that little one with no ornaments hardly."

"Yeah, super." Her mind raced to the job of procuring decorations for this "greatest, most beautiful" tree in the world. Lights, balls, tinsel, garland… The list went on.

As if reading her mind, Liam said, "About those ornaments. I picked up a few in town and brought them with me. And a couple of strings of lights, as well. I can help you set it up." He stared at Jude and apparently correctly interpreted her frown. "Of course you'll want to add your own touches," he added.

"The nice thing about this tree," he continued. "It's alive, planted in dirt. So we can keep it around in your yard after the season."

That would certainly make her tree-loving sister, Carrie, happy. But had Liam completely forgotten that she'd agreed to see him only on a professional level? Why was he suddenly acting like (a) they were one happy family doing family things, or (b) she was a charity case who couldn't afford a little holiday cheer in her house. Either way, his gesture had made her son ecstatic and that was its own reward.

She spoke in a clipped, forced-calm way. "Liam, may I see you outside for a moment?"

"Sure. I can use a hand with the boxes in my car."

"I'll help, too," Wesley said.

"No, you stay here, honey. Make sure Mutt doesn't think he's suddenly in the Black Forest and forgets why he goes outside."

When they'd left the house, she said, "You really shouldn't have done this, Liam."

"Just part of my m.o.," he said. "The other night you said there were many things I shouldn't do."

"Please, let's not go over that again. All I meant was that it's not your responsibility to get us a tree."

"No, of course it isn't." He smiled. "And when I saw it in your house, I realized it is a bit big."

"A bit?"

"You'll get used to it. Decorate it and then, when the season is over, plant it. In a year it will be bigger than the barn." When he decided she truly didn't appreciate his humor, he sobered. "Look, Jude, it's Christmas."

"I know that, but we have a tree!"

"From what Wes told me, it's not even big enough to put a present under."

"Okay. So now we have one that can accommodate an entire toy store!" She huffed, saw her breath, and shivered. "In case you didn't notice, I could barely open my door enough to send you outside just now!"

He smiled! And shrugged out of his jacket. "Here, take this. I at least have on a shirt and a sweater." He draped the coat over her shoulders, and two kinds of warmth enveloped her. Only one had to do with the jacket.

"I'm sorry if I overstepped," he said. "Wait a minute. I'm not sorry. I wanted to do this. Christmas is only a week away."

She knew she wasn't going to make him take the tree away. Wesley was already falling in love with the prickly monster. And perhaps it would be nice to have a fully grown evergreen in her yard. Once the decision was made, she glanced toward his car where the ropes that had held the tree on the top were dangling from the roof. "What decorations did you get?" she asked.

He started toward the car. "You'll love them. Among other things, I got Western-themed ones—horses, sleighs, cowboy boots and hats."

Okay, this tree would have some redeeming qualities. "No goat decorations?" she said.

He laughed. "They weren't in stock. I ordered some."

She came up behind him and put her hand on his shoulder. "You know, Liam, my concern is about more than just a tree."

He was serious when he turned around. "I know that."

"Wesley is completely taken with you. He talks about you all the time. He can't wait to see you. And since Sunday night, he has been raving nonstop about all the cool things you do. You've become a major force in his life whether you want to be or not. I can't have him thinking that those dangerous activities are in his future. There is no way that, as long as I hold some influence over him, I would allow him to do any of those things."

"I get it, and it's your call." Liam grasped her arms. "I'll talk to him, Jude. I'll emphasize how much training is involved for what we do. I'll make it sound like we have weeks of homework in advance of the actual act. He won't think it's so glamorous then."

She nodded. That might help and put Liam's endeavors in the realm of a six-year-old's grim reality. But Wesley's connection to Liam probably wouldn't be altered. Kids were messy. They misbehaved. They ate in the car, they brought home strange animals. And Liam hadn't "signed up" for a relationship with kid duties.

He kissed the top of her head. "It's Christmas, Jude. Let's spruce up a spruce."

She smiled, feeling for the first time this season that it actually was Christmas. "A Douglas fir!"

IT TRULY WAS a beautiful tree. Once Liam and Jude had moved the furniture around, there was enough room for the evergreen. Wesley enjoyed every moment of decorating, getting a kick out of the cowboy decorations and even some special ornaments of the night sky that Liam had managed to find.

They'd only stopped long enough to eat pizza delivered by the only shop in town familiar with the location of the barn at Dancing Falls. Jude found a bottle of wine in her cupboard, and Wesley was allowed his weekly quota of soda.

Now Wesley was in bed. A fire crackled on the hearth, and the scent of one overly large, magnificent Douglas fir filled the living room. Jude and Liam sat on the sofa. The TV wasn't on. The tree lights were entertaining enough. Soft, light classical music accompanied the sound of the fire. And the bottle of wine was empty on the coffee table.

Jude sighed with contentment. All was certainly not right with her world, but this moment couldn't have been any more perfect. "Thank you, Liam. Wesley loves the tree."

He tightened his arm around her shoulders. "You're welcome."

"But don't think that if Wes calls you and says he wants a swimming pool in the backyard, you can send in an excavator."

He chuckled. "I get it. Talk to you first."

"That's the plan from now on."

His voice lowered as he spoke in her ear. "So, are we good now, Jude? All that stuff from the other night is over and forgotten?"

He couldn't be that naive. As comfortable as this cold night, a warm fire and a wonderful tree made them feel, the underlying problem still existed. If all she wanted was a casual relationship, one where she didn't love too much, then this would be fine. She could see Liam occasionally. He could go off on his exploits, and whatever happened had no power to destroy her heart again.

But she already loved too much, and that was the problem.

"Liam…" She paused. She didn't know how to answer him. She didn't want to utter the words that would tell him how she felt and end the moment, maybe forever.

After an extended silence, he sat straight, turned to see into her eyes. "Tell me what your fears are all about, Jude. It's the only way we can move forward. Tell me about Paul."

Five years earlier

PAUL HAD BEEN gone for two weeks. *No, that's not true,* she kept telling herself. He'd been gone for months. But two weeks ago, he'd been killed by some insidious bomb, and now he was dead. Jude's days were endless hours of trying to be a mother to the child who would never know his father, trying to convince her worried parents that she was fine, trying to shower and eat and get dressed.

When her father brought the FedEx box from the big house, Jude wanted to scream at him to take it away. The return address from a foreign army post convinced her that she didn't want to see what was inside. In his most comforting voice, Martin told her opening the box might help her.

It didn't.

The contents were now in a locked box on her closet shelf, up high where Wesley couldn't get to them until she felt the time was right. For days she considered throwing the items away, but, in the end, she kept them so her son might know something about his father that her bitterness prevented her from ever telling him.

On that horrible day when the box was delivered, while her father held her young son, Jude went through the items one by one. Paul's wallet with her picture first, their son's birth picture second. The wallet had contained thirteen dollars in American money. He'd just received a paycheck and, as usual, had sent the majority to her. Maybe he'd intended to get a beer with the money. Or shaving supplies, or maybe a stake to play cards for dimes and quarters. She didn't know what soldiers did with their money.

There was a rabbit's foot. Silly, but he'd gotten it as a child and he always carried it. His cell phone, a flip type that no one even used anymore. One playing card, an ace of hearts. She didn't know why he carried that. There were other odd items. A polished stone, a menu written in Arabic, a label from a Budweiser bottle. She knew alcohol was not sold in Arab countries and imagined the symbol of an American beer was a reminder of home.

Along with these things, she made a copy of his last email and put it in the box. *Going to accompany a small division delivering supplies tomorrow, Judie. I'll be fine. The road has been checked for explosives. Just a reminder, sweet thing, I love you with all my heart except for that part reserved for Wesley. Tell him his daddy loves him. And remember... I will come home to you soon.*

Damn you, Paul, she'd thought at the time—the reaction she always seemed to have when she read his promises. *Damn you for leaving me. And, even worse, damn you for dying. Why did you have to be a hero? Heroes often don't come home. And what do the ones who love them have to show for this heroism? A rabbit's foot and a Budweiser label.*

She'd handed the box to her father and clutched her son to her chest. "Put it away, Daddy. I never want to see these things again. Lock them up."

He'd stood, tucked the box under his arm. "I'm sorry this has caused you such pain," he'd said. "I'd hoped that looking at these things would make you see what happened in a new light. But, Jude, honey, you can be proud of the man…"

"Don't even say it, Daddy!" she'd ground out through gritted teeth. "He shouldn't have gone. He should be here now! Any pride I might have felt is wasted on a dead man."

Weeks later her father brought the box back to her along with his earnest suggestion that the items belonged here, with her. She put the box on the closet shelf. She never opened it again, and her resentment grew like black mold in her bloodstream, and her guilt for feeling this way consumed her. Pride for the hero did not warm her bed at night. She was over the cruel machinations of men and the inexplicable reasons they found for doing unreasonable things.

SHE STARED INTO Liam's soft brown eyes, and her next breath caught in her throat as if there wasn't enough air in the room to fill her lungs. And slowly, deliberately, she began to tell him about Paul ending with the story of her greatest loss.

Liam listened with what seemed to be his

entire self. He didn't move, hardly blinked, didn't even appear to breathe. He let Jude tell her story her own way without asking questions. And because he kept himself in the background of the events of her life, she was able to get through it.

Chronologically and almost unemotionally, she presented the facts of what had happened beginning when she first met Paul. She explained Paul's announcement on the night he told her he'd enlisted, the night that changed everything. And she explained her reaction. And somehow she even managed to tell about the day the army chaplain came to her house and later, when the box arrived.

When she was finished, Liam gently put his hand on her shoulder. "I'm so sorry, Jude," he said.

She blinked when her eyes began to burn. "I guess what made it even worse is that I waited my whole life for Paul. I didn't know it, of course, but the day I met him I just knew he was the one. I immediately decided that there was no better man for me than Paul O'Leary. He had been born to be with me."

Though her bottom lip trembled, she smiled. "I was never popular," she said. "Alex had several brainy boyfriends, ones who were wired to succeed. And Carrie… She had all sorts of boyfriends from the cutest to the most athletic. All she had to do was bat her long eyelashes, and the guys came running. I was the wild one who attracted the wrong guys, the ones who dared me, got me into trouble, but never really saw me as serious girlfriend potential.

"My mother told me to try and be less intimidating. 'You don't have to win every argument, Jude,' she'd said. 'You don't have to win at every game. Life isn't always about competition.' It was good advice. I just didn't know how to implement it. I was always fighting. Fighting to be noticed. Fighting to protect some poor creature. Fighting for a cause. Mom said I scared the right kind of boys away. Maybe she knew what she was talking about. But in the end, the right guy did find a way into my life, and my future was set. I could quit fighting. I'd been noticed."

Liam took her hand. "Believe me, honey, you are still being noticed. No one could ignore a beautiful bridesmaid in tennis shoes."

She managed to smile at the image she

must have presented that night, fighting even then to prove she was not part of the crowd. "You're just being nice, but I appreciate it even so."

"I'm not being nice. I believe my fall for Jude O'Leary began that night on the country club balcony, and it has been an unpredictable ride ever since. It hasn't been easy, but it hasn't been boring. And now I want a future with you, Jude, for as long as we want to be together. But I also know that our life is not about just the two of us. There seems to be always four people in the room—you, me, Wesley and Paul."

"And what about Wesley? He has to be my first concern and he already is infatuated by you. He admires you, hangs on your every word. Are you willing to give up your summer adventures to stay with us?"

"I know how you feel, and we need to talk about Wesley and your concerns."

"Are you?" she said again. "I can't let him follow you in all that you do."

"One problem at a time, okay?" He sighed. "Wesley's a good kid and I think we'll work it out, but first, I don't know what to do about Paul."

"What do you mean?"

"I now know who he was, how you met, why you loved him. I know how you felt about him from the day you first saw him. But I'm not sure how you feel about him now. And of all the stumbling blocks that exist between us—differences about the foundation, distance between where we live, your feelings that I might corrupt Wes…" He smiled. "I think your feeling for Paul is the one we need to conquer. I don't expect you to forget him. I don't even expect you to release him from your heart, but if it's going to work between you and me, you have to make room for someone else."

She blinked through gathering moisture in her eyes, but gave him a steady gaze. "I will always love him, but I don't believe I will ever forgive him." She twisted her hands in her lap. "I know that sounds selfish, but he volunteered, Liam. He wanted to join the army. He didn't have to go. He wanted to. He didn't even discuss it with me. And when he told me, I realized I'd never known this part of him at all, not the man he truly was. And that's the part I can never forgive."

Liam released a deep sigh. "It's impossible for me to judge a man I've never met. I do know you, Jude. And the way I see it, you have to do one thing to get on with your life."

"One thing?" Could the confusion and bitterness of the last few years be cured by the application of only one thing?

"Yep. You have to forgive Paul. You have to accept the man he was and let it go. He will never be able to explain himself to you. He will never be able to make you understand why he enlisted. He will never tell you about the last moments of his life and why he made the decisions he made. I understand that you want those answers. But, Jude, you can't have them, so you have to let them go unanswered. To do that you have to remember the man who loved you and forgive the man who hurt you."

He covered her hands until she stopped twisting her fingers. Then he raised one palm to his lips and gently kissed it. "Can you do that?" he asked.

"I don't know. The idea of forgiveness has become one with my feelings of guilt. How can I feel this way about a hero, a man who gave his life to save others? What kind of horrible person am I to resent a man who died for his country? But I do resent him. He didn't have to be a hero, any more than you have to risk everything you do every summer..."

She took a moment to quell the trembling in her stomach. "I don't know if my son and I can be a part of your life, Liam, if you put these dangerous exploits above our needs. If I can't trust you to stay safe and put my concerns above those of your friends, how can I trust you in other things?"

He remained silent for long moments, her hand still in his. Finally he said, "Jude, what is danger anyway? Does it only exist in a war zone, or on a mountainside or on the Appalachian Trail? Honey, danger is all around us. It exists in our cars every time we take the wheel. It exists in crowded classrooms where kids are petri dishes for germs. It exists in the barn where that cranky horse of yours scares everyone. Heck, this beautiful Douglas fir could catch fire tonight. Danger is everywhere, but you can't stop living. You can't barricade yourself in these four rooms."

She wanted his words to change her. She wanted them to make sense, and they did, but they couldn't alter her thinking. "A person can still make choices, Liam, and your choices are not mine and never will be. And your choices are not right for my son, and I will never compromise about that. He thinks what you do is fun and exciting. He's too young to know any better."

He stroked the hair where it fell to her shoulder. "Jude, honey, what I do *is* fun and exciting, but I approach every activity with caution and common sense. To some people diving headfirst off the high board is fun. But would you do it without knowing how deep the water is? It's fun to ride the river rapids, but would you do it without a life jacket?"

She bit her lip, knowing that what she was going to say would destroy all of Liam's arguments. "And I suppose the thought of war is exciting to some, but would you go if you didn't have to, if you had a wife and child on the way?"

She took her hand from his and touched his cheek. "I'm sorry, Liam. You are a good man. I care very much for you. But I can't pretend that I will support your efforts to challenge death every summer. I can't go through the loss of someone I..." She stopped, knowing what words were about to slip from her mouth

"...someone who is close to me," she said. "This time, I don't think I would survive."

He layered his hand over the one that still touched his cheek. "It's okay, Jude. Let's not talk about it anymore tonight. Let's just agree that it's a beautiful tree."

When her lips curled into a grin, she felt renewed. "Yes, it is. I love it, and Wesley is thrilled."

"That's enough for tonight, then," Liam said. "But if you think I'm giving up on us, then you don't know me too well. You, Jude O'Leary, are the most hardheaded, fascinating, wonderful woman I have ever known. And perhaps the most wounded, but I hope, I pray, that can be made right."

Her face flushed with warm, intense emotion. And when he bent to kiss her, the warmth spread throughout her entire body. She kissed him back, telling him in her own way, thanks for listening, for understanding. She didn't have any answers tonight, but for now, she had Liam.

CHAPTER EIGHTEEN

Two years ago, for his Christmas gift, one of Martin's patients gave him a police scanner unit. Many nights he listened to the calls coming in to the local station. The activity kept him informed on his neighborhood and made him more aware of potential problems.

On Saturday, five days before Christmas, he heard a report that gave him great concern. A patrol unit had been sent to Aurora's Attic Bed-and-Breakfast. Hearing the report, Martin was reminded of a few months before when his friend had been robbed by teenage delinquents who had never been caught. Could those same boys have returned, and if so, why would they target the house again? And were they aware that her son was currently living there? And, most alarming, what if Aurora and William had surprised the thieves and been injured?

Only one way to find the answers. So Martin headed over to the century-old Victorian to see what had happened. When he pulled up in front of Aurora's wide porch, he saw two patrolmen getting into their cruiser. Recognizing one of them, Martin called out, "Dirk, what's happened? Everything okay here?"

"Yeah, Dr. Foster. Some stuff went missing, but we got a full report. Looks like the perpetrator has left town, but I'll make sure a unit comes by here a few times during the night."

Bundled in a thick pink chenille robe, Aurora came onto the porch. Martin got out of his car.

"Why am I not surprised to see you?" she said. "You always seem to know when something's not right over here."

"Thank goodness you're all right, Aurora," he said. "Was it the same kids from before? Is William okay?"

She held the door open. "You might as well come in. I'll fix coffee."

He entered the nicely appointed parlor, looked around and didn't see Aurora's son. "Where's William?" he asked.

"Probably halfway to the West Virginia border by now," she answered.

He shrugged out of his jacket, tossed it on the sofa. "What are you saying? Why wasn't he here when you got robbed?"

"I wasn't robbed, Marty. At least not in the way you're thinking. Let's use William's words and just say that he *borrowed* a few things he'd convinced himself he couldn't live without."

Martin sat in the nearest easy chair but was too stunned to feel comfortable. "Are you telling me your son stole from you?"

She took a seat close to him. "I can understand your surprise, but believe me, this is par for the course with William and me." She ran her fingers through the twisted strands of red hair that framed her face. "For years William has made a habit of taking from me when I wasn't willing to hand over what he thought he needed."

Martin quickly recalled prior conversations about William. Aurora hadn't wanted Martin to meet her son, claiming there was always tension between the two of them. Martin had thought that strange at the time. "What did he take, Aurora?"

"Some jewelry. I don't have much that's worth a whole lot, but I have saved a few good pieces over the years. When William arrived, I hid them under a drawer liner in my dresser. But he found them. Unfortunately he also found an envelope with five thousand dollars in it."

"You keep that much money in your house?"

She shrugged. "I've always been a cash type of person. I never know when money will be needed to pay for a delivery, a subcontractor or a refund to an unhappy guest. Just yesterday I noticed that my stash was running low and I went to the bank to replenish it." She frowned. "Now I wish I hadn't. William would have gotten only a few hundred." She crossed her legs, pulling the robe tight around her thighs. "I'd given him a week to get himself together, but ended up extending his stay for a couple more days. He seemed better, and he'd been helping me. But I should have known he'd eventually resort to his old game."

Martin inched forward in the chair. "Better? What do you mean better?"

She widened her eyes in a gesture that told him what he'd suspected. "Oh. You mean he seemed clean."

Martin reached over and covered Aurora's hand. "I'm so sorry. You don't deserve this kind of treatment from anyone, especially someone from your family. You've worked so hard to get this place up and running."

She smiled, slipped her hand from under his. "You make it sound like I'm giving up, Marty. Far from it. This is just a setback. I've suffered worse. Things are slow now with Christmas almost here, but once Happy Valley opens up and the skiers come, I'll have business. More than I can handle."

She was probably right. The beginner slopes of the nearby ski resort brought lots of enthusiastic learners to this part of Ohio. His admiration for Aurora grew. She had obviously considered her profit potential before investing in the old house as a bed-and-breakfast. She knew skiers could be reliable return guests.

"Aurora," he began. "If I'm out of bounds, just say so, but how long has William had a drug problem?"

She stood. "Follow me to the kitchen, Marty. If we're going to get into all these details, I'd better get that coffee brewing. We'll sit at the kitchen table and I'll tell you the long, and not very nice, story."

An hour and two cups of coffee later, Martin had a pretty clear idea of the difficult life Aurora had led. She'd married a man who turned to alcohol when he couldn't succeed as a husband or provider for his family.

"Phil wasn't a bad man," she'd said, defending him. "He just wasn't motivated, or really very bright. But the worst part of his alcoholism was that his addictive nature seemed to have been inherited by our son. I've read that addictive tendencies can transfer from one generation to the next. Only with William, it wasn't so much booze as drugs."

She tried to smile, wasn't successful and took another long swig of coffee. "Like father, like son," she said. "The apple doesn't fall far from the tree. I've heard them all through the years. I tried to keep the family together, but in the end I couldn't save Phil. He didn't want to be saved. But I thought William had a chance, so I didn't give up on him."

Martin stared into brilliant green eyes that held such determination, such strength. "How did you keep it all together?" he asked. "You had to maintain a home, your faith that everything would be all right with William, not to mention your dignity."

She gave him a resigned smile. "There came a time when my dignity didn't matter so much."

"But what about finances? I'm assuming you couldn't rely on a paycheck from Phil to keep you going."

"Oh, heavens no. But I'm not poor, Marty. You know I paid cash for this house. I was an executive assistant for a big commercial real estate firm in Chicago. Indispensable, they called me, and I expect I was. At least I kept getting raises and decent Christmas bonuses. I suppose I'm a businesswoman at heart, though my business savvy definitely didn't apply to my relationship with my son."

She sighed. "How was I able to do my job so well at the firm and then screw up so badly at home…?"

Martin understood. He'd known others like Aurora, people with good hearts and sometimes narrow judgment. "He was your son, Aurora," he said. "Rules of common sense often don't apply to family."

She nodded. "William had a way of getting to my emotions. He knew just which strings to pull. I lent him money when he convinced me he was clean. I paid for his rehab stays. I visited him weekly, encouraged him, loved him." She wiped a finger under her eye. "I still do, but I can't help him anymore. I knew I shouldn't have let him in my house last week, but there he was, sitting in the cold on the porch in that light jacket with that junker car in the parking lot. I looked at him and all I could see was my baby boy with that winning smile."

Martin knew all too well what it felt like to want to give your children whatever they wanted. Sometimes it was just so darn hard to say no even when you knew it was the right answer. But he'd been blessed with good girls and a caring, loving wife for many years. How difficult it must have been for Aurora to try to hold her family together, to keep up with the grind of a high-pressure job, with nothing but her hopes and a will to succeed.

"You're an amazing woman, Aurora," he said. "You've been a good friend to me and my girls and I believe in you."

"Well, thanks, Marty. I appreciate that. But we've established a two-way street of trust. I believe in you, too. I wonder, though. Do you still believe in me after I tell you I sent the police after my son?"

"Absolutely."

"I've done it before—had William arrested. When I couldn't think of another way to get him into rehab, I'd use the law. But this time he has five thousand dollars, so I don't think they'll find him. Unless they…"

Martin knew what she couldn't say. *Unless they find his body.* What a nightmare to live with such uncertainty about someone you loved with all your heart.

"I wish I could do more to help you, Aurora."

She stood, indicating he should leave. "You're doing all you can do, Marty, circumstances being what they are. You're being my friend, maybe the best friend I've ever had."

He clasped his hands together. "But it's not enough…"

"Go home, Marty. I'll be fine."

He walked to the door of the kitchen but stopped and turned back to look at her one more time. She glanced up, her eyes moist but her smile back in place. She waved her fingers in a dismissive way. "Go on, shoo."

She didn't say anything else, and he left.

WHEN LIAM HAD talked to Jude on Tuesday, their relationship seemed back on track. Not exactly a track he wanted, but at least they were speaking. There was hope. Liam didn't kid himself about where Jude stood with regard to his adventures, and perhaps for the moment, not bringing up the topic for a while was best.

Jude told him she'd received an email answer from a humanitarian group in Costa Rica. The group, according to her request, agreed to pay half the shipping costs for her goats.

"That's super," he'd said. "What's needed to get the process moving?"

"I'll contact a live animal transporter and have the goats taken to Baltimore, where they can be loaded on a ship for Central America."

"Good for you," he'd said. "But Eloise stays?"

Jude had laughed. "Yes. She can't be trusted on a long voyage. She'd eat through the side of the boat and try to swim home." She'd paused a moment before saying, "I wouldn't have been able to do all this without your advice, Liam. I really owe you, and so does my dad. Which reminds me, there's a check here for you."

"Tear it up," he'd said. "My pleasure. And speaking of pleasure, can I come over tomorrow?"

"I'd love it if you would."

"I can bring a new-release movie and sub sandwiches."

"Okay. Make sure the movie is kid-appropriate."

When they'd disconnected, Liam considered that just the sound of Jude's voice lifted his spirits, made him grateful he'd been able to help her. But his feelings went far beyond his ability to offer advice. He was crazy about a woman who seemed determined to make him crazy by making him feel guilty about something completely innocent that he looked forward to every summer.

Who would have thought he'd ever fall for a woman like Jude. Sophisticated? Not at all. Knowledgeable about clothes and fashion? Not her. Educated with diplomas on her wall? No, she didn't need diplomas to find her own kind of success. She was good-hearted, caring—qualities that often made a diploma superfluous in defining a worthwhile life.

But what was he going to do about her fear of losing him over his exploits? He wasn't going to give up what he looked forward to every year. He didn't want to disappoint the best friends he'd ever had. These friends, these adventures had become part of his life. But how, in good conscience, could he disappoint Jude? Especially if the life he wanted with her wasn't going to happen if he continued participating in risks she disapproved of.

Pushing aside the accounts he'd been working on in his office, he took a sip of coffee and thought about what he would do. What was a marriage anyway? And how did the *M* word suddenly pop into his mind? Was he thinking about marrying Jude? Was he ready to assume the responsibilities of looking after a six-year-old? Would Jude even allow him to have an active part in Wesley's life?

He'd been married before. Two years of a relationship that hadn't worked almost from the beginning. He and Cheryl had been married but separate, both leading their own busy lives, following their own individual interests.

He often went out with his buddies. She arranged girls' nights with other high-powered career-minded friends. Cheryl had never once complained about his summer activities. She never once expressed concern. It was enough if she'd say, "Do you have everything you need? Okay, see you in a couple of weeks."

He hadn't considered whether her attitude about his exploits made him lucky or not. He was free to do what he wanted. What man wouldn't be grateful? What husband wanted a woman worrying over him? Well, maybe Liam did. His marriage had ended with a slow-burning fizzle until it just eventually turned to ash. And, oddly, when they both agreed it was over, not much changed in his life.

No one could say that Jude didn't care. Yes, her fears were irrational. He knew all precautions were taken to guarantee his safety on these trips. He and his three friends weren't the only guys who took minimal risks for the sake of manly companionship. He knew he'd return to her, and he wanted her to trust him. But she couldn't. So what was he going to do to earn the love and trust of the woman he wanted?

And how was he going to convince her, and himself, that he could be the positive role model she wanted for her son? And did he even want the job? If only there were a fool-proof test of a man's heart to determine if he was truly ready to be a father. Liam had never given the notion much thought. His life was running along pretty much as he wanted it to. Could he make sacrifices for the son of the woman he loved?

His phone rang and he checked the caller ID. Lenny, the friend who was going on the Mount Dunwoody climb. He called once a week to double-check on the other three guys who'd promised to take the five-thousand-foot trek up the mountain.

"Hey, Len," Liam said. "How's it going?"

"If it were any better, I'd have to be twins," Lenny quipped. "Just calling to see if you've made our reservations at the lodge for the week before the climb."

Liam had completely forgotten his assignment for the past week. "Oh, sorry, buddy. I haven't done that yet."

"No problem. There's still time. I understand the beginning of June isn't their busiest season. Still a slight chance of snow at the highest elevation."

Liam thought of his friends and recalled the times he'd shared with these special three guys in the past. They'd established traditions and strong bonds. And then he thought of a future with Jude, the traditions they could build together. And suddenly words he never thought he'd utter came pouring out.

"Uh, Lenny, I'm afraid I have some bad news."

"What's that?"

"Something has come up. I can't make it this year."

Lenny chuckled. "Yeah, right."

"No, really, Len. I'm not going."

"What? Are you kidding me, Manning? You can't back out. You're the one who wanted this climb in the first place. I've made all the arrangements with four of us in mind. We'll each have specific jobs."

"You can do it with three," Liam said. "In fact, it might be easier to only have to watch out for two other guys."

"That's not the point, and you know it. We do these things together. We're a team. Unless someone's dying in June, you can't not show."

"No one's dying," Liam said. "But my reason is important. I'm going to beg off this time."

"When the other guys hear this, they're going to be royally pissed. You'll probably get some phone calls."

"I'll handle them if I do."

"What's this reason? It had better be good."

Suddenly Liam's temper began to flare. Now he had to explain himself? "Not that I'm obligated to tell you everything," he said, "but a friend here needs me at that time. I want to be here for her."

"Her?" Lenny's voice rose in anger. "You're bailing on us for a chick?"

Liam didn't know intimate details of the marriages of two of the guys who had wives. But he figured those relationships had to be similar to the one he'd shared with Cheryl. Neither friend ever complained about his wife not going along with his plans. Maybe, like Cheryl, they didn't care enough. He was at a crossroad with Jude right now. The pathway he chose could decide his future.

"She's a woman, yeah," he said. "I can't explain it to you, but you'll just have to accept my decision."

Lenny sighed. His voice calmed. "Okay, I will. I know you, Manning, and if you say this is important, then it's important. But we'll miss you."

"Same here. Thanks for understanding."

Lenny chuckled. "I wouldn't go so far as

to say I understand, but good luck with whatever's going on with you. I'll let you know how the climb went."

"I'll be anxious to hear."

Liam disconnected. Tomorrow would be a life-changing day for him. Meanwhile, he was looking forward to subs and a movie tonight.

CHAPTER NINETEEN

AFTER REPORTING AT the radio station on Wednesday morning, Jude went to Main Street of Fox Creek and strolled the hundred-year-old storefronts. She finished her Christmas shopping and went home and wrapped packages until she called Carrie. "When are you leaving Michigan?" she asked. "Christmas is in two days."

"I know. You're not going to like what I have to tell you, Judie."

"Why? What's wrong?"

"I won't be home for Christmas."

"Sure you won't." It was meant as a sarcastic comeback.

"No, really. I'm in the middle of a project here and the results need constant monitoring. I'm not comfortable turning the experiments over to anyone else. My crew—and I use the term loosely, since there are only three of them—all have families. I don't have the heart to ask one of them to stay here and test the waters of Lake Chimanga."

"But, Carrie, you can't miss Christmas!" Jude said. "You've never missed Christmas."

"I know and I'm sorry. But, Jude, I was just home for Thanksgiving, and I'll come as soon as I can even if it's January before I get there. But my work is just too important. Hundreds of birch trees are depending on the results."

"Trees! Once again you're sacrificing your family for a bunch of trees."

Carrie laughed. "What can I say? I love you both. But right now the trees need me more."

"Have you told Daddy this? He's counting on everyone being here. Alex, Daniel and Lizzie arrive on the twenty-fourth."

"I'm going to call him when I hang up with you. I hope he'll understand."

Jude tried to hide her disappointment. Christmas wouldn't be the same without the whole family together. She sniffed, rubbed her nose. "I guess I'll just have to return all your presents."

"Don't you dare! I said I'd be there, just not on Christmas. You leave all my presents under the tree."

"Carrie, we won't even have a tree when

you get home. Rosie will have taken it apart and returned it to the attic. And besides all that, who will make the red velvet Christmas cake? Who can I count on to spike the eggnog? For heaven's sake, Care, who will play the piano?"

Carrie giggled. "You're surprising me, Jude. I never knew you were so fond of traditions. I mean, I always thought Christmas was just another day you had to feed the menagerie."

"It's different this year," Jude said, feeling suddenly wistful. Maybe it was the gigantic Douglas fir taking up half the living room. Maybe it was the man who gave it to them, the man who was coming over today with a movie.

As if reading her mind, Carrie said, "I can tell it's different. I'm thinking it's quite possible my big sister is in love. If that's the case, honey, you won't need me to make this a picture-perfect holiday."

Truly Jude always needed Carrie, maybe this Christmas more than any other. Alex was bright and helpful and gave sound advice. But Carrie, she was the one who could whittle log-sized problems into toothpicks with a single phrase. Carrie didn't take life too seriously and she never let anyone around her bring down her mood. Their mother used to say, "Carrie could charm a rattlesnake into tying her shoelaces."

None of the girls really understood the literal meaning of that sentence, but they still knew what their mother was saying. And now Jude needed her sister in the worst way. She needed to talk to her about Liam, about his penchant to challenge death, about how she loved him in spite of it but couldn't live with his decisions. She wanted to tell Carrie what she'd bought Liam for the holiday. Bottom line, she needed Carrie for Christmas.

"Don't be upset with me, Judie," Carrie said. "I couldn't stand it if you were mad at me. This is just something I have to do, and you'll have a wonderful Christmas with Daddy and Wesley and…" She let out a mischievous cough "… Liam Manning."

Jude couldn't remember a time when she was ever seriously angry with Carrie. Her sister just had a way of making sure that when the dust of her mistakes settled, everyone liked her again, even if she'd screwed up royally.

"I'm not mad at you, Care Bear," Jude said. "But I'll miss you."

"Same here. But I'll call Christmas Day."

"And you'll call Daddy now?"

"Yes, I will. Gotta go now, Jude. I love you."

"Love you, too."

Jude disconnected and tried to turn her thoughts to the rest of her day. She was looking forward to seeing Liam, but Carrie's announcement had certainly dampened her spirits. The day was gloomy and overcast, so Jude went over to their very large, very pretty Christmas tree and plugged in the lights. The gifts she'd ordered for Wesley had arrived at the big house. She'd chosen gifts for her father, sisters, niece and Aurora. It would be a good Christmas after all. Besides, who could be melancholy with two hundred blinking colors brightening the room?

A HALF HOUR LATER, Martin pulled up in front of the barn and stormed up the stairs to Jude's apartment.

"Daddy, what's wrong?" Jude asked, though she knew.

"Your sister, that's what's wrong. She's not coming for Christmas."

"I know, but we'll have a nice family time anyway. Alex and Lizzie will be here."

"And I'm here!" Wesley chimed in. "We can play with all my new stuff, Grandpa."

Martin grinned. "You're right, Wes. We sure can. It'll be a holly, jolly time after all."

Jude sensed that her dad really needed some cheering up. What better way to accomplish that than to make him feel needed. Besides, she did need his advice about Liam. Thankfully Wes remembered a project he'd been working on and headed for his bedroom.

Jude sat next to Martin on the sofa. "Daddy, I need advice, and, well, you're a guy, and this is a guy thing."

A worried look crossed his face. "I'm thinking this is about a much younger guy, Jude, maybe Liam Manning's age. I'm only good at giving old guy advice."

She smiled. "Stop calling yourself old. You're in the prime of life."

"Thank you, sweetheart. I'm going to choose to believe you're right. Now, what's going on between you and Liam?"

She let out a long breath, squared her shoulders and began. "I really like him, Daddy. I never thought I would feel this way about any man again, but I think about him all the time. He has turned my life upside down, made me start to consider those long-term goals you wanted me to set."

"That's great. I'm happy to hear it, but why do I sense a big *but* coming next?"

She grinned sheepishly. "You know me too well. Here's the thing…"

She told Martin about having dinner at Liam's, seeing the pictures of what she'd come to think of as his "wall of risk." She explained her reaction to Liam's activities in terms of her fear of losing him as well as her fear about Wesley wanting to follow in his footsteps.

"If I give my heart again, and it's broken again, I don't think I could go on. The last five years haven't been happy, I know that, but I've come to live with my loss and grief. I've guarded my heart so carefully that until Liam, I truly believed that feeling nothing for someone was so much better than feeling too much.

"Liam tells me I'm acting irrationally. I get what he means. To him, these trips are part of life, the thrill of male bonding and a sense of accomplishment. To me, his adventures are unnecessary and dangerous."

She reached over and took her father's hand. "I love him, Daddy. I don't want to lose him. I don't want to tell him goodbye because I can't live with his choices. But I don't want to see him leave me and never come back. I don't know what to do."

Martin sat perfectly still for a few moments. Then he breathed deeply, turned to look directly into her eyes and said, "There are many ways to lose someone, Jude. A person can walk away and never come back. He can do something stupid or adventurous or whatever you want to call it, and die. Sure, it's possible." His eyes clouded with his own grief. "Or the love of your life can become ill and waste away just a few feet from the arms that still ache to hold her."

"Oh, Daddy..."

"Your mother is lost to me, Jude, just as much as if she'd died, but does that mean I'm sorry I ever loved her in the first place?"

"I know your answer to that," Jude said.

"Of course you do. I wouldn't give up a moment of those wonderful years with Maggie even though I've lost her now." He patted Jude's hand where it lay over his. "Every time you open your heart, Jude, you risk hurt, but, and maybe this is just an old guy's opinion, it's a risk worth taking."

She nodded slowly, letting his words sink in.

"You've been through a lot, my dear Judie, but you're strong and alive and doing good things every day for those around you. It's your own personal satisfaction that has suffered. So here's what you have to decide before it's too late…"

She waited as he gathered his thoughts.

He cleared his throat. "Is loving Liam worth the chance that you might lose him? Or is giving him up because of your fears now worth the chance that you'll never love again?" Martin smiled, held his palms in front of him as if he were balancing something. "Love or fear. I know what my answer would be."

Jude leaned over and wrapped her arms around her father's neck. "Daddy, I love you. Thank you."

His voice was raspy when he spoke again. "You're welcome. I don't know what your mother would say to you, but I gave this my best shot."

Martin rose from the sofa. "Guess I'll

get going. I've a mind to make this the best Christmas ever."

Jude walked to the door with him. "I believe you'll do it, too."

When he'd left, she thought about the decision she faced. Her father had narrowed down her choices to two. Choosing between them shouldn't be so difficult, should it?

CHAPTER TWENTY

WESLEY CAME OUT of his room a few minutes later. "Where's Grandpa?"

"He went to his house."

"Oh. When's Liam going to get here?"

"Wesley, how many times are you going to ask me that question?"

"Until he gets here."

Wesley began circling the coffee table with his arms out to his side and the sound of an engine bubbling from his lips.

"Wesley, would you stop that please. You're making a racket. And what are you doing anyway?"

"I'm an airplane, Mom," he said, continuing to circle and now flapping his arms. "When Liam gets here I'm going to ask him to take me up in a plane so I can jump out with a pair of chutes."

Stay calm, Jude. Wesley is just a little boy. "First of all, it's parachute, not pair of chutes.

Second of all, it's going to be a long time, if ever, when you jump from a plane with Liam or anybody else."

Wesley stopped circling and skidded to a stop in front of her. "But it looks so cool. You saw the picture on Liam's wall. He was smiling."

"I'm not at all sure that was a smile," she said. "I think it was the force of the wind pushing his lips back. Or maybe he was scared and that was a scream." Amazed that she could talk about this without heightened anxiety creeping into her voice, Jude realized that she had to handle this discussion carefully.

He looked up at her with his beautiful blue eyes wide and determined. "I'm not afraid of stuff. I want to do it, and I'm asking Liam to take me."

She pulled two chairs away from the dining table. "Sit down, Wesley. We need to get some things straight."

She sat and waited for him to take the other chair. "Honey, I am your mother. I love you, and it's my job to protect you and make certain you don't do anything that could hurt you. That's good, isn't it?"

He shrugged. "I don't know. Liam does lots

of things that are fun and 'venturous. Doesn't he have a mom?"

"Yes, he does, but he's a grown man. I don't suppose he has to listen to his mother like you do."

"When can I stop listening?"

"That's hard to say. Growing up takes a long time. You have to get taller and bigger and learn everything you can at school. Then you have to show good judgment. Do you know what that means?"

"Nope."

"It means you have to show everybody that you can make wise decisions. And I'm afraid that jumping out of airplanes at the age of six is not a wise decision."

"So I can never do it?"

She sat straight and held his gaze. "When you're older, you can do what you like, but I hope you'll think about the things you want to do with that good judgment I was talking about. As for me, I hope you never jump out of an airplane."

His face remained placid for a moment and then his emotions changed. He scrunched up his eyes as a frown formed on his lips. Jude was aware of his leg bouncing under the table.

Her son was acting as if someone had just lit a firecracker inside him and he was ready to explode.

He stood up. "I have good judgment now!" he shouted. "All you want me to do is stay here and take water to the horses and put the goats back in their pen."

"Wesley, honey—"

"I'm sick of that stuff. And it's mean for you to make me do it. I want to do different stuff, better stuff."

Wesley had never spoken to her like this. She'd never once thought that he wasn't happy working with the animals. She'd always assumed that he wanted to do these chores. "Have you felt like this before today?" she asked.

"Yeah. People tell me I'm a cowboy and I hate it! I don't want to be a cowboy. Why doesn't anybody ever ask me what I want to be?"

Jude blinked several times. She'd always loved animals, dedicated much of her life to them. So had Paul. He'd been an expert rider and seemed to have learned basic veterinary skills without ever going to college. Love of animals was one of the traits that drew her to Paul from the beginning. She'd assumed Wesley would inherit this love.

She calmed enough to keep her voice from shaking. "Wes, I never knew you felt this way. You don't have to be a cowboy. You can be whatever you want."

"When? I have to grow up and have stupid judgment first!"

"Yes, that's right. Until then you'll continue to live here, and I'll continue to rely on you for whatever help you can give me. But when you're older, when you're a young man, you can choose to do or be something else. But, honey, while you're my little boy, you won't be jumping from airplanes."

"You're never going to let me do things!" he said. "How old do I have to be to do what I want?"

"I'll know the answer to that when you make decisions that prove to me that you're ready to be a man."

His bottom lip trembled. "I am old enough, and I'll show you! Maybe I'll just go and live with Liam."

She stood and took a step toward him. How had this conversation backfired so badly? At least she was grateful to learn about the resentment Wes had been feeling. "We're a team here, Wesley. We belong together and that's the way it is for now."

He sniffed. "Can I go outside?"

"It's chilly. Put your jacket on."

He grabbed his coat from the hook and slipped it on.

"And your hat."

He yanked the knitted cap over his ears. "Can I go now?"

"Yes, but stay close. Don't leave the yard."

The door slammed behind him and he clomped down the stairs. Jude collapsed on the sofa and replayed the last few minutes in her mind. No matter what her father said, she still had to protect her son from growing up too fast or thinking she would allow him to pursue activities that were strictly out of bounds. Could she in all honesty, and as a good parent, look the other way when Liam took off for his adventures, knowing the influence he had over Wesley?

Surely Wesley would come back inside soon, the frown replaced with a big smile. It wasn't in a child's nature to stay grumpy for long. And Liam was coming over. That should make her son happy. But in the meantime, the sparkly Douglas fir didn't seem nearly so cheerful. And the decision she'd been so close to making seemed as distant as ever.

JUDE WENT IN her room to change her clothes. She didn't see Wesley enter the barn. She didn't notice when he took a cotton rope from the tack room. She couldn't hear his voice when he approached the stall where Titan was kept and spoke to the horse. She didn't know when Wesley opened the stall door.

CHAPTER TWENTY-ONE

LIAM PULLED UP to the barn and turned off his engine. He had started to reach into the backseat for the sandwiches he'd picked up on the way over when, out of the corner of his eye, he spotted Wesley. A sharp pain sliced into his chest. He blinked hard. It couldn't be. Wesley had the wild Thoroughbred, Titan, on the end of a rope, and the two of them were in the open paddock. Jude wouldn't have allowed this.

Liam quickly exited his car and ran to the fence surrounding the grazing area. "Wesley!" he called. "What are you doing?"

Wes tugged on the rope, trying to pull the horse into the center of the paddock. Titan wasn't willing to cooperate and reared up on his hind legs. Wesley wrapped the rope around his wrist. "I'm showing Mom that I'm big enough to do things, like tame this wild ol' horse!"

With his adrenaline pumping, Liam hopped over the fence, his hands raised. "No, don't do that. Drop the rope and come over here to me."

Wesley continued to struggle with the huge animal. "I'm gonna get on him, Liam. Then Mom'll see that I can make my own decisions."

Fearful of further irritating the horse, Liam took a few cautious steps toward Wesley. "I don't know what's going on, Wes, but this isn't the way to prove anything to your mom. You need to let go of the rope now."

All at once Titan chose that moment to begin a sort of crazed gallop toward the other side of the paddock. Wesley went down to the ground. "I can't let go, Liam!" he shouted. "My wrist is caught!"

The next moments were a blur. Wesley was dragged on the hard ground as he was pulled along at the whim of a thousand-pound animal. He tried to dig his boot heels into the dirt, but Titan obviously only found the obstacle a fuel to his natural temperament. He shook his large head and picked up speed.

Liam raced across the paddock and made several unsuccessful grabs for the rope before his fingers finally wrapped around the cotton braid. He had to get Wesley free. Already the boy's wrist was turning a sickening blue color. As Liam struggled to loosen the loop around Wesley's wrist, the horse reared up in a threatening way, not once but repeatedly. Liam dodged the hooves that came dangerously close to his head. In the back of his mind, he thought he heard Jude's voice coming from the stairs—panicked and scared.

Running alongside the horse and boy, Liam finally managed to free Wesley's hand. He lunged for Wesley as the boy lay on the ground. The horse went up on his hind legs again, and Liam bent over and pushed Wes toward the fence and safety. "Run, Wes!" he hollered. "Get out of here!"

That was the last Liam knew as the hoof of a raging animal came crashing down against his temple. A white-hot pain slashed into his skull as he hit the winter ground hard and his world went black.

JUDE FLEW DOWN the stairs when she heard commotion outside. She landed on the ground just as Liam released her son from the rope. Wesley got to his feet, stumbled and took off toward her. A scream stayed in her throat as she was caught in the grip of the worst fear she'd ever known.

She pulled Wesley under the lowest fence rail and dragged him a few feet from the paddock, then went back immediately to help Liam. But it was too late. She saw the powerful hoof connect with the side of his head and Liam crumple to the ground as if he were made of straw. She heard Wesley scream but couldn't go back to him now. She darted between the fence rails and captured the rope dragging behind the horse, who circled the paddock with a dangerous fire in his eyes as he headed for his wounded target.

It took all Jude's strength and her loudest, most commanding voice to get the animal under control enough to send him into the barn. She slid the barn door closed and ran back to the paddock. Liam still hadn't moved. And now Wesley was crying hysterically.

"I killed Liam, Mommy," he wailed. "I killed him."

Crouching beside Liam, Jude felt for a pulse in his neck. Thank God. The faint sign of life was there. But blood oozed from Liam's temple and his ear, and his color had gone ashen.

"Wes, get my cell phone. It's on the cof-fee table."

The child didn't move. His eyes were round with terror, and he was on his hands and knees crying as she'd never heard him cry in his life. "I killed him, Mama!"

"No, you didn't. He's not dead. Can you hear me, Wes? You've got to run upstairs and get my cell phone. Go now!"

He gasped, made it to his feet and ran up the stairs.

"Dial 911," Jude called when he came bar-reling down again. "Then hand me the phone." She didn't know what to do. She needed help. Should she be giving him mouth-to-mouth? Should she cover him? Was he going into shock? Should she raise his head? She wished her father were here, but he was at the hos-pital. She'd never felt so inadequate in her life. She wasn't prepared for the magnitude of what she realized was a life-or-death situ-ation.

As calmly as she could, she related the de-tails to the emergency operator. Good grief, she didn't even have an address to give the woman. "Tell them to drive around back until they see the barn," was all she could say. "And hurry.

"Hang in there, Liam, help is on its way." She kept talking to him, stroking his arm, interspersing prayers as the words came to her.

"He's not moving, Mama," Wesley said.

She'd almost forgotten about her son. He'd come into the paddock and sat on his knees a few feet away, his eyes transfixed on Liam. When Jude saw the streaks of tears down his face, she reached for him. "He'll be okay, Wesley."

"It's all my fault," he said. "I'm sorry. I was just—"

"Don't talk about that now, honey," she said, noticing for the first time the bruises coloring his wrist. "Do you hurt anywhere badly, Wes?"

He looked at his wrist, which might very well be broken, sniffed again and said, "No."

How many times had she told him never to go near Titan? How many warnings? How many threats had she made in case he even thought about disobeying her? And for what? In the end, he was still a six-year-old child, angry and determined to find his way. She stared at her distraught son trying to remain brave and knew with shocking clarity he could have been killed today. Liam saved his life. She rested her cheek lightly against Liam's chest, trying to find comfort in the weak rise and fall of his lungs. A moment later she realized her tears had soaked his shirt.

At the first faint wail of a siren, Jude got to her feet. Supporting her trembling body against the fence, she waved her arms, bringing the ambulance closer.

THANK GOODNESS THE EMTs were skilled, calm and precise. Of course none of the three medics were in love with the victim. Through the blur in her brain, she recognized medical terms.

Blood pressure dropping…

Bring a collar…

Need a back board…

Not nearly soon enough for Jude, Liam was loaded into the ambulance for his ride to Cuyahoga Medical Center.

"Will he be all right?" she asked one of the techs.

"I can't tell you that, ma'am," he said. "But he's in good hands now and we'll be in constant contact with the ER doctors on the trip."

"I'm going to follow you," she said. "My son has an injury to his wrist."

"Let me take a quick look at it," the medic said. Wes winced when the fellow took his hand. "That should be x-rayed." He confirmed what Jude had already suspected. "He'll be okay in the car with you, but take it easy on the drive." The EMT stared into her eyes. "You look a bit shaky to be driving."

"I'll be fine."

The ambulance left with cargo that had become as precious as life to Jude. How was it possible that after five years of denying herself true happiness, she could find herself in love again—when she'd sworn she'd never love another man? And now that man, the one who'd brought her out of her shadowy life, could die.

She bundled Wesley into her truck, and they followed the ambulance down the drive to the main road. In moments, however, the ambulance was way ahead of them, sirens blaring, until the red taillights were only blinking red orbs in a wintry sky. Neither Jude nor Wesley spoke until Wes finally swallowed hard and said, "He'll be okay, won't he, Mom?"

"I hope so, honey. For now we must believe that he will be."

"I hate that mean old horse!"

Jude questioned whether this was the right time to discuss what had happened with her son, but he seemed to want to talk about it. "Wesley, baby, why did you take Titan from his stall? What were you thinking?"

He hiccupped between almost every word, but she got the gist of what he tried to say. "I wanted to prove to you that I was big enough to make my own decisions. If I'd tamed Titan, you would have thought so, right?"

She glanced over at him. "Oh, sweetheart, even if everything had gone well today, it takes more than one victory to make a man. It takes years and experience, and lots of learning. The right decision would have been to listen to me about that horse and never let him out."

His eyes welled with tears again in his grief-swollen face. "I think it's time for us to find Titan a new home," she said. "Somewhere on a bigger place maybe, where there are no children."

"But you want to keep Titan, don't you, Mom? You wanted to make his life better."

"Yes, I thought I did, but now I realize I was wrong. Every day I kept Titan on this farm, I was taking a risk..." She stopped, recognizing the word she'd thought about and said so often in the last weeks. "You're not the only one to blame, Wesley. I'm to blame, too, for keeping a dangerous animal around you." She tried to smile, to take the guilt away from her son. "I never should have trusted that grumpy ol' horse anywhere around the number-one guy in my life."

He gulped air. "So if Liam dies, we're both to blame?"

She understood he needed her to take some of the awesome responsibility from his shoulders and transfer it to hers. And she owed him that. "I suppose, but I don't think he's going to die."

"He can't," Wesley mumbled. "He's the best friend I ever had."

Jude bit her lip. *I know what you mean. He's the best friend I ever had, too.*

WHEN JUDE PULLED into the emergency entrance of the medical center, the ambulance that had brought Liam was empty, its large double doors gaping open in the back. She experienced a measure of calm knowing he was being treated. She parked as close to the entrance as possible and walked with Wesley into the emergency room. A triage nurse examined him quickly.

"We heard you were coming in," she said. "Let's get a picture of that wrist."

"You'll be okay with the nurse," Jude said to Wesley. "I'm going to go upstairs and find Grandpa."

While Wesley went back to X-ray, Jude went to the third floor and her father's office. He was just leaving surgery and met her in the hallway. His normally placid face became pinched with concern.

"What are you doing here?" he asked. "You okay? Is it Wesley?"

"He…he's having an X-ray."

She dissolved into tears and Martin spoke to a nurse about sending the results of Wesley's X-ray stat. Then he escorted Jude into his office and closed the doors. Somehow she managed to tell him the details of the most frightening experience of her life.

"Wesley will be fine," he assured her. "Annette at the desk will tell the nurses in X-ray to bring him up here when they're finished."

He gave her a comforting stare. "What can I get you? Coffee?" He slid open his desk drawer. "Something from my emergency stash?"

"No, I'm okay," she said. "But Liam…"

"I'll find out what I can, honey, but in the meantime, we've got to call Lawrence and Alicia."

Liam's parents! Jude sank farther into her chair. How would they take this news? "Yes, we should," she said.

"Let me do that. If you want to wait outside…"

"Yes, I would."

Martin took her to a chair in the visitors' lobby and returned to his office. A few minutes later, he came to find her. "They're on the way to the hospital," he said. "Understandably they're quite shaken up." He focused on a spot down the hall. "Look who's here," he said, his voice suddenly chipper.

Wesley, his wrist wrapped in a bandage and his arm in a sling, hurried toward them. "Look what I got on my arm," he said.

"That's dandy, Wes," Martin said, and turned his attention to the nurse who'd brought Wes upstairs. "What's the news?"

"A sprain," the young woman said. "But he needs to keep the arm immobile for a few days. He should be okay with doses of a children's pain medication as needed."

Martin turned his attention back to Jude. "Why don't I take you both home? Actually why don't I take you to my house? I think that would be a good idea at least for tonight."

"I don't want to leave," Jude said.

In a low voice, Martin assured her that leaving would be okay. "I doubt we'll know anything about Liam tonight."

"Dad, I'd appreciate it if you'd take Wesley to your house, but I'm staying for a while."

"I want to stay, too," Wesley said. "I want to know how Liam is, and I want to show him my sling."

"I understand, Wes," Jude said. "But right now, I want you to go home with Grandpa. When the medicine they gave you wears off, your wrist will probably hurt. Grandpa's the best one to take care of you if it does."

"Do I have to go?"

"Yes, you do."

"Come on, sport," Martin said. "I've got to get my coat from my office." He stopped midway down the hall. "I'm thinking I might not be able to make it home without some ice cream. What do you say?"

Within a minute they were gone, and Jude took the elevator down to Emergency. She stopped the first nurse she saw. "How is Liam Manning? He was brought in with a head injury."

"He's having a CT scan," the nurse said. "And a neurosurgeon will be seeing him next."

"A neurosurgeon? Why? Do they suspect a brain injury?"

The nurse patted her arm. "It's customary for head injuries. Don't jump to conclusions."

"Could I speak with the doctor after he's seen Liam?"

"Are you immediate family?"

"No, but I'm a very good friend. The accident happened at my house, and I'm quite worried about him." The nurse didn't seem inclined to grant Jude's request, so she played the one card she had to persuade her. "I'm also Dr. Foster's daughter, if that makes any difference."

The nurse smiled. "We all love Dr. Foster around here. Let me see what I can do."

A few minutes later, a doctor came into the

waiting room, saw her sitting in a chair and came over. "Are you Martin's daughter?" he asked.

"Yes. How's Liam?"

The doctor held out his hand. "I'm Frank Baker, the staff neurosurgeon. I've just read Liam's scan."

Jude shook his hand. "And?"

"I wish I could say that he just had a simple concussion, but I'm afraid it's more serious than that."

"He doesn't have a concussion?"

"Well, yes, he does, but his concussion is a grade three, the most severe possible. I would feel more confident about Liam's recovery if that's all we discovered."

"What do you mean? Hasn't Liam regained consciousness?"

"No, he hasn't, and the scan showed a significant bleed in the brain, which could cause a clot between the brain and the skull. If that happens, we would have to operate to relieve the pressure."

Jude's heart lurched in her chest. "A bleed. An operation on his brain? How dangerous would that be?"

"Of course there is risk, but I'm hoping

we don't have to do surgery. Right now, even though Liam is still not awake, we have induced a coma to give the brain time to heal. Any sudden body movements could cause further injury to the affected area, so it's essential we keep the patient immobile."

Jude could only nod. She didn't trust her voice to form recognizable words.

"If the swelling goes down, we'll probably only need to keep him in the coma for a few days. Then we'll give him the chance to wake up on his own." The doctor frowned. "If he does, we'll follow up with another CT scan with the hope of discovering the bleeding has stopped."

"Can…can I see him?" Jude asked.

"Not right now. He's being taken up to ICU where he can be properly monitored. As I explained, he wouldn't know you were here anyway."

Commotion at the entrance to the ER caused the doctor and Jude to glance in that direction. Lawrence Manning strode through the doors, accompanied by a woman Jude assumed was his ex-wife. She'd only seen Alicia Manning one time, twenty years ago, but the qualities of this tall, striking woman were hard to forget. Wrapped in an ankle-length coat with the fur collar turned up around her neck, Alicia looked as if she could command the entire operation of the hospital. Still, Jude's heart ached for her. Signs of stress were definitely etched on her pale face.

"Hi, Frank," Lawrence said, walking immediately to the doctor. "Did they call you in to see Liam?"

Dr. Baker explained the details he'd just related to Jude. With each retelling, both parents' faces grew more concerned. Alicia took a tissue from her purse and wiped her eyes.

"I've got to sit down, Larry," she said. She turned toward the waiting room chairs, passed a quick glance in Jude's direction and took a seat. If she recognized Jude, she didn't say anything.

Jude went over to her and put her hand on Alicia's coat sleeve. "Mrs. Manning, I'm so sorry about what happened."

"You're sorry? Why are you sorry? Who are you?"

"We've met before," Jude said. "I'm Martin Foster's daughter."

Alicia's eyes widened in what could only be horror. "The middle daughter? The one

Liam took to the planetarium? That's who you are?"

"Yes, but..."

Understanding dawned as a spark of fire in Alicia's eyes. "Of course. This all makes sense now. He's been seeing you, hasn't he? It was your horse! You're the reason my son is right now in a coma. We don't know if he'll live or die!"

Jude felt her throat start to close. She coughed. "Mrs. Manning, we can't think that way. We have to believe Liam will be okay."

"*We?* What do you mean *we*? You don't even belong here. You don't matter to Liam."

"I don't think that's true," Jude said. "And anyway, Liam matters to me. He matters a lot."

"I told him not to get involved with you," Alicia said. "I warned him about your antics, your brushes with the law. You have been a disgrace to your father for years and now you may have killed my son."

Jude blinked back burning tears. She wanted to run out, but that wasn't her way, so she tried again. "It was an accident, Mrs. Manning." Her voice began to tremble. She swallowed and continued. "Liam was coming to the rescue of my young son. Liam saved his life. He was a hero."

Alicia's voice rose to an angry growl. "What good is a dead hero, Miss Foster? I'd rather have a live son than a dead hero. I would think you, of all people, would understand that."

Her words settled like hot acid in Jude's stomach. How many times had she said and thought those same words—*what good is a dead hero?* Would she have wanted Liam to stand by while her son was trampled by a maniac horse, or was she glad he jumped in and saved him? What had once seemed so black and white to Jude was now shades of gray. She needed to think through these feelings, but now, at this moment, her mind and her heart were too full to handle more emotion.

Finished with his discussion with Dr. Baker, Lawrence Manning came over to the seats. "What is wrong over here?" he asked. "Keep your voice down, Alicia. This is a hospital, after all."

Alicia glared up at her ex-husband. "You think I don't know that, Larry! You think I'm not aware every second that my son is fighting for his life in this place?" Casting one brief, hateful look at Jude, she said, "I want her out of here. She's not family. She's nobody, except that she's responsible for our son lying in a coma upstairs."

"Mrs. Manning," Jude began. "Respectfully I'm not leaving until I know how Liam is."

Alicia started to rise, but Lawrence held up his hand. "Miss Foster—"

"Mrs. O'Leary," Jude said.

"Oh yes. I do apologize. Out of consideration for the years of friendship with your father, I'm simply going to ask you to leave at this time. I don't want to get security involved, but I could because you are not family. And you can see how upset Mrs. Manning is. Your being here only adds to the tension."

Gripping the arms of her chair, Alicia said, "Yes, go! And don't come back."

Jude didn't move from her chair. "This is a public place, Mrs. Manning, Dr. Manning. I'm sorry if you don't want me here, but despite your threat, there's really nothing you can do about it."

Lawrence spoke in a soothing voice. "Jude—it's Jude, right?"

She nodded.

"I beg you, please…"

Taking a swift appraisal of her options, Jude relented. She didn't need another medical emergency on her conscience, and Mrs. Manning looked as if she might have a stroke any minute. "Save your breath, Dr. Manning, I'm going. I hope your son recovers very soon."

Without another word being spoken, she left the emergency room and went to her truck. Giving her heartbeat a few moments to return to a normal rhythm, she took several deep breaths, put her key in the ignition and drove home.

JUDE SPENT THE next day and a half calling the hospital and talking to whoever would listen about Liam's condition. Each time she learned the same thing. His condition hadn't changed. He was still in a coma.

She tried to put the worry out of her mind and let Christmas happen with her son. At least the news early on Christmas morning about Liam had been more hopeful. The doctors had determined that the swelling in his brain had gone down, and they'd taken him off the induced coma medications.

Alex, Daniel and Lizzie had arrived on Christmas Eve, brightening Jude's spirits.

The family opened gifts, played games and ended up snuggling around Martin's great stone fireplace. Jude and Wesley slept over so everyone could be near Maggie and make her part of the celebration as they had done for the last few years. Maggie was shown every gadget, goodie and fashionable sweater that had been wrapped and given with love. And she received her share of kisses while her daughters relived memories of Christmases past.

Jude was determined not to spoil the holiday for her family. She didn't know what she would do with the solid gold belt buckle she'd had made for Liam, the one with the symbol of Dancing Falls engraved on its shiny surface. Liam probably would not want to be reminded of her beloved home ever again.

On Christmas morning, Wesley was delighted to discover that Santa had indeed found Fox Creek, Ohio. And the jolly man had managed to stuff into his sleigh a red two-wheeler, countless LEGOs and enough books about astronomy to keep Wes busy for a long time. At least he kept up a good front as if he believed all that were true. Secretly he cuddled up against his mother on the sofa, smiled and said, "Thanks for all the great stuff, Mom."

Alex and Jude were making the traditional goose dinner when Aurora arrived looking festive in a red velvet skirt with a white sweater. She came right into the kitchen to lend a hand, but when she found preparations well under way, she asked Jude if they could have a little talk.

"Somewhere private," she said.

"That would be outside," Jude suggested. "Everywhere else is a madhouse. Will you be too cold?"

"Nonsense. The sun is out, and besides, I was raised in Chicago! But let's get our jackets just in case."

The two women met a minute later on the patio. Jude handed Aurora her gift.

"Yours is inside," Aurora said.

"That's all right. Go ahead and open it."

Aurora removed the tissue and took out a colorful knit scarf. "It's beautiful. I love it." To prove her appreciation, she wound the scarf around her neck.

"It's handmade by a woman in Bees Creek," Jude said. "I've always thought she did lovely work."

"Thank you, dear."

"Now, what did you want to talk to me about?"

Aurora smiled. "First of all, merry Christmas."

"Thanks. You, too. I'm glad you came for dinner."

Aurora lifted Jude's hand. "Is it, Jude?"

"Is it what?"

"Merry?"

"Well… Carrie's not here and…other things."

"I hope you won't be angry with your father, but he told me about what happened here a few days ago. Poor Liam, but thankfully he came at just the right time."

"I keep replaying in my mind that awful scene and what could have happened if Liam hadn't shown up when he did. He didn't even stop to think. He just ran into the paddock risking his life for Wesley's."

"That's often the way heroic deeds are done, isn't it?" Aurora said. "A person acts without thinking to save someone else when he could lose his own life. It makes a person wonder…"

"Yes. It does." *About Liam. About Paul…*

"Kind of makes you understand how the

family of those men Paul saved must be feeling, how much gratitude they have toward him."

Jude nodded. How amazing that Aurora's thoughts mirrored her own right now. Throughout this day Jude had thought several times about the men Paul saved and the fact that because of him they were sharing Christmas with their loved ones. Slowly, over the last hours, the bitterness she'd always carried in her heart had begun to fade. "But then in my mind's eye," she said, "I see Liam in the hospital bed."

"Why in 'your mind's eye,' Jude? Haven't you been to see him?"

"I was there the first night, but I've only called the nurses' station since then. Liam's parents asked that I not return. They blame me for what happened and I understand that."

"Hogwash," Aurora said. "You can't control the actions of a horse. You want to be with Liam, don't you?"

"M…more than anything."

"Then go to the hospital," Aurora said. "There is nothing quite so sad as a missed opportunity, and yours is today. There is no reason why you shouldn't be with the man you…"

Aurora chuckled. "Forgive me for blurting out something you may not even realize yet yourself."

"That I love Liam? Oh, I realize it, Aurora, and not being able to see him is killing me."

Aurora looked out over the expanse of lawn at the back of the house. A dusting of snow had already covered the grass, and more was forecast for later. In fact, there had been talks of a blizzard, one the likes of which the Great Lakes snow belt hadn't seen yet this season. "Your father has told me many things about you girls and your loves," she said, her voice dreamy. "I have determined a few things for myself, but mostly I agree with Marty."

"Oh? What has he told you about me?" Jude almost cringed.

"That you're a fighter and a believer in good, and that anyone who might try to convince you that you're wrong had better have a darn good reason for saying so."

"My stubbornness about my convictions has gotten me in trouble several times, Aurora."

"Well, if you want my opinion, now is not the time to abandon that fighting spirit. If you want to be at Liam's bedside, then go to him,

Jude. Don't let anyone bully you into retreating from that room. You deserve to be there, and I have a hunch that of all the people who have visited him in the last few days, you're the one he's waiting for."

"Do you really think so?"

Aurora cradled Jude's hand against her cheek. "I've had some pretty strong opinions about you and Liam since Alex's wedding, and no one could convince me that they were simply the rambling thoughts of an old woman."

Jude smiled. "There is nothing old about you, Aurora." She stood. "About dinner..."

"I'll take over for you. And I'll save you a plate for later." She laid Jude's hand on her lap and added, "That's enough hand-holding between us for now. There's another hand that needs to be held. Now go before the snow gets any worse. Nothing is prettier than a snowy Christmas unless you have to be out in it."

Jude leaned over and kissed Aurora's cheek. "Thank you, Aurora, for believing in me with all my faults."

Aurora chuckled. "You have faults? The only one I'm concerned even the least little bit about is maybe your reluctance to forgive the mistakes of the past." She shrugged. "But then I guess we're all like that, aren't we? They may be heavy, but we tend to carry our grudges nevertheless."

Jude stood, smiled down at Aurora, who she thought had the most sincere, kindest way of telling someone to get on with her life. "We should all forgive," Jude said. "And I promise to try.

She scurried into the house and grabbed her car keys.

"Where are you going, Mom?" Wesley asked from the living room floor where he and Lizzie were building a LEGO castle.

"Just out for a while, sweetheart." She lifted him up by his shoulders and gave him a big kiss on his forehead. "Merry Christmas, Wes!"

Looking completely confused, he giggled. "You, too, Mama."

MARTIN CAME INTO the kitchen after Jude had left. "What's going on?" he asked Aurora. "Where's Jude off to?"

Aurora took his arm and led him back to the living room. "I think she's going to try and perform a Christmas miracle," she said.

Martin grumbled under his breath, "Why is the father always the last to know?"

THE ENTRANCE TO Cuyahoga Medical Center was trimmed in garland and white lights. Inside, carols played softly in the public area. Jude wondered if the same cheerful music would surround those people whose illnesses were critical—those in the ICU unit.

She took the elevator to the third floor. A few people passed her in the hallway carrying bright bouquets of red carnations. Some had colorfully wrapped gifts. She wished she had something for Liam. She turned a corner and saw the Mannings seated in the waiting area. She straightened her spine, reminded herself that she was truly a fighter and walked briskly toward them.

Unfortunately Jude's determined footsteps were nothing like the muffled sounds of the medical staff in their soft-soled shoes. Her rarely worn dressy pumps echoed on the tile floor, and Lawrence and Alicia were quickly on their feet.

"What are you doing here?" Alicia demanded in a harsh whisper.

Lawrence put a hand on her shoulder. "Don't start," he said.

"How is Liam?" Jude asked.

"He's holding his own," Dr. Manning said. "We're hoping he'll regain consciousness soon."

Alicia shrugged off her husband's controlling hand. "There, Jude, now you know. You can go."

"I've come to see Liam," Jude said. "And I won't leave until I've done that. I am grateful to him for so many things, but the most important is the fact that he very likely saved my son's life." She took a deep breath. "And besides all that, I happen to be in love with him."

Alicia's eyes widened in shock. Dr. Manning responded with a resigned nod.

Jude continued. "I think, just maybe, if Liam is the forgiving man I believe him to be, he might actually love me, too."

She squared her shoulders into fighter stance. "I think that about covers it, so I'm going in now."

Alicia opened her mouth but snapped it shut again when Lawrence glared her into silence. "Go ahead, Jude," he said. "Maybe you'll have better luck than we've had."

The glass door to Liam's room whished open with a soothing hiss that did nothing to calm Jude's nerves. She clasped her hands tightly over her abdomen to still her trembling fingers. The vibrant man she'd come to love was lying motionless in a bed a few feet away. She couldn't lose her resolve now.

Her insecurities vanished when she approached the bed, for there was Liam, the man she knew, the one she loved. His sandy hair lay smoothed back from his forehead. His eyes were closed as if he were simply resting, his mouth full but slack with the release of tension that only comes with deep sleep. But this was not just deep sleep, she reminded herself.

A dusting of beard covered his lower face, and Jude longed to touch it, to smooth away the faint creases of care and pain on his face. But then she saw the bandage on his temple where his hair had been shaved, and remorse for what had happened to him on her farm consumed her.

She pulled up a chair and sat close to his bedside. Laying her hand lightly on his forearm, she said, "Hi, Liam, it's me, Jude. I'm sorry for what happened to you, so terribly sorry. I know you're going to be all right just as soon as the doctors figure out why you're not waking up."

She moved her hand down to lightly grasp his. "You have to wake up, Liam. I can't bear it if you don't. I have to tell you how grateful I am that you showed up at Dancing Falls when you did. You saved Wesley, you know. He was out in that paddock with that wild horse because he wanted to prove something to me, but what I learned that day wasn't about Wesley as much as it was about you.

"I've been thinking a lot lately, mostly about how selfish and narrow-minded I've been." Jude moved her chair even closer, wanting to remove as much distance between her and Liam as she could. Her knees touched the metal bed rails. "It's Christmas today," she said. "The Douglas fir is quite beautiful. Wesley is excited about his gifts, though he keeps asking about you. He wishes you'd been with us this morning. I have a gift for you, though I don't know how appropriate it will be now." She smiled. "Here's a hint. You can melt it down and make a pair of cuff links if you like."

Liam's fingers flexed against Jude's palm, a featherlight but distinct pressure, and a sudden and intense warmth flooded her. "Talk to me, please," she said. "Yell at me if you want. I was wrong, Liam, about so many things. You were right. So much of our journey is just a series of risks, but we have to take them or life isn't worth living. You're going to be okay. You're going to come back and continue on with your life. You'll go on many adventures and do many exciting things."

With the tips of his fingers Liam continued trying to communicate, sending ripples of tender shock up her arms. She squeezed his hand. His fingers pressed more deeply into her flesh. Bolstered with renewed hope, she emptied her soul to a man she hoped could hear the words she needed to say.

"I remember your words. Danger lurks everywhere, but knowing that cannot take away our joy of living. I thought about all those exploits of yours, the ones that take place a mile aboveground, and the ones that happen a thousand feet into the ocean, and I realized that the only time you were hurt was when you were standing on solid Dancing Falls land, the one place on earth that I've always thought was my safe haven. You didn't have time to prepare for your act of heroism, and that's exactly what it was. You are Wesley's hero, and mine, too.

"When you wake up, I'm going to tell you how much I love you. And then I'm going to make some changes. I've decided to put some pictures away and take a special box down from the closet shelf and give it to Wes. I'm not going to be controlled by fear and guilt anymore. You have taught me that loving someone again doesn't take quite as much courage as I thought it would. In fact, it's as simple as opening your heart and believing. And I believe that if you love me back, you'll come home to me. That's all that matters."

She pushed back from the bed. "I don't want to tire you, sweetheart. I could talk forever and tell you so many things, but there will be time enough when you're better." She stood, leaned over the bed and kissed his cheek. "I love you, Liam. Rest now so you can come back to all of us who feel the same way about you." She stroked her hand over his hair. "Merry Christmas."

She was nearly to the door when she heard a gravelly voice speak her name. "Jude…"

Rushing back, she grabbed on to the arm he had managed to raise above the bed rail. "Oh, Liam, I've been blubbering by your bed for the last half hour. Did you hear any of it? I love you. That's what I said."

His eyelids fluttered, opened. Jude cried, hugging his hand to her chest.

"Wesley? How…?"

"He's fine, perfectly fine."

A small smile curved his lips. "That day, I came to tell you something…" he said.

"Never mind. It can wait."

"Something else, too," he said. "That day, with Wes, I passed a test…important one."

"A test? Why, yes, you passed a test of bravery. But you already knew you are brave."

"No. A test about Wesley. I would have done anything to…"

His voice faltered, but Jude understood what he was trying to say. "You love the little guy, don't you?" she said.

He swallowed, nodded. "New Year's Eve…"

A bubble of near hysterical laughter burst from her lips. "What about New Year's Eve?"

"You have a date?"

She laughed and sobbed at the same time. "I hope so."

He licked his dry lips. "Plans. I'm going to propose."

She squealed in a most unladylike way. "To me?"

He smiled.

"I'll be there," she said. "Wherever you want me to be. And now I'm going to get a nurse and your parents."

"You'll come back?"

She returned to his bedside and held his hand tightly. "Of course I will. And I now know that what we have each day we are together is what's important. I'm going to love you more every morning as if it were a new beginning. I will cherish the times we have together without worrying about the future.

"I promise to come back to you, Jude. Always."

"You know what, Liam? It's enough if you promise to try. Knowing that, I will treasure each and every moment we have together."

EPILOGUE

CLOSE TO DUSK on Christmas Day, Martin stood at the kitchen window looking out on the snow-covered yard. The flurries had finally stopped, but not before dumping a good five inches on Fox Creek roads. Luckily he'd seen the snowplows out a half hour ago, and as long as they'd removed the accumulation, they could lay down salt. Jude would get home safely.

"It's beautiful, isn't it?"

The voice from behind him didn't startle him. In fact, he'd grown quite used to Aurora's soothing words. "Yes, it is. Imagine what it must be like up by the lake tonight."

"They always get the worst of it." After a few moments, she said, "What's wrong, Marty? You seem out of sorts all of a sudden. It was a delicious dinner."

"Oh yeah, it was great. You ladies outdid yourselves."

"Then what? I know your grandchildren

are happy. Lizzie has tried on her new sweaters, and Wesley is sleeping on the couch, exhausted. Alex and Daniel are cuddled up like the newlyweds they are."

He smiled. "All's right with the world this Christmas. But I wish Carrie were here. She's never missed Christmas. And now Jude is off at the hospital..."

"No, she's not," came a voice from the doorway. "She's home."

"Jude!" Aurora rushed over to greet her. "We're glad you made it home before it became totally dark. How did things go?"

The smile on Jude's face should have told them everything they needed to know. "Liam's awake," she said. "He's talking and smiling and making plans."

"That's great, Jude," Martin said. "What plans?"

"He's going to ask me to marry him, and I'm going to say yes."

Aurora hugged her. Martin shook his head. "What's with you kids today? In my day a man just came out and asked, or he didn't. He didn't make plans to ask." The words were accompanied by a twinkle in Martin's eyes.

"It's fine, Daddy," Jude said. "I figure he just didn't think a hospital room was very romantic, so he set up the proposal for New Year's Eve, wherever we may be."

He opened his arms. "Come here, baby girl. I couldn't be losing you to a nicer fella." As he hugged her, he focused on Aurora's comforting smile, as if she were saying, *Now see? Everything is perfect, or nearly.*

"Where will you two live?" he asked. "I hope you'll stay here. What will you do with all the animals? Have you told Wesley yet?"

"Details, Daddy," she said, laughing. "It'll all work out."

She stepped away from him. "I'm going to go tell Wes now."

"How will he take the news?" Martin asked.

Jude grinned. "He's been wanting Liam to move in with us for weeks now."

When she'd left the room, Martin walked up to Aurora.

"Get ready for another wedding, Marty."

He gave her a great big smile. "Two down and one to go."

* * * * *

Don't miss Carrie's story coming in early 2017 from acclaimed author Cynthia Thomason and Harlequin Heartwarming!

LARGER-PRINT BOOKS!

GET 2 FREE LARGER-PRINT NOVELS PLUS 2 FREE MYSTERY GIFTS

Love Inspired®

SUSPENSE
RIVETING INSPIRATIONAL ROMANCE

Larger-print novels are now available...

WESTERN WP PROMISES

YES! Please send me **The Western Promises Collection** in Larger Print. This collection begins with 3 FREE books and 2 FREE gifts (gifts valued at approx. $14.00 retail) in the first shipment, along with the other first 4 books from the collection! If I do not cancel, I will receive 8 monthly shipments until I have the entire 51-book Western Promises collection. I will receive 2 or 3 FREE books in each shipment and I will pay just $4.99 US/ $5.89 CDN for each of the other four books in each shipment, plus $2.99 for shipping and handling per shipment. *If I decide to keep the entire collection, I'll have paid for only 32 books, because 19 books are FREE! I understand that accepting the 3 free books and gifts places me under no obligation to buy anything. I can always return a shipment and cancel at any time. My free books and gifts are mine to keep no matter what I decide.

272 HCN 3070 472 HCN 3070

Name	(PLEASE PRINT)	
Address		Apt. #
City	State/Prov.	Zip/Postal Code

Signature (if under 18, a parent or guardian must sign)

Mail to the **Reader Service:**

IN U.S.A.: P.O. Box 1867, Buffalo, NY 14240-1867
IN CANADA: P.O. Box 609, Fort Erie, Ontario L2A 5X3

* Terms and prices subject to change without notice. Prices do not include applicable taxes. Sales tax applicable in N.Y. Canadian residents will be charged applicable taxes. This offer is limited to one order per household. All orders subject to approval. Credit or debit balances in a customer's account(s) may be offset by any other outstanding balance owed by or to the customer. Please allow 4 to 6 weeks for delivery. Offer available while quantities last. Offer not available to Quebec residents.

WPBPA16R

LARGER-PRINT BOOKS!
GET 2 FREE LARGER-PRINT NOVELS PLUS
2 FREE GIFTS!

◆ HARLEQUIN®

super romance®

More Story...More Romance

YES! Please send me 2 FREE LARGER-PRINT Harlequin® Superromance® novels and my 2 FREE gifts (gifts are worth about $10). After receiving them, if I don't wish to receive any more books, I can return the shipping statement marked "cancel." If I don't cancel, I will receive 4 brand-new novels every month and be billed just $5.94 per book in the U.S. or $6.24 per book in Canada. That's a savings of at least 12% off the cover price! It's quite a bargain! Shipping and handling is just 50¢ per book in the U.S. or 75¢ per book in Canada.* I understand that accepting the 2 free books and gifts places me under no obligation to buy anything. I can always return a shipment and cancel at any time. Even if I never buy another book, the two free books and gifts are mine to keep forever.

132/332 HDN GHVC

Name _____ (PLEASE PRINT) _____

Address _____ Apt. # _____

City _____ State/Prov. _____ Zip/Postal Code _____

Signature (if under 18, a parent or guardian must sign) _____

Mail to the **Reader Service:**
IN U.S.A.: P.O. Box 1867, Buffalo, NY 14240-1867
IN CANADA: P.O. Box 609, Fort Erie, Ontario L2A 5X3

Want to try two free books from another line?
Call 1-800-873-8635 today or visit www.ReaderService.com.

* Terms and prices subject to change without notice. Prices do not include applicable taxes. Sales tax applicable in N.Y. Canadian residents will be charged applicable taxes. Offer not valid in Quebec. This offer is limited to one order per household. Not valid for current subscribers to Harlequin Superromance Larger-Print books. All orders subject to credit approval. Credit or debit balances in a customer's account(s) may be offset by any other outstanding balance owed by or to the customer. Please allow 4 to 6 weeks for delivery. Offer available while quantities last.

Your Privacy—The Reader Service is committed to protecting your privacy. Our Privacy Policy is available online at www.ReaderService.com or upon request from the Reader Service.

We make a portion of our mailing list available to reputable third parties that offer products we believe may interest you. If you prefer that we not exchange your name with third parties, or if you wish to clarify or modify your communication preferences, please visit us at www.ReaderService.com/consumerschoice or write to us at Reader Service Preference Service, P.O. Box 9062, Buffalo, NY 14240-9062. Include your complete name and address.

HSRLP15

READERSERVICE.COM

Manage your account online!

- Review your order history
- Manage your payments
- Update your address

We've designed the Reader Service website just for you.

Enjoy all the features!

- Discover new series available to you, and read excerpts from any series.
- Respond to mailings and special monthly offers.
- Connect with favorite authors at the blog.
- Browse the Bonus Bucks catalog and online-only exculsives.
- Share your feedback.

Visit us at:
ReaderService.com